# Caught!

Footsteps! Someone was coming!

As quietly as I could, I shut the cabinet and looked around for somewhere to hide.

Against the wall were some metal mesh sliding walls, like the ones that held the paintings on Stack 7. I slipped behind them and stood as flat and still as possible, trying to look like a painting.

I was only just in time. Peering around a picture frame and through the mesh, I saw Ms. Minnian, the skinny, bespectacled librarian, come striding down the aisle in her flat, pointy shoes. She stopped right in front of the cabinet where I'd just put the boots.

She opened the cabinet and took out the boots. She stroked them with her fingertips, frowning, then brought them to her nose for a sniff. Still frowning, she lifted her head and sniffed the air.

I had a horrible feeling she was sniffing for *me*.

I froze and held my breath.

# the GRIMM Legacy

## POLLY SHULMAN

SCHOLASTIC INC.
New York  Toronto  London  Auckland
Sydney  Mexico City  New Delhi  Hong Kong

ISBN 978-0-545-43652-6

Copyright © 2010 by Polly Shulman. All rights reserved.
Published by Scholastic Inc., 557 Broadway, New York, NY 10012, by arrangement with Puffin Books, a division of Penguin Young Readers Group, a member of Penguin Group (USA) Inc. SCHOLASTIC and associated logos are trademarks and/or registered trademarks of Scholastic Inc.

12 11 10 9 8 7 6 5 4 3 2          12 13 14 15 16 17/0

Printed in the U.S.A.          40

First Scholastic printing, January 2012

Design by Katrina Damkoehler
Text set in Bembo

*To Mom and Scott, with love and thanks.*

# Contents

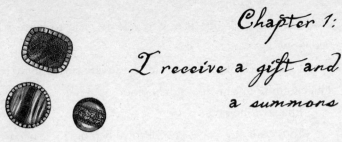

## Chapter 1:
## I receive a gift and
## a summons

Snow fell hard: big, sticky flakes that got under my coat collar where the top button was missing. The weather had delayed my subway, and I was worried I would be late for class.

In front of school, a homeless woman was struggling with a shopping cart. A passing taxi sent out a freezing wave of gray slush, causing the woman and cart to topple over into the gutter.

I had to help. Her hands were icy claws as I pulled her to her feet. She felt much lighter than she looked in her bulky rags. "Thank you," she said, shaking snow off the blanket that had covered her shoulders. Underneath she wore a T-shirt stuffed with newspaper. And on her feet, to my horror, I saw sandals.

The late bell was about to sound, but I couldn't abandon someone wearing sandals in the middle of a snowstorm—not when I had a spare pair of shoes with me. I helped her set the cart back on its wheels, then took my gym sneakers out of my bag. "Here," I said. "Can you use these?" They probably wouldn't fit—I have embarrassingly large feet. But at least they would be better than sandals.

The woman took them and turned them over, studying the soles. She held the right sneaker close to her face and peered inside, seeming to sniff at it. The left she held to her ear like a telephone.

At last she looked at me. Her eyes were surprisingly bright, a pale, luminous gray like storm clouds.

"Thanks," she said.

"You want my socks too? Probably not, they need to be washed." As soon as I'd said it, I realized it was a pretty insensitive thing to say—people with nowhere to live don't have much opportunity to do laundry. Probably they're used to dirty socks.

"Thanks," said the woman again, starting to smell the socks but evidently thinking better of it. "Wait," she said as I turned toward school. She rummaged through the bags in the cart as the snow continued to tumble down and melt in my collar. I was getting impatient, but I waited till the woman found what she was looking for and held it out to me. "Keep it safe."

"Um, thanks."

It was a number 2 pencil—the ordinary yellow kind, with a pink eraser, like you use for the SATs. I put it in my book bag, pulled my scarf tighter, and turned toward the school door.

"Hurry, Elizabeth, you're late," said a grim voice. My social studies teacher, Mr. Mauskopf, was holding the door open for me. He was my favorite teacher, despite his intimidating sternness.

The homeless woman gave him a little wave, and Mr. Mauskopf nodded back as the door swung shut behind us. I thanked him and hurried to my locker, hearing the late bell chime.

The day went downhill from there. Ms. Sandoz made me play volleyball barefoot when she saw I didn't have my sneakers, and charming Sadie Cane and Jessica Farmer spent the period playing Accidentally Stomp on the New Girl's Toes. Then in social studies Mr. Mauskopf announced a research paper due right after New Year's, effectively eliminating the vacation.

"Choose wisely, Elizabeth," he said as he handed me the list of possible topics.

My stepsister Hannah called me that evening to ask me to mail her her black lace top. She'd handed it down to me when she left for college, but with Hannah, gifts rarely stayed given for long.

"What are you up to?" she asked.

"Working on ideas for my social studies research paper. European history, with Mr. Mauskopf."

"I remember Mauskopf—what a weirdo! Does he still wear that green bow tie? And give out demerits if he catches you looking at the clock?"

"Yup." I quoted him: "'Time will pass—but will you?'"

Hannah laughed. "What are you writing about?"

"The Brothers Grimm."

"The fairy-tale guys? For Mauskopf? Are you crazy?"

"It was on his list of suggested topics."

"Don't be a little goose. I bet he just put it on there as a test, to see who would be dumb enough to think fairy tales are history. Hey, I probably still have my term paper from that class. You can use it if you like. I'll trade it for—hm—your good headphones."

"No, thanks," I said.

"You sure? It's about the Paris Commune."

"That's cheating. Anyway, Mr. Mauskopf would notice."

"Suit yourself. Send me that lace top tomorrow, okay? I need it by Saturday." She hung up.

I chewed at the end of my pencil—the one the homeless woman had given me—and stared at the topic I'd circled, wondering whether to follow Hannah's advice about switching topics. Mr. Mauskopf took history very seriously, and fairy tales don't sound that serious. But if he didn't want us writing about the Brothers Grimm, why put them on the topic list?

Fairy tales were a big part of my childhood. I used to sit in my mother's lap while she read them out loud and pretend I could read along—until, after a while, I found I actually could. Later, in the hospital when Mom was too sick to hold a book, it was my turn to read our favorites out loud.

The stories all had happy endings. But they didn't keep Mom from dying.

If she were alive now, I thought, she would definitely approve of my learning more about the men who wrote them. I decided to stick to my choice.

Strange as it sounds, once I decided I found myself actually looking forward to the term paper—it would give me something interesting to do. Vacation was going to be lonely since my best friend, Nicole, had moved to California. I hadn't made any new friends in the four months I'd been at my new school, Fisher, and the girls I used to hang out with were too busy with ballet to pay much attention to me anymore.

I missed my ballet classes, but Dad said we couldn't afford them now that he had to pay for my stepsisters' college tuition, and I was never going to be a professional dancer anyway—I wasn't obsessed enough, and my feet were too big.

• • •

Fairy tales might not be history, but as I learned in the hours I spent in the library over Christmas break, Wilhelm and Jacob Grimm were historians. They didn't invent their fairy tales—they collected them, writing down the folk tales and stories they heard from friends and servants, aristocrats and innkeepers' daughters.

Their first collection of stories was meant for grown-ups and I could see why—they're way too bloody and creepy for children. Even the heroes go around boiling people in oil and feeding them red-hot coals. Imagine Disney making a musical version of "The Girl Without Hands," a story about a girl whose widowed father chops off her hands when she refuses to marry him!

I thought I'd done a pretty good job when I finished the paper, but I still felt nervous when I handed it in. Mr. Mauskopf is a tough grader.

A few days after we returned from vacation, Mr. Mauskopf stopped me in the hall, pointing a long forefinger at the end of an outstretched arm. He always seemed to have twice as many elbows and knuckles as other people. "Elizabeth! Come see me at lunch," he said. "My office."

Was I in trouble? Had my paper creeped him out? Was Hannah right—had I failed some kind of test?

The door to the social studies department office was open, so I knocked on the door frame. Mr. Mauskopf waved me in. "Sit down," he said.

I perched on the edge of a chair.

He handed me my paper, folded in half along the vertical

axis. Comments in his signature brown ink twined across the back. I took a breath and willed myself to look at the grade.

"Nice work, Elizabeth," he said. Was that a smile on his face? Almost.

I opened the paper. He had given me an A. I leaned back, my heart pounding with relief. "Thank you."

"What made you choose this topic?"

"I don't know—I always loved fairy tales. They seem so—so realistic."

"Realistic? That's quite an unusual view," said Mr. Mauskopf with a hint of a smile.

"You're right." I felt dumb. "What I mean is, all the terrible things that happen in fairy tales seem real. Or not real, but genuine. Life is unfair, and the bad guys keep winning and good people die. But I like how that's not always the end of it. Like when the mother dies and turns into a tree and keeps helping her daughter, or when the boy who everybody thinks is an idiot figures out how to outwit the giant. Evil is real, but so is good. They always say fairy tales are simplistic, black and white, but I don't think so. I think they're *complicated*. That's what I love about them."

"I see." Mr. Mauskopf consulted his planner. "You're new this year, aren't you?"

I nodded. "I used to go to Chase, but both my stepsisters are in college now, so the tuition . . ." I stopped, a little embarrassed to be discussing my family finances.

"Ah, so you have stepsisters," Mr. Mauskopf said. "I hope they aren't the evil Grimm kind?"

"A little," I replied. Veronica's a lot older, and Hannah—

Hannah hated sharing her room with me after my father and I moved in. Hannah liked having someone to boss around the way Veronica bossed her. Hannah was always taking my things and never letting me use hers. But I couldn't say any of that—it seemed too disloyal. "My stepsister Hannah was in your class— Hannah Vane," I said instead.

"Say no more," said Mr. Mauskopf. He gave me the ghost of a smile, as if we were sharing a joke. Then he asked, "Did you ever replace your sneakers?"

"My sneakers?"

"I recall seeing you give away your sneakers—very generous of you."

"I haven't had a chance," I told him. I didn't want to get into our embarrassing financial situation again.

"I see." He cleared his throat. "Well, Elizabeth, this is all very satisfactory. Would you like a job?"

"A job? What kind of a job?"

"An after-school job. A friend of mine at the New-York Circulating Material Repository tells me they have an opening. It's a great place. I worked there myself when I was your age."

I tried to imagine him at my age, but the bow tie got in the way. "Is that like a library?"

"'Like a library.' Exactly. Well put."

"Yeah—yes, please. I'd like that," I said. A job meant money for things like new gym shoes, and it wasn't like I had a crammed social schedule.

Everybody at Fisher had known each other for aeons. It was already taking them a long time to warm up to me, the new girl. Then I made the mistake of sticking up for Mallory Mason when some of the cool girls were making up songs about her weight and her braces. Worst of all, Ms. Stanhope, the assistant principal, overheard me and used me as an example of "compassionate leadership" in her next "class chat." After that, nobody wanted to have anything to do with me except Mallory herself. But I didn't actually like her.

Who knows? Maybe if I took the library job, I would make friends there.

Plucking his fountain pen from his breast pocket, Mr. Mauskopf wrote a number on a slip of paper, folded it vertically, and handed it to me pinched between his index and middle fingers. "Call and ask for Dr. Rust," he said.

"Thank you, Mr. Mauskopf." The bell rang, and I hurried to my next class.

That afternoon when I got home, I went straight to my room, avoiding the living room so Cathy, my stepmother, wouldn't rope me into doing errands or force me to listen to her bragging about my stepsisters.

I wished my father were home so I could tell him about my new job. Not that he listened to me much these days.

Instead, I told Francie, my doll. I know it sounds babyish, but she was my mom's doll, and sometimes talking to her makes me feel a tiny bit like I'm talking to Mom.

Francie smiled at me encouragingly. Of course, she always smiles since her smile is sewn on—but I still took it as a good sign.

Francie is the only one of Mom's doll collection that Cathy let me keep after Hannah chipped Lieselotte's nose. Lieselotte was the crown of Mom's collection. She's a bisque doll, made in Germany over one hundred and fifty years ago and worth a lot of money.

"I'll just put these away until you're old enough to take care of them properly," Cathy had said when she packed the dolls away.

I knew back then it wasn't worth protesting. Cathy always sided with her own daughters. At first I used to complain to my father, but he would just say, "I need you to get along with your stepsisters. I know you can. You're my little peacemaker. You have a big, generous heart, just like your mother." So I told Cathy I didn't break Lieselotte, but I didn't say who did.

"If you're not old enough to take responsibility, you're certainly not old enough to play with dolls this valuable," said Cathy. "Now, don't start crying—here, you can keep this one; it's not worth anything. Even *you* can't do much damage to a rag doll. You'll thank me when you're older." She handed me Francie and shut the lid on Lieselotte's look of faint, aristocratic surprise.

"Time to make a phone call, Francie?" I asked.

She smiled a yes.

I called the number on the slip of paper.

"Lee Rust," said the person who answered.

"Hi, Dr. Rust? I—this is Elizabeth Rew, and my social studies teacher, Mr. Mauskopf, said to call you about a job?"

"Ah, yes, Elizabeth. Stan said you would be calling. I'm glad to hear from you."

Stan? So Mr. Mauskopf had a first name?

"Can you come in for an interview next Thursday after school?"

"All right. Where do I go?" I asked.

Dr. Rust gave me an address not far from my school, east of Central Park. "Ask for me at the front desk; they'll send you up."

The discreet brass plaque beside the door said *The New-York Circulating Material Repository.* From the outside, it looked like a standard Manhattan brownstone, the last in a long row. Next door was a big old mansion, the kind that are now mostly consulates or museums. That place would have made an impressive library, I thought as I walked up the steps to the repository and pulled open the heavy doors. It was just the sort of place I used to go to with my father, before he met Cathy. We used to spend every rainy weekend in museums and libraries. Especially the less famous ones, like the Museum of the City of New York and the New-York Historical Society, with their odd collections of things—old china and tinsmiths' tools and models of what the city looked like before the Revolution. We would play a game: pick out which painting (or clock, or chair, or photograph, or whatever) would have been Mom's favorite.

I hadn't been to a museum with my dad in years, but when I opened the doors, the slightly dusty smell brought it all flooding back. I felt as if I'd stepped back through time into a place that was once my home.

Through some trick of geometry, the entrance opened out into a large rectangular room apparently wider than the building that held it. At the far end was a massive desk, elaborately carved in dark wood.

A guy my age was sitting behind it.

But not just any guy—Marc Merritt, the tallest, coolest, best forward our basketball team had ever known. I had once seen him sink an apple core into the wastebasket in the teachers' lounge from his seat across the corridor in study hall, with both doors partly closed. He looked like a taller, African American version of Jet Li, and he moved like him too, with the same acrobatic quickness. He was in Mr. Mauskopf's other social studies section, and we had health ed together. Most of the girls at Fisher had crushes on him. I would too, if I didn't think it would be presumptuous . . . Well, to be honest, I did anyway. I was pretty sure he had no idea who I was.

"Hi, I'm here to see Dr. Rust?" I said.

"All right. Who should I say is here?"

"Elizabeth Rew."

Marc Merritt picked up the receiver of an old-fashioned telephone, the kind with a dial. "Elizabeth Rew here to see you, Doc. . . . Sure. . . . No, till six today. . . . All right." He pointed a long arm—longer than Mr. Mauskopf's, even—toward a fancy brass elevator door. "Fifth floor, take a left, through the arch. You'll see it."

When I stepped out of the elevator, corridors branched away in three directions. I couldn't imagine how they fit it all in one narrow brownstone. I went down three steps through an arch to a small, book-lined room.

Dr. Rust was slight and wiry, with thick, shaggy hair just on the brown side of red and a billion freckles.

"Elizabeth. I'm glad to meet you." We shook hands. "Please, have a seat. How is Stan?"

Strict but fair. Stern-looking, but with an underlying twinkle in his eye. Oddly dressed. "Fine," I said.

"Still keeping that great beast in that tiny apartment, is he?"

"I guess? I've never been to his apartment."

"Well. Let's see, you're in Stan's European history class, yes?"

"That's right."

"Good, good. Stan's never sent us a bad page. He says you're hardworking and warmhearted, with an independent mind—which is high praise from Stan, believe me. So this is really a formality, but just to be thorough, do you do the dishes at home?"

What kind of a question was that? "Yes, most of the time." One more bad thing about my stepsisters going away to college—I was the only kid left to do chores.

"About how often?"

"Most days. Five or six times a week, probably."

"And how many have you broken this year?"

"Dishes?"

"Yes, dishes, glasses, that sort of thing."

"None. Why?"

"Oh, we can never be too careful. When was the last time you lost your keys?"

"I never lose my keys."

"Excellent. All right, sort these, please." Dr. Rust handed me a box of buttons.

"Sort them? Sort them how?"

"Well, that's up to you, isn't it?"

This had to be the strangest interview I'd ever heard of. Was I going to lose the job because Dr. Rust didn't like the way I sorted buttons?

I poured them out on the desk and turned them all faceup.

There were large wooden disks and tiny pearls, shiny square buttons made of red or blue or yellow plastic, sparkly star-shaped ones with rhinestones that looked as if they would shred their buttonholes, little knots of rope, a set of silver buttons each engraved with a different flower, tiny rabbits carved from coral, plain transparent plastic buttons for inside waistbands, big glass things like mini doorknobs, a heavy gold button studded with what looked like real diamonds.

I grouped them by material: metal; wood and other plant products; bone, shell, and other animal parts; stone; plastic and other man-made materials, including glass. Then I divided each category into subgroups, also by material. Within the subgroups, I ranked them by weight.

"I see. Where would you put this?" Dr. Rust handed me a metal button, the kind with a loop on the back rather than holes. The front part had a piece of woven cloth of some sort, set behind glass.

I hesitated. Should it go in metals, in man-made materials for the glass, or in plants for the cloth? Maybe the cloth was wool, though, which would put it in animal parts. "Am I allowed to ask a question?" I said.

"Of course. Always ask questions. As the Akan proverb says, 'The one who asks questions does not lose his way.'"

"Where's Akan?"

"The Akan people are from west Africa. They have a remarkably rich proverb tradition. Perhaps because they believe in asking questions."

"Oh. Okay—what's the button made of?"

"Excellent question. Gold, rock crystal, and human hair."

Not man-made materials, then; maybe stone. Other than that, the answer didn't help me much. By weight, the button was mostly gold, so maybe it should go in with the metals? But I had put the diamond-looking one in stone, not metal. I decided to classify the new button by its weirdest component and put it in the animal pile.

"Interesting," said Dr. Rust. "Sort them again."

I scrambled them and resorted, making an elaborate grid of size and color. It started with red at the top and ran through the rainbow down to violet at the bottom, with extra rows for black and white. From left to right, it started with tiny collar buttons and finished with vast badges.

"Where would you put this?" Dr. Rust handed me a zipper.

A zipper! "Why didn't you give me this the last time?" I said in dismay. "I could have put it with the metals."

Was it my imagination, or had Dr. Rust's freckles moved? Hadn't the large one over the left eye been over the right eye earlier?

I scrambled the buttons again and started over. This time I sorted them by shape. I put the zipper with the toggles and a rectangular button carved with zigzags. I didn't like that solution, but it was better than nothing.

Dr. Rust raised an eyebrow (no large freckle anywhere near now) and asked, "Which do you think is the most valuable?"

I considered the diamond one but picked an enameled peacock with blue gems in its tail. Dr. Rust seemed pleased.

"The oldest?"

I had no idea. I picked one of the silver ones.

"The most beautiful?"

I was getting a little impatient with all this. I picked one of the plastic ones, in a lovely shade of green. Dr. Rust didn't seem quite to believe me. "The most powerful?"

"How can a button be powerful?"

"Oh, I think you'll find over time that every object here has its own unique qualities. You'll find that the materials in our collections speak to you."

Did that mean I'd gotten the job?

Still, some of the buttons did seem to draw me more than others. I chose a black glass button with a disturbing geometry. Dr. Rust picked it up and examined it closely for a long time while I watched the freckles, trying to catch them moving. Wasn't that butterfly shape of freckles on the left side just a minute ago?

"Well, Elizabeth, this has been most illuminating, but we both have a lot of work waiting," said Dr. Rust at last, as if *I* had been the one staring endlessly at a button. "Can you start next week? Here, I think you'd better have this."

Someone opened the door just as Dr. Rust handed me one last button. It matched the buttons on my coat—it might have been my missing top button.

"And here's Marc, right on time."

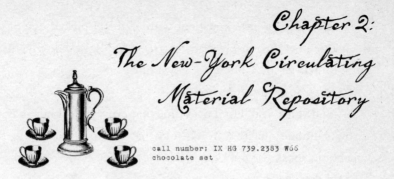

# Chapter 2:
## The New-York Circulating Material Repository

call number: IX HG 739.2383 W66
chocolate set

Marc stood in the doorway.

"You two know each other, right?" said Dr. Rust.

"Yeah, we met downstairs," said Marc.

"Actually, we're in health ed together," I said. "With Ms. Reider."

Marc had the grace to look embarrassed.

"Good," said Dr. Rust. "Take Elizabeth up to Stack 9 and show her the ropes."

"But the ropes are on Stack 2."

"I meant metaphorically."

Could it be possible—did Marc wink at me? The great and famous Marc Merritt winking at *me*? If so, he did it very quickly.

"And send Martha Callender a pneum," continued Dr. Rust. "She'll want to do her orientation thing and work out the schedules. Glad to have you with us, Elizabeth. We've been shorthanded lately—we can really use the help. If you have any questions, you know where to find me."

I had a billion questions, in fact, but I followed Marc down the hallway and through a door marked *Staff Only.*

"What's a stack?" I asked.

"A floor where the holdings are stored."

"And what's a pneum?"

"Pneumatic tube carrier," said Marc.

"Okay, what's a pneumatic tube carrier, then?"

"You'll see. Watch your head here."

We went through a low door—Marc had to duck, but my head was in no danger—and up a staircase, flight after flight after flight. The brownstone couldn't possibly have so many floors—we must have gone way past the roof, into some sort of penthouse addition. I was panting hard, but Marc looked as cool as ever, like the black king in my chess set.

At last he opened a door marked *Stack 9*. We stepped out into the middle of a long room with rows of cabinets stretching away on both sides. Near the door was a pair of desks facing a trio of elevators: a tiny one the size of a microwave, another the size of a dishwasher, and a third the size of a small refrigerator. Beyond them thick pipes snaked off in several directions. These were painted white, black, and red, and each had a small oblong door at elbow height. One of the pipes ended like a bathtub faucet over a wire basket.

"The staging area is basically headquarters on each floor," said Marc. "You can hang up your coat over there." He took a white slip of paper from a tray of different-colored slips, wrote something on it, and folded it in half.

As I stood looking around, one of the pipes began to cough and thump, as if a tiny elephant were panicking inside. Something hurtled out of the open end of the pipe and landed with a thud in the wire basket beneath. Marc held it up to show me: a transparent plastic tube like a skinny soda can, with thick felt padding on both ends.

"See? A pneum."

The pneum had a sliding panel in its side. Marc slid it open, reached into the pneum, extracted a piece of paper, and replaced it with the note he'd written. He pulled open a door in one of the pipes. I heard a soft roaring, like a wind in a canyon. He slipped in the pneum and let the door clap shut. The pipe banged as the pneum shot through it.

"Where did it go?" I asked.

"Upstairs to the pneum routing station."

"How does it work?"

"The pipes are full of pressurized air. It's like a tiny hurricane inside the pipe. The air pushes the pneums through the pipes, all around the building."

"So you could send that pneum anywhere?"

"It goes where the pipe takes it. You have to pick a pipe that's going where you want to send the pneum. I better run that call slip," he said. "Wait here. If Ms. Callender shows up, tell her I'll be right back." He headed off down a row of file cabinets.

I hung up my coat, wandered over to a cabinet stenciled with letters and numbers, and peeked in. Inside I saw shelves of teacups. The next cabinet had shelves of coffee mugs. From time to time I heard a pneum gallop through the pipes in the ceiling.

Soon Marc came back with a pair of packages each the size of a shoe box. He put the first one in the smallest elevator, shut the door, and pressed a button.

"Was that a book?" I asked.

"What? No, it's a chocolate pot. Sorry, I should have showed you. The patron requested a hot-chocolate set. Here's the cream and sugar." He opened the second box and showed me a fancy, swirly cream pitcher and sugar bowl packed in fluffy stuff, like cotton. He delicately tucked the fluff back around the set.

"Can I ask you a question?" I asked.

"Uh-huh. Like Doc says, 'The one who asks questions does not lose his way,'" he answered in a credible imitation of Dr. Rust's high-low voice.

"Okay, so this job. What am I supposed to be doing? Am I like a dishwasher?"

"A dishwasher!" He hooted with laughter. "Why would you be a dishwasher?"

I bristled. Being laughed at was bad enough—being laughed at by Marc Merritt felt doubly bad. Besides, it didn't seem like such an unreasonable question to me. "Well, Dr. Rust asked me how often I do the dishes and if I break a lot of china. And there's all this china around. What *is* the job, if I'm not washing dishes?"

"You're a page."

That made less sense than a dishwasher. Was he making fun of me? "You mean a medieval page, like an entry-level knight? Are there swords and dragons hidden away in some of these cabinets?"

He hooted again, but I didn't feel as bad. At least this time you could argue he was laughing at my joke. "A library page," he said. "When a call slip comes, you go get the item the patron requested. Did you ever use the reference library on Forty-second Street? You know how they keep the books locked up and bring them to you when you request them? Did you ever wonder who gets the books? That's the pages."

"Okay, so if this is a library, where are all the books?"

"Books? There's some on Stack 6. Most of them are in the Document Room or the Reference Room. And, you know, here and there."

Not many books? "What kind of a library is this?"

Before he could answer, the staircase door opened and a woman walked in. "Hi, Marc," she said. "Elizabeth, right? I'm Martha Callender." She tucked a lock of straight brown hair behind a little round ear. Everything about her, in fact, was round: her cheeks, her figure, her collar, the big buttons on her jacket, even her haircut, which roundly framed her round face and kept getting in her round eyes.

"Welcome, welcome! It's great to have you here," she told me. "We've been very shorthanded—we lost two pages in the last two months—and Stan told Dr. Rust you're a hard worker."

"I love his class. It's worth working hard in," I said, flattered.

"I bet he's a great teacher. How is he doing? And the Beast?"

"Mr. Mauskopf is fine. I've never, um, met the Beast."

"No? Well, that's something for you to look forward to." She beamed at me. "Did Marc give you the grand tour?"

"Not yet, I was running a call slip," said Marc.

"Okay," she said. "I'll show you around, then. Did you have any questions to begin with?"

"Yes," I said. "What is this place?"

"I'm not sure what you mean—which place? Stack 9? The Stack 9 staging area?"

"No, I mean the whole institution, the repository."

I didn't expect a real answer. Whatever this place was, it seemed to be full of people who told you to ask questions and then declined to answer them.

But Ms. Callender took a breath and began. "The New-York Circulating Material Repository is the oldest subscription library of its kind in the country. We've existed in one form or another since 1745, when three clock makers began sharing some of their more specialized tools. That collection became the core of the repository in 1837, when a group of amateur astronomers pooled their resources and opened shop. Our first home was on St. John's Park, near Greenwich Street, but we moved uptown to East Twenty-fourth Street in 1852 and to our current location in 1921. Of course, we've expanded into the adjoining buildings since then. In fact, most of the stacks are part of the 1958 expansion. Lee's office is in the original 1921 bequest, though."

Informative, but not very enlightening. "Are the subscribers the people who come here to borrow books or whatever?" I asked.

"Books?" She looked taken aback. "No, not really. There are plenty of other libraries for that. I hope you're not going to be disappointed, honey—if it's books you're after, I can put you in touch with Jill Kaufmann at the Lion Library. They can always use pages."

Was I imagining things, or was Marc smirking a little?

"No, it's just—Mr. Mauskopf said there was a job at a library, so I just assumed, you know, I would be working with books. If it's not books, what is it?"

"What? Objects, of course. We're just like a circulating book library but with far more varied collections."

"What kind of collections? Collections of what?"

She took a breath and began again. It sounded as if she'd given this speech many times too. "Some of the more popular types of items we loan out these days include musical instruments, sports equipment, and specialized cooking tools. Many New Yorkers like to give the occasional fondue party, for example, but they don't want to devote the cupboard space to a lot of fondue pots. Or if you're thinking of learning to play the piccolo, you might borrow one to see how you like it. In the late nineteenth century, specialized silver services were very popular. In the 1970s, it was wood lathes. Lately there's been a run on—oh dear!" She broke off as a girl around my age appeared from between a pair of cabinets with a slip of paper in her hand. "There's another one, I bet."

"Excuse me, Ms. Callender. Dr. Rust is out and there's a patron who needs to borrow something from the Grimm Collection. Can you handle the deposit?" asked the girl.

"Of course. Thanks, Anjali." Ms. Callender turned to me. "I'm sorry, hon, we'll have to finish up later. Here, I need you to fill out these forms. You can leave them with Anjali when you're done, and I'll see you—let's see, when's your first shift? Tuesday. I'm so glad to have you with us, honey—it'll be a big help. And I hope you'll come to love the repository as much as we do." She shook my hand vigorously and vanished between a pair of cabinets.

"She seems friendly," I said.

"Ms. Callender? She's a honey," said Anjali.

Marc grinned at her.

I sat down at one of the heavy oak desks to fill out my forms.

Anjali leaned against it. She was medium height, with cascades of black hair, amber-tan skin, and brown eyes under perfectly arched eyebrows. I had always wanted eyebrows like that. Mine are straight and kind of plain.

"I'm Elizabeth Rew," I said.

"Nice to meet you, Elizabeth. I'm Anjali Rao."

"Hey, can I ask a question?" I asked.

Anjali and Marc intoned in unison, "The one who asks questions does not lose his way!" Then they smiled at each other.

"What's the Grimm Collection?"

The smiles vanished and they glanced at each other. "Don't worry about that for now," said Anjali.

"Oh. Okay," I said, feeling a little snubbed. There was an awkward silence. "So," I tried again, "what do they pay us around here?"

"Eighty-five percent of minimum wage," said Marc.

"How can they call it the minimum, then?" I objected.

"It doesn't seem fair, does it? We're students, so they're allowed to pay us less," said Anjali.

I thought about it. "I guess it could be worse."

"You could get more flipping burgers—but then you'd have to flip burgers," said Marc. "This place smells a lot better."

"Except Stack 8," said Anjali.

They both snorted. I wanted to ask what Stack 8 was, but I didn't want to risk being told to mind my own business again.

"So, Elizabeth," said Anjali, "where did you put the memorial button?"

"The what?"

"The button with human hair."

"It's downstairs with Dr. Rust."

"No, I mean what category did you put it in?"

"With the things made of animal parts. Why, where did you put it?" I asked Anjali.

"Mid-nineteenth century. But now I think it should have gone in eighteenth. Doesn't matter, I still got the job. What about the barrette?"

"What barrette? There was no barrette, just buttons. Oh, and a zipper."

"A zipper! How interesting. I wonder what that means. What about you, Merritt, did you get a zipper or a barrette? Do you remember?"

"I got a belt buckle and an electric switch," said Marc. "And the memorial button."

"Really? That's two extras besides the button box. I only got one."

"Yeah, I don't think Doc was too happy when I put the belt buckle in with the nails. I think the electric switch was like giving me a second chance to prove myself."

"What nails?" I said.

"Oh, you didn't get any nails?" said Anjali. "I did. They were in the button box."

A pneum thumped into the basket. She went to get it.

"Are you on 9 with us now?" Marc asked her. "I thought you were down in the Dungeon today."

"I am, but it's okay, I'm on break. I have another ten minutes." She handed Marc the slip. "Do you think Doc ever flunks anybody for sorting the buttons wrong?"

"Wrong how?" asked Marc.

"I don't know, maybe if you did something really obvious, like lining them up by size."

Marc looked a little embarrassed; I wondered whether he'd lined the buttons up by size. I knew how he felt—I'd done it myself. Well, I'd used size and color together, but close enough.

He studied the slip and headed off down the room. I gazed after him, admiring his walk.

"So you go to Fisher with Merritt?" asked Anjali.

"Yes, where do you go?"

"Miss Wharton's School," she said. It was a fancy all-girls' private school near Fisher. When I went to Chase, we used to be in the same sports league for the girls' teams. I wondered whether she would be stuck up—Miss Wharton's had that reputation. But she seemed nice enough so far.

I finished the forms and handed them to her. "That's it, I guess. How do I get out of here? This building's a little confusing, and I don't have a great sense of direction," I said.

"Just take the elevator to the lobby."

I looked at the three little elevators doubtfully. "What elevator?" I asked.

Anjali laughed. "Oh, did Merritt make you climb up all those stairs? He's such a he-man! I didn't mean the dumbwaiters—I meant the real, live, person-size elevator. Come on, I'll show you."

I put on my coat and followed her through a fire door. "I'm glad you're here. It's about time they finally hired somebody," she said.

That made two people today who'd told me they were glad

to have me around—the first two in years. I had a feeling I was going to like this place.

"It's been extra busy since Mona disappeared, and sort of spooky," Anjali whispered.

"Someone disappeared?" I asked.

"Mona Chen, one of the pages."

"Where'd she go?"

"I don't know. Ms. Callender thinks she went back to Taiwan with her family, but she never said good-bye, and that's not like her. Marc and I are trying to find out what happened to her. We think it may have something to do with . . ." She stopped.

"With what?"

"I'm sorry. Never mind. You're going to think I'm crazy. And I don't want to scare you away before you've even started! But I did think I should warn you."

"Warn me about what? Scare me how?" There was something almost gothic about this place, with the mysterious collection Anjali and Marc wouldn't tell me about and now a disappearing page. I was less scared than intrigued.

Anjali paused. "Well, there are some wild rumors about a— about a flying creature that's been following some of the patrons and pages around. They even say it snatched a repository object right out of a patron's hands."

"A flying creature? What do you mean?" This did sound crazy. Was Anjali fooling with me? She looked serious.

"I've heard it's like a giant bird," Anjali said. "At least that's what they say. I don't know if it's true. But then Mona disappeared, and she was really scared about the bird and so I thought . . ."

"Wait," I said. "Have you seen this bird yourself?"

She shook her head. "I don't think so. But sometimes I get the feeling something's watching me."

"That sounds pretty scary," I said, not knowing how seriously to take her.

"Yeah, well . . ." She punched the elevator call button. "I don't mean to freak you out. Just, watch out for . . ." Anjali looked at me and smiled.

"For enormous birds that steal objects and kidnap pages," I finished.

"Yeah, I know it sounds nuts. But after you work at this place for a while, you'll start to get used to some pretty unlikely stuff."

The elevator arrived and I got in. "See you Tuesday!"

"See you Tuesday, have a good weekend!"

Anjali waved as the doors closed. New friend or weirdo? I wondered. She seemed nice, anyway. It wouldn't be so bad, I decided, if she turned out to be both.

## Chapter 3:
## A suspicious page

Dad was home alone when I got back from the repository.

"Hi, sweetheart," he said. "Are you just getting home from school?"

"School got out hours ago, Dad. Today I was interviewing for my new job," I said. "Remember? I told you about it last week."

"Oh, that's right. Where is it again, the Historical Society?"

"No, the New-York Circulating Material Repository," I reminded him. Dad used to remember things I told him, back when it was just the two of us.

"That's that private museum with the beautiful stained-glass windows," he said. "They're famous. I've always meant to go see them."

"It's wonderful. You would love it; it's your kind of place. You should come, especially now that I work there. I bet I could show you around, give you a tour," I said.

We heard Cathy's key in the front door and she burst into the room.

"Michael! Come look at the colors I'm considering for the bedroom." Cathy was constantly repainting the apartment and was never quite satisfied with the results.

"Sure." He followed her out.

"So you'll come with me to the repository, Dad?" I asked.

"We'll talk about it later, Elizabeth," he said. I wondered if we ever would.

I went to my room and did my homework, rushing through my French so I could take my time with social studies. I wanted to read praise in Mr. Mauskopf's brown ink when I got the homework back—*well argued* instead of *sloppy thinking*. I wanted to deserve it.

At lunch the next day, I stood with my tray listening to the roar of the cafeteria and feeling even more lonely than usual. I looked around for someone to sit with. I saw Mallory Mason across the room. If only I liked her! She would certainly be willing to sit with me, but I didn't want to be her friend—she was as mean as the kids who picked on her, just less powerful. And sitting with her would spoil my chances of making other friends.

I looked around for other possibilities and spotted Katie Sanduski, a girl from my French class, but she had a book propped up against her backpack. She looked pretty absorbed.

At a table by the window, three girls from math class were talking and laughing and throwing the occasional corn chip at each other.

Should I interrupt Katie's reading? Should I try to insert myself into the merry chip-tossing trio?

Katie, I decided. Interrupting one person should be easier than interrupting three. But just as I made up my mind, Katie closed her book and got up to bus her tray.

Nothing else for it, then. Maddie, Samantha, and Jo. Gathering my courage, I threaded my way toward them. Before I could reach them, though, three more girls—ones I didn't know—descended on the table with shrieks and claimed the last three spots.

I turned aside and sat at the nearest empty seat. A couple kids glanced at me, then glanced away. A puddle of spilled soda divided me from them. I ate as quickly as I could and left the cafeteria.

I was ten minutes early to social studies. Peeking through the window in the door, I saw Mr. Mauskopf sitting at his desk alone.

He saw me too. "Come in, Elizabeth," he said, beckoning with his long arm.

"Hi, Mr. Mauskopf." I shut the door behind me. "Want my homework?"

"Thank you. So? Did you take the job at the repository?"

I nodded. "I start Tuesday."

"And how do you find it so far?"

"Pretty interesting," I said. *Weird* was the word I really meant, but I didn't quite feel comfortable saying so to Mr. Mauskopf. "All those zillions of objects. The people there seem really nice. Ms. Callender's so friendly. And the building is cool too, with the marble floors and all the fancy carved doors. It's so much bigger on the inside than it looks on the outside."

"Did you see the famous Tiffany windows?"

"No, my dad mentioned them, but I haven't seen them yet. Where are they?"

"In the Main Examination Room."

"Oh. Is that in, like, the medical section?"

Mr. Mauskopf laughed, although I wasn't aware I'd made a joke. "Make sure you see them next time," he said. "They're spectacular."

Then the rest of the kids came back from lunch and class began.

That afternoon I wished more than ever that I had some friends at school, since there was no one to notice the big event of the day: the great Marc Merritt greeting me in the hallway. At least, I think it's fair to call it a greeting; he didn't say anything, he just nodded at me.

I took that as permission to say, "Hi, Marc." He was with some of his tall friends, though, so I didn't press it. I heard him explain, "Girl from health ed," as they walked on.

When I got to the library on Tuesday, Anjali was sitting behind the circulation desk. She sent me upstairs to find Ms. Callender on Stack 6, where the librarians—all except Dr. Rust—had their offices.

Ms. Callender showed me the time clock, a boxy machine mounted on the wall next to a rack of cards with names on them. I found my card and stuck it in the clock's jaw. The machine chomped down violently, stamping it with the time.

"I'm going to start you off on 2, which is textiles—Textiles and Garb," said Ms. Callender, punching the elevator button. "Stack 2 was always one of my favorites back when I was a page. If you feel the urge to try things on, well, I won't tell. I never could resist when I was your age. Just stick to cotton, linen, and wool—they're pretty sturdy—and make sure you pick the right sizes so you don't rip anything." She winked at me.

We went out through a fire door into a long, dim room, like Stack 9, only much more gloomy. "Why's it so dark here?" I asked.

"We keep the textiles below ground level because of the light. Daylight is terrible for most fibers. It can make them fade or even fall apart. There are desk lamps, though, if you want to read. And the ladies' room on this floor has a full-length mirror."

The aisles between the cabinets stretched out into darkness. I heard footsteps echoing a long way off. "It's spooky," I said.

Ms. Callender smiled, making her round cheeks bunch up into apples. "You think so?" she said. "Most of the pages find Stack 1 the spookiest. Now, the first thing to remember: always wash your hands and wear gloves. The oils and acids on your skin can damage the cloth." There was a sink near the dumbwaiters, along with a supply cabinet full of cotton gloves, padded hangers, tissue paper, and cardboard boxes stamped *Archival*.

"I don't get it," I said, washing my hands. "This is a circulating library, right? So people are checking out the clothing and wearing it. That's got to be worse for it than me touching it with my hands."

"Yes, you're right. Technically, almost all of our holdings circulate," she said. "But that doesn't mean people can just do what they like with whatever they borrow—they have to return it in the same condition they received it in or they pay degradation fines. And the most valuable objects require a deposit."

"How much do you have to pay if you get finger acid on something?"

"It depends what you're handling. Not much if it's just a T-shirt, more if it's something like Lincoln's hat or Marie Antoinette's wig. With the important holdings, we have so many restrictions that nobody really borrows them but museums, and they certainly don't wear them. We have an actuary on staff to figure it all out."

"Marie Antoinette's wig! Can I see that?"

"Sure." Ms. Callender touched a button and a dim light illuminated one of the aisles. We walked down it to a door marked *V, which she unlocked. "This is the Stack 2 Valuables Room— *V for *Valuables,*" she said. The room was crammed with labeled cabinets. She unlocked one and showed me rows of wigs on what looked like china heads. There were blond ones and black ones, wigs with intricate braids and simple buns, long curly wigs like the ones judges wear on British TV shows.

"I won't take it out, but that one's the queen's," said Ms. Callender, pointing to a white wig. It was tall and rather plain.

"Wow! Was she wearing it when she had her head cut off?" I asked. I looked for bloodstains but didn't see any.

"No, no," said Ms. Callender. "Ugh! No, that's just one of her simpler weekday wigs. She gave it to a lady in waiting, who escaped the revolution disguised as a wig maker and made it to England, where she married a fur trader from Vermont. One of their descendants donated it in the 1960s. He got a tax write-off."

"That's amazing! Where's Lincoln's hat—can I see that too?"

"Maybe another time. Ask me again when we're not busy, okay, honey? Now let me show you how to run a call slip."

Ms. Callender locked up the *V Room carefully and we went back out to the Stack 2 staging area, where the sink and elevators were. A guy about my age was inspecting a call slip under one of the desk lamps.

"Hello, Aaron," said Ms. Callender. "This is Elizabeth. I'm showing her how to run slips. Mind if we take that?"

"Not at all," he said, handing her the paper. She spread it on the desk.

It read:

```
Call number: II T&G 391.440944 L46
Description: Ladies' parasol, silk, steel,
and bamboo, vegetable ivory handle.
French, Lendemain Frères, 1888
Patron: Matilda Johnson
Affiliation: TriBeCa Studio
```

"For your purposes, the most important part is the call number," said Ms. Callender. "It tells you where to find the object. We use a modified Dewey decimal system to organize the collection, like a conventional book library. The objects are grouped by subject. The first segment of the call number, the prefix—II T&G in this case—identifies the stack and collection: Stack 2, Textiles and Garb. After the prefix comes the Dewey decimal number."

"So where's II T&G 391.440944 L46?"

"You can check the wall map. Fifth row east. This way." I followed her down another dim aisle between cabinets labeled with call numbers.

When we reached the right row, Ms. Callender stopped and

twisted a dial on the wall, like a kitchen timer. A light came on in the aisle. "The lights are on timers to save energy," said Ms. Callender. "That way you don't have to worry if you forget to turn them off behind you."

She opened the cabinet door and pulled a small umbrella out of a cubbyhole. "Always double-check to make sure you have the right object," she said, opening the umbrella gently. She inspected the handle and read a cardboard tag. "This is it." We headed back toward the desks.

Ms. Callender marked the call slip with her initials and sent the umbrella up to the Main Examination Room in the medium-size dumbwaiter. "That's the basic idea," she said. "For today, you can shadow Aaron—he'll tell you what to do. And let me know if you run into any trouble."

Aaron was reading a book at one of the desks. "So you're the new girl," he said, looking up.

"I'm Elizabeth Rew," I said.

"Aaron Rosendorn."

"How long have you worked here?" I asked.

"Two years."

"You must like it, then," I said.

"Yeah."

"What's your favorite thing about it? Do you have a favorite collection?"

"What do you mean?" His eyes narrowed.

"I don't know—there are different collections here, right? The textiles on this stack and the china upstairs. Or I heard someone say something about the Grimm Collection, whatever that is. Do you have a favorite?"

He frowned. The light from the reading lamp threw shadows on his high cheekbones and around his nose, giving him an arrogant expression—or maybe that was just how he looked. "Why do you want to know?" he asked. He sounded either stuck up or paranoid.

"No reason—I was just making conversation. Is it a big secret or something?"

"No, not really," he said. "This is one of the world's great repositories. It's an honor to work here." He looked at me for a few seconds like he was sizing me up. "How did you get the job?"

Was he implying I didn't deserve it? "My social studies teacher, Mr. Mauskopf. He used to work here himself when he was our age. He knows Dr. Rust and Ms. Callender."

"Where do you go to school?"

"Fisher."

"Oh, with Marc Merritt." Now he sounded even more suspicious and disapproving. What was wrong with this guy? Everyone else here seemed so friendly.

"Yes, Marc's in my class," I said.

"How nice for you," said Aaron. What an unpleasant person, I thought.

A pneum came rattling through the pipes and thumped into the basket. Aaron pulled out the slip and handed it to me. "Let's see how you handle this," he said.

"You sure you trust me?" I was a little surprised at my own sarcastic tone. This guy really got under my skin.

"Not yet. That's the point. The last page, the one you're replacing—she was a disaster. I'm a senior page. I have responsibilities. I need to see how you work."

"Was that Mona?"

"No, Zandra. What do you know about Mona?"

"Nothing, really—just that Anjali told me she disappeared. Who's Zandra, and why was she a disaster?"

"Never mind Zandra. She was a disorganized mess-up and a liar and a thief, and now she's gone. Let's see if you're better."

Wow, I thought, this guy could be related to my stepsisters. "Fine," I said. I read the slip, a request for a Chinese headdress. I found the right cabinet easily enough, despite the dim room. But when I reached up for the elaborate headdress, Aaron hovered so close I was afraid he was going to step on my feet. I tilted the headdress to slide it off the shelf.

"Careful! It's fragile; those bobbles are glass," he said.

"Back off, you're making me nervous," I snapped. "I'm not going to hurt it." I lifted it down. "See? Safe and sound."

"All right," said Aaron. "I just had to make sure."

I checked the label and carried the headdress down the hall to the staging area, where Aaron showed me how to file the call slip.

The next request was from someone named John Weinstein from Dark on Monday Productions. He wanted to borrow a doublet.

"Who are these people, and why are they borrowing these things?" I asked.

"This guy's from a theater company, so chances are he's

getting ideas for costumes. Probably Shakespeare. They always borrow doublets when they do Shakespeare," he said. This time he stood back and let me take the doublet out of the cabinet without comment.

We ran a few more slips—my favorite was a delicate mask, with feathers curling around the upper half of the face. Aaron watched me closely, but he didn't find anything to criticize. He was pretty intense, but I was impressed at how seriously he took his job.

When it was time to take my break, Ms. Callender took me upstairs to see the Main Examination Room. "This is where patrons come to get the items they requested," she said. "They can sit and work at the tables."

"Like the main room in the library," I said.

"Exactly."

It was a striking space, with tall ceilings, massive, imposing tables, and an elaborately carved staging area where Anjali and the other pages and librarians were bustling around, putting away slips and stacking pneums. I finally got a chance to see the Tiffany windows, but since it was a gloomy afternoon, I couldn't make out any shapes or patterns in them.

I sat at one of the tables and did homework, then went back downstairs to Stack 2 when my break was over.

One patron requested antique Navajo rugs from New Mexico and kilim rugs from Turkey. They were heavy—it took both me and Aaron to carry them. We spread them out on the big table to check their condition before sending them upstairs in the big dumbwaiter.

"Look at how similar these two patterns are, with those triangles and diamonds and rectangles," I said. "They're from different continents, but they look like the weavers knew each other."

"That's just because of how they're woven," said Aaron. "The yarns cross each other at right angles, so it's easier to make straight lines than curves."

"Yes, but it's more than that," I said. "The colors are completely different, but look at those zigzags and that border. And the rug from Iran we sent up before looks nothing like either one of them."

"I see what you mean," said Aaron. "I wonder what made them choose the same patterns."

"I wish we could go back in time and ask them," I said.

"Me too."

Aaron was much nicer when he was talking about rugs than when he was scolding me about not breaking things, I thought.

Around five, the fire door opened and Anjali came in, pushing a large cart full of objects. "Returns!" she called.

Aaron went running over to help her.

They wheeled the cart over to the center of the stack, Aaron pushing and Anjali steadying it.

"How's it going, Elizabeth?" she asked. "Having fun?"

"Yes, thanks."

"Good. Don't let Aaron work you too hard." She winked at me and vanished through the stack door. Aaron stared after her with a look of naked longing.

"She seems nice," I said, to break the silence.

He turned to me as if he'd forgotten I was there. "What? Yeah . . . yeah, she's very . . . nice," he said.

Seeing the transformation in Aaron made me wonder how it would feel to have someone—even a not-so-nice guy like Aaron—look at me the way he looked at Anjali.

I hoped that someday I would find out.

desk lamp

That Saturday the arctic weather softened slightly. I was walking in Central Park after my morning shift at the repository when a bear came bounding toward me across the snow. I froze.

Not a bear, I saw as it got closer, but a bear-sized shaggy dog making the frozen air echo with its barks.

"Griffin, stay!"

The dog skidded to a stop in front of me. I took a step back. It was wagging its tail—that was reassuring. It put its huge wet paws on my shoulders and tried to lick my face.

"Do I know you?" I asked the dog, trying to duck away.

"Down, Griffin! Don't knock Elizabeth over!" said a familiar stern voice. It was Mr. Mauskopf. He snapped his long fingers at the dog.

This, then, must be the Beast.

The dog subsided onto its haunches, put its head to one side, turned its ears forward, and looked up at me with eyes as big as saucers. It didn't have to look up very far; we were practically at eye level. It raised a big, hairy paw and offered it to me.

"How do you do?" I said, shaking the paw. It felt as heavy as a sack of onions.

The Beast took that as an invitation to put its paws on my shoulders again.

"Down, Griffin! I said down!" barked Mr. Mauskopf. The dog subsided again. "He seems to like you."

"Good dog," I said, amused. For all his famous sternness, Mr. Mauskopf didn't seem to be too good at making his dog obey. He must be more of a softy than he let on. I patted Griffin's lumpy, shaggy brown shoulder. He put his tongue out and wagged his entire hindquarters.

"Nice day for a walk," Mr. Mauskopf said.

"At least it's warmer than yesterday. I just finished my shift at the repository."

"Yes, I've been wanting to talk to you about that. How are things there?"

"I love it. It's like getting to take things out of museum display cases and actually touch them."

Mr. Mauskopf smiled. "I remember that excitement," he said. "Before I started working at the repository, I never thought much about objects. To me a spoon was just a spoon. Then my supervisor put me on Stack 9, and I saw those thousands of spoons, all different sizes and shapes and patterns and uses. I realized they didn't just appear by magic. Someone had thought about each one and decided what it should be like, what shape, what to make it out of. It was like a whole new world opening up. I think that's when I became interested in history."

"I know what you mean," I said. "Ms. Callender showed me Marie Antoinette's wig. It makes you realize that Marie Antoinette actually existed."

He nodded. "And what does she have you doing? Martha

Callender, I mean, not Marie Antoinette." Wow, a joke from Mr. Mauskopf!

"Mostly running call slips, reshelving, that sort of thing."

"Good, good." A pause; Mr. Mauskopf glanced at the Beast. Griffin gave a single bark, almost as if he and Mr. Mauskopf were exchanging words. Mr. Mauskopf turned back to me. "Tell me, have you seen anything to alarm you?" he asked.

"To alarm me? What do you mean?" Was he talking about the gigantic bird?

"My friends at the repository tell me there's something . . . not quite right. I wondered if you'd noticed anything that could be helpful."

"What's not right? One of the pages—Anjali—she told me she'd heard about a . . ." It sounded so unlikely. Could I really tell Mr. Mauskopf? Wouldn't he think I was an idiot to believe it?

"A what?"

Well, I'd started—no stopping now. "An enormous bird. It's supposed to be following people around and stealing things."

To my surprise, Mr. Mauskopf nodded gravely. "Yes, I've heard that too. Have you seen this bird?"

"No . . ."

"Did the page who told you about the bird see it? Anjali was her name, right?"

"She said she didn't."

"Hm. And have you seen or heard anything else that concerns you?"

"Well . . . I heard that there was a page who got fired."

Mr. Mauskopf paused, as if trying to decide how much to say. "That's right. Dr. Rust had to fire one of the pages. She tried to take a vase without signing for it or leaving a deposit. But that's not all. Apparently, some more objects have disappeared since Zandra was let go, and I've heard of objects similar to the ones in the repository turning up in private collections."

"Do they think another page is still stealing stuff?" This was alarming. "Or is it the bird, like Anjali said?"

"Nobody is quite sure what is happening. I have trouble believing that a gigantic bird, even if it exists, could get into the repository on its own and steal things. There must be people involved. So keep your eyes open for anything suspicious, and if anybody approaches you and asks you to remove any items outside of proper channels or even if you just get an uncomfortable feeling, please come to me or Lee Rust right away. Okay?"

"Okay," I said. I had an uncomfortable feeling right now about the whole thing, in fact, but I didn't think that was what he meant.

"Thank you, Elizabeth." He turned to go.

"Hey, wait a minute, Mr. Mauskopf. Can I ask you a question?"

"Certainly. As the Akan proverb says, always ask questions."

"Why are you and the librarians always quoting Akan proverbs, anyway?"

"Oh, that. It's sort of a private joke. One of the pages when I worked there was descended from the Akan people—your friend Marc Merritt's uncle, in fact. He liked to quote the proverbs, and the rest of us picked up the habit. I've always thought the proverbs chimed nicely with the Grimm stories. Was that your question?"

"No, but it's connected—to the Grimm stories, at least.

What is the Grimm Collection? Does it have anything to do with the Grimm fairy tales?"

"The Grimm Collection! Did one of the librarians tell you about that?"

"I overheard one of the pages talking about it with Ms. Callender, and then everybody got all weird when I asked about it."

"Ah. Well, then I'd better let Dr. Rust explain. Don't worry, if you do a good job at the repository, you'll learn about all that soon enough. I have every confidence . . . Griffin, stop! Griffin! I'm sorry, Elizabeth, I . . . must run . . ." Mr. Mauskopf crashed through the snow after the big dog, who was urgently pursuing some important matter.

The following Tuesday, I planned to leave school as quickly as possible, hoping to get to the repository and see Dr. Rust before my shift started. But I passed the gym on my way out and paused to watch the basketball team practicing. The coach was making Marc do defensive drills with three of the guys.

Marc looked as if there were wings on his feet, he moved so lightly and stayed aloft so long. He even smiled at me from mid-air before he turned to snatch the ball out from under Jamal Carter's nose, making my heart jump too. I smiled back, but he was no longer looking at me.

When I got outside, it was snowing hard, flakes creeping under my coat collar where the top button was still missing. I really needed to sew on the new one, but I wasn't that good at sewing. I put my head down, turning it as little as possible to keep from exposing my neck as I hurried to the library. I shouldered the heavy door open. Through my steamy glasses I saw Anjali behind the circulation desk again. She waved me upstairs.

Marc was at the time clock, punching in ahead of me.

"Hey, Marc. Didn't I just pass you in the gym? How'd you get here so quickly?" I asked, sticking my card in the clock to be chomped.

"I walk fast."

"That fast? You hadn't even finished basketball practice."

"Long legs," he said dismissively, heading for the stairs.

Was I prying? Had I annoyed him? I put my card back in the rack, kicking myself.

Ms. Callender sent me down to Stack 2. "It's going to be a slow night with this weather," she said. "You might as well sweep the shelves."

"Okay—is there a broom down there, or a brush or something?"

She laughed, her cheeks bunching up into balls. "It's not that kind of sweeping. Ask a page to show you. Marc or Aaron. Gumdrop?"

"What?" Was this a new endearment—had she gotten tired of "honey"?

"Gumdrop?" She held out a bag.

"Oh, thanks." I took a green one and rode the elevator down, chewing.

When I got to Stack 2, Aaron was at his usual desk, reading; Marc was nowhere in sight.

"Hi, Aaron. Where's Marc?"

"Downstairs, why?"

"Ms. Callender said one of you should show me how to sweep the shelves."

Aaron looked irritated. "And you'd prefer Merritt, is that it?"

"No, I just—he came down the stairs ahead of me; I thought he'd be here."

"Great. Another member of the Marc Merritt fan club."

"No . . . well, of course I think he's cool and all, but I'm not actually in the fan club," I said.

Aaron gave me a look that, in other lighting, would probably have suggested that he couldn't believe he was stuck on Stack 2 with such an idiot. Under the desk lamp's dramatic highlights and shadows, though, it suggested that he was an ogre about to eat me.

"I mean," I explained, "most of the kids in the fan club are a lot younger."

The highlights and shadows shifted. Now he looked like an ogre who was going to choke up the idiot he had eaten.

"Some of their little sisters are in it too," I said.

"You can't be serious! You mean there's an actual Marc Merritt fan club?" he said.

I was starting to get irritated myself. "Of course there is. I'm sure you could join, since you take such an interest. All those girls would probably enjoy having an older guy around, even if it's just you."

Aaron stood up and said coldly, "Sweeping the shelves means making sure there's nothing out of place. Check the labels and look for gaps between items or for anything that doesn't belong where it is. Make a note of any anomalies you find. You start on that end and I'll start on this." He strode off into the darkness.

• • •

I spent a painstaking hour examining shoes, rows and rows of them, enough to keep every homeless toe in the city toasty. Did you know that in seventeenth-century France shoes were one-shape-fits-both-left-and-right? Or that ancient Egyptians gave their mummies shoes made of papyrus and palm leaves? Or that in fourteenth-century Poland, shoe toes grew so long and pointy that fashionable gentlemen looked like they were wearing snakes on their feet?

I didn't find anything out of place in the shoe section. There was a gap where a patron had borrowed a pair of size 12-D pumps, but I found a call slip for it on file.

Checking a row of platform shoes from Renaissance Venice, I turned the corner and was surprised to find Marc Merritt with a pair of brown work boots in his hand.

"Oh, so you *are* working on this stack today?" I said.

"No, I'm down in the Dungeon," he said.

"What's the Dungeon?"

"Stack 1."

"So what are you doing up here, then?"

"Returning these."

"Oh, okay. Want me to file your call slip?"

"No, I . . . I didn't fill one out. I just borrowed them for a little while—my shoes got wet and my feet were cold. I figured nobody would notice they were gone. Don't tell, okay?"

"Sure." I wondered whether this was one of those suspicious requests Mr. Mauskopf wanted me to look out for. Surely not—after all, Mr. Mauskopf knew Marc himself and had recommended him for the job. He'd even said he was friends with Marc's uncle.

If anything suspicious was going on with Marc, he would surely know more about it than I would. Besides, this was *Marc Merritt,* asking *me* for a favor! How could I refuse?

"Thanks, Elizabeth." Marc hurried off.

A few cabinets later I found a terrible jumble in a section of leggings and chaps. I started to sort them out, but I couldn't figure out the documentation, so I bit back my pride and asked Aaron.

"Wow, this is pretty bad," he said. "It looks like my brother's room when he can't find his sneakers. Let's take this mess up front and sort it out where there's better light." He piled the tangle of garments on a hand truck and pushed it to the work area by the dumbwaiters.

"Try to find labels for these things," he said. "I'm going to see who took these out last." He started flipping through cards in the circulation file. He snorted. "Thought so!"

"What?" I asked.

"The last request for II T&G 391.4636 B37 was run by MM—Marc Merritt. Same with II T&G 391.413 A44."

"That doesn't mean he put them back wrong," I pointed out. "They could have been returned weeks later."

"Well, they weren't. They were returned the same day."

"Does it say who reshelved them?"

"No, we don't record that."

"Then why do you assume it was Marc?"

"Why do you assume it wasn't? He was on this stack that day."

"Somebody else could have been with him."

"Could have been. There's no evidence they were, though."

"There's no evidence they weren't, either. And somebody could have scrambled the stuff later too. Who knows when it happened? Maybe it was that page who got fired."

"The evidence points where the evidence points."

"What do you have against Marc?"

"I don't have anything against him personally. I just don't get why everybody melts around him just because he's a basketball star. It's like you think he can't do any wrong. You ignore all the squirrelly stuff he does." Aaron was clearly getting upset.

Well, so was I. "What squirrelly stuff? And who's everybody? You mean Anjali?"

"No, I mean everybody! You girls are the worst, but the librarians are almost as bad. I don't like the way he's always sneaking around the Grimm Collection."

"No?" I asked. "So what's in the Grimm Collection?"

Aaron looked even more upset. "Forget I said that!" he snapped. "I should have kept my mouth shut. I'm taking my break now. Leave this stuff. I'll get a librarian to come check it out." He stalked off through the fire door.

I thought about what he'd said. In fact, the business with Marc and the boots *had* been kind of squirrelly. And if Marc had been careless about filling out a call slip for the boots, couldn't he have been careless about reshelving the leggings and chaps too?

On the other hand, he'd brought the borrowed boots back right away, which was pretty responsible of him. Probably this was all about Aaron's jealousy.

That was understandable. I would be jealous too if I were a guy.

But what was this Grimm Collection, and why was it making Aaron so upset?

The stack door opened and an unfamiliar librarian came in. She was tall and skinny, with glasses and hair in a bun; she looked like a stereotype of a librarian. She was the first one I'd ever seen who looked like that.

"Elizabeth, right? I'm Lucy Minnian," she said. "Aaron tells me you have a mess to sort out."

"Yes, I was sweeping the shelves and I found all this."

She poked at the tangle, then whistled under her breath. "I'd better send Lee down," she said. She went out.

After a while, Dr. Rust came in. "What's the trouble here?"

"I found all this stuff misshelved."

"Hm . . . looks like the work of that Zandra Blair. She left a trail of chaos wherever she went. It took us a while to figure out she was the one doing it—she was great at shifting the blame. I'm glad to have seen the last of her! Let's see, were there any labels with these?"

"Not that I could find."

Dr. Rust began sorting through the chaps, separating the tangled straps. "I wish we could use something more up-to-date, like radio tags. Then we wouldn't lose things on the shelves for years when they get misshelved."

"Why don't you, then?" I asked. "Too expensive?"

"No, we could probably find the funds for it. But the board of governors is conservative about technology—they call it 'modern magic.'"

"What's wrong with that? Modern magic sounds good to me."

"Me too. But they prefer the old kind." Dr. Rust held a pair of leather leggings up to one ear with a hand, as if listening for a secret, then scribbled something on a white tag and tied it to a buckle. I looked carefully to see if I could catch the freckles moving, but it was too dark to make them out.

Dr. Rust seemed to listen to another pair of chaps, gave it a shake, and listened again.

"So, Dr. Rust, can I ask you a qu—," I began, but stopped. I knew what the answer would be.

"Of course. Always ask qu's."

"What's the Grimm Collection?"

Dr. Rust put down the last garment and looked at me seriously for a long time, then said at last, "Stan Mauskopf has never sent us a bad page."

Was that supposed to be an answer? "I really appreciate his good opinion. I'll do everything I can to live up to it," I said.

"I'm sure you will. Yes, I really do think you will." Dr. Rust took a deep breath. "The Grimm Collection is one of the Special Collections on Stack 1—probably the most special of the Special Collections. The original holdings came to the library in 1892 as a legacy from Friedhilde Hassenpflug, a grandniece of Jacob and Wilhelm Grimm."

"I know who they are. I just wrote a paper about the Brothers Grimm for Mr. Mauskopf."

"Of course. So you know about their collections of *märchen*— folk tales or fairy tales. But stories weren't the only thing they collected. They also assembled a remarkable group of objects."

"Oh, that's cool! I knew the Brothers Grimm were historians, but I hadn't heard they were interested in the history of—of objects, of *stuff* too."

Dr. Rust nodded. "Yes, it's called material culture. The study of how physical objects relate to society and history. It's relatively new as an academic discipline, but in a sense it's always been central to our mission at the repository. It didn't exist per se at the time of the Grimms—they were visionaries in so many ways. We're very fortunate to have the privilege of caring for their collection."

"What kind of objects did they collect?"

"Things mentioned in the *märchen*."

"What do you mean, like Cinderella's slippers?"

"Something like that." Did I detect a trace of longing in Dr. Rust's voice? "We don't have Cinderella's actual slippers, but that's the idea."

I was relieved to hear Dr. Rust wasn't crazy enough to claim they had Cinderella's actual slippers. That would be going a little too far. "What *do* you have, then?" I asked.

"Oh, spindles and straw and beans and tears. A glass coffin. A golden egg. A number of things. The Grimms were serious and thorough collectors, and of course we've added to the collection a great deal over the years, objects associated with other fairy-tale and folklore traditions. I'm especially proud of our French holdings—we have the best collection outside the Archives Extraordinaires in Paris. And there's some important material related to the *Arabian Nights* in the Grimm Collection too."

"I would love to see that."

"One of these days, perhaps. We like to get to know our

pages for a while before we let them work with the Special Collections. Some of those objects are quite . . . powerful."

If these were really the objects that inspired the famous fairy tales, then *powerful* was a good word, I thought. I tried to imagine what it would feel like to touch the spindle that inspired the story of Sleeping Beauty. When I was six, my mother took me to see Tchaikovsky's *Sleeping Beauty* at Lincoln Center—that's when I fell in love with ballet and fairy tales. How I wished my mother were still alive! I would love to see the look on her face when I told her about the collection.

If only I'd known about the collection when I was writing my paper for Mr. Mauskopf's class! I wondered what he thought about all this. I hoped I would get to see the collection soon. I would have to work hard and show Doc and the others that I was trustworthy.

"Well, that sounds amazing. I would love to work down there," I said.

"Patience," said Dr. Rust. "In the words of the Akan proverb, 'One eats an elephant one bite at a time.'"

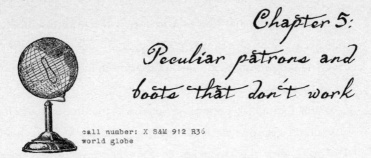

## Chapter 5:
## Peculiar patrons and
## boots that don't work

I got my first paycheck two weeks later—enough to replace my sneakers and even a few clothes I'd missed after Hannah left for college. I was working three shifts a week, two after school and one on Saturday.

I spent the next few shifts on Stack 5 (V T: Tools), Stack 4 (IV M: Music), and Stack 7 (VII FA: Fine Arts). It was fun to roll out the racks of paintings and see the mosaic of styles side by side. Cubist portraits rubbed elbows with sentimental domestic scenes and heroic landscapes. The sculpture was very heavy, which made it harder to deal with. Fortunately, Ms. Callender assigned us to the stacks in pairs, so there was always someone to help me, usually Marc or a quiet, burly guy named Josh.

After a few weeks at the repository, I found myself looking at everything differently—ordinary things, like chairs and windows and hot dog stands. I noticed their shapes; I noticed what they were made of. I noticed how they worked. I noticed the different doors in my neighborhood, the carved oak doors on the brownstones and the lacy iron gates on the apartment buildings and the graffitied metal gates on the shops. Objects would remind me suddenly of other objects, often ones in the collection: the fountain in front of the Plaza Hotel was like an egg cup on Stack 9, my father's bicycle helmet had the same built-for-speed curves as a record player on Stack 4. I felt as if I had new eyes. My father himself still hadn't found time to come visit. His loss, I told myself.

After I caught a potentially serious error on Stack 9—Josh was about to misshelve a lead-smelting cauldron from Stack 5 (V T: Tools) with the saucepans in the kitchenwares section on Stack 9 (IX HG: Household Goods)—Ms. Callender decided I was ready for the Main Examination Room, the MER.

My first shift there was on a cold, bright Saturday. I'd never been in the MER on a sunny day. When I opened the door from the dim hallway, I could hardly believe I was in the same building, or any building at all. Sunlight poured in all around me, filtered through leaves and blossoms and bare tree branches. It sparkled off streams and waterfalls and snowdrifts. It gleamed on wet rocks and the wings of blackbirds.

After a moment, I realized what I was looking at: not an enchanted grove, but the famous Tiffany windows. All four sides of the MER were paneled with forest scenes. To the north was winter, with frost-rimed rocks and black branches against a bright sky. To the east, spring: crocuses, the barest glimmer of green, blossoming trees dropping petals that seemed to twist and float. To the south, summer: layer upon layer of green, with birds peeking out here and there and a pair of deer stooping to drink from the mossy stream. And to the west, fall in all its blazing yellows and reds. It was the most beautiful thing I'd ever seen.

After a minute I noticed Ms. Callender beckoning from the center of the room, where the dumbwaiters and pneumatic tubes came together behind the magnificent carved wood partition.

She smiled at my expression. "Pretty, aren't they? I love it up here. Tiffany really knew what he was doing," she said.

"It's gorgeous." I thought of my father again. His loss, that was for sure!

"Well, let's get you to work. You can sit at the desk today to get the hang of things. You'll be giving the patrons their items when the pages send them from the various stacks. And every half hour, you'll do a collection round—take the cart through the room and pick up any items the patrons are done with."

I expected a library hush in the MER, but it was fairly noisy, especially in the carved staging cage where we three pages were working. The radiators hissed like lovesick lizards, the dumbwaiters chimed when they arrived, and the pneums came thumping and banging into their baskets like baby meteorites, while all around us the windows shimmered and glowed. I kept staring at them and losing track of my work.

Sarah, a plump blond page, sat on a swivel stool by a long, knotted row of pneumatic pipes, at least a dozen of them. Whenever a pneum fell into the basket at her elbow, she would pop it into one of the pipes, scooting up and down the row on her wheeled stool to find the right pipe—each one led to a different stack. She worked so fast it made me dizzy to watch her. I was glad I didn't have her job.

It was fascinating to see the patrons in person. I remembered some of their names from the call slips I'd run in the stacks downstairs. They all wore white cotton gloves, which made them look strangely formal.

The man from Dark on Monday Productions came to claim another doublet. He was shorter than I'd imagined.

In the back of the room, under the winter windows, a couple of homeless-looking people had settled in. One of them had half a dozen shopping bags and was dozing, head down at the table.

"Is sleeping allowed?" I asked Ms. Callender.

She glanced over. "It's fine—that's just Grace Farr. Sometimes people come in to get warm in the winter. You can let them sleep unless they're snoring and bothering the other patrons. If you have any trouble, ask Anjali for help—or send me a pneum. I'll be downstairs on Stack 6. But you won't have trouble with Grace. She's a friend."

"That's good," I said. I was glad they had a place to get warm.

After half an hour, Anjali sent me out with a cart to collect the items the patrons had finished with. The rumbling woke the sleeping patron—Grace Farr—as I went past her. She looked up at me and I recognized her pale gray eyes. She was the woman with the shopping cart, the one I'd given my sneakers to! "Hello," I said, startled.

"Hello again." She winked. Then she put her head back down on the table, and I continued my rounds.

My favorite patrons were a pair of elderly men in threadbare but well-pressed suits. They requested a magnificent eighteenth-century Russian chess set, carved from walrus ivory, and took it to a corner table under the autumn windows, where they spent the rest of my shift playing an intense game.

One patron, a short man with a neatly cropped beard, was doing some sort of work with globes. He requested half a dozen and lined them up in the middle of one of the long tables under a lamp, where he twirled them this way and that, peering at the continents through a magnifying glass and taking notes. He seemed at home in the MER. He would stop to exchange a word or two with the chess players on his way to retrieve a new globe. He kept looking over at Anjali.

"What's with the globes? Is that guy a cartographer?" I asked her.

"He's an antiques dealer. He kind of gives me the creeps, the way he's always staring at me."

"Yeah, I noticed that too. Creepy. What's he doing with the globes?"

"Probably trying to figure out whether some antique globe he's trying to sell is real, or where it's from, or what to charge for it," Anjali said.

The man kept looking over in our direction with a little thoughtful frown. Not quite like he was admiring Anjali the way guys so often did—more like he was evaluating a painting he was thinking about buying.

After I'd been working for an hour or so, a patron came to pick up a pair of boots that looked a lot like the ones Marc had borrowed the day his feet got wet. In fact, they looked so similar I thought they must be the same ones. I checked the call number, expecting it to be from Stack 2, Textiles and Garb, but it started with I ★GC, a designation I hadn't seen before.

Soon the patron brought them back. "Excuse me—you gave me the wrong boots."

I checked the label, which was tied to the laces: I ★GC

391.413 S94. "No," I said. "The label matches the call number on your call slip."

"Well, they must be mislabeled. They don't work."

"What do you mean they don't work?" I said. "You mean they don't fit?"

"They fit fine, they just don't *work*."

"How can boots not work?"

He peered at me. "I think I'd better speak to a librarian. Could you get me your supervisor, please?"

"Okay." I took the boots over to Anjali. "Where do they keep the phone around here?" I asked her. "I need Ms. Callender."

"Ask Sarah to send her a pneum. Why, what's up?"

"Some patron's insisting these boots were mislabeled. It's weird. He says they don't work."

"What? Show me." Anjali sounded alarmed. I handed her the boots. "Oh, let's not bother Ms. Callender about this," she said hurriedly. "You can handle things without me for a few minutes, can't you? I'll be right back." She went to the window and spoke to the patron, then hurried out.

I had a hard time keeping up with the arriving objects. One dumbwaiter would ping while I was taking something out of another, then the third would chime and open. Things kept piling up as I ran back and forth between the dumbwaiters and the desk. I wondered how Anjali had managed it all so gracefully.

A line formed at the window, and the patrons started murmuring, a soft but threatening noise. The little man with the beard frowned at me when I let one of the globes slip and hit the base against the desk. I was relieved when Anjali came back with a pair of boots in her hand.

"Good, you're back—I was starting to panic. Are those the right boots?"

"Yes, they were misshelved."

"So that's a different pair?" They looked the same to me.

She nodded and beckoned to the boot patron, who took the new boots and sniffed at them.

After a muttered conversation with Anjali that I couldn't hear over the conveyor belt, he left with the boots, apparently satisfied.

"Everything cool?" I asked Anjali.

"Yes, it's fine now," she said. "You don't need to bother Ms. Callender about it. I straightened it out."

"Okay," I said.

When Ms. Callender came in with Marc, Anjali looked momentarily worried, but she relaxed when he smiled at her reassuringly.

Ms. Callender consulted her clipboard. "Marc, you're on dumbwaiters. Sarah, man the window, okay, hon? And Anjali, would you mind showing Elizabeth how to handle the tubes? I'll be on 6 if you run into any difficulties."

Anjali pointed me to the stool where Sarah had been sitting. She pulled up another wheeled stool in front of the tangle of tubes, where the pneums were hammering down.

"We're basically operating a switchboard," she told me. "All the pneum stations all over the building have a tube that leads here to us. A few of them are connected directly to each other, but most of them aren't, so if someone wants to send a pneum from Stack 4, say, to Stack 7, it has to go through us."

"That sounds like a lot of work," I said.

"It is. We have to send them on quickly or the whole system backs up, and it's easy to make a mistake. But don't worry too much—if you send a pneum to the wrong stack, they'll just send it back here."

The job was exhausting yet exhilarating, like a video game. I had a thousand rules to remember. Anything in a red pneum went to Stack 6, where the librarians had their offices. Blue pneums went straight to Dr. Rust. Pneums carrying call slips went to the appropriate stack. I had to memorize which stack held which collection. Tools were on Stack 5, household items on 9, fungibles on 8.

"What on earth is a fungible?" I asked Anjali.

"Something that needs a lot of replacing."

"You mean things like lightbulbs and paper towels?"

"No, that's ephemera, on Stack 3. Well, the paper towels are. Lightbulbs are in various places. Some are on 5, Tools and Scientific Instruments; some are on 9, Household Goods."

"Oh, okay. But what are fungibles?"

"Plants and animals."

"What? You're kidding! Is this like a zoo or something? Can people check out, like, a giraffe?"

"I doubt it," said Anjali with a grin. "I don't think we have any giraffes in the collection. If we did, they'd be in the annex anyway."

"What's the annex?"

"Off-site oversize storage. Those are call slips that start with ★A. Like, here's one—oops, no, that's a ★V."

"What's a ★V?"

"Valuable items. They're kept on the same stack as the rest of the things in their category. Pages aren't allowed to run those slips. Only librarians have the keys, so send ★V call slips to Stack 6."

"Oh, right—like Marie Antoinette's wig?" I asked. "Ms. Callender showed me, in a locked room on Stack 2."

"Exactly."

I routed a request for a teapot to Stack 9, one for a guitar to Stack 4, and three for hats to Stack 2.

It took me a while to get the hang of the tubes themselves. I kept snapping the doors on my thumb. Eventually, though, I fell into a sort of meditative rhythm. My hands flew peacefully from basket to tube. The hiss and clatter and creak of the machines began to feel like forest sounds: the rush of a waterfall, the rustle of leaves, the chatter of squirrels. Out of the corners of my eyes, I seemed to see things moving in the stained-glass windows— birds, branches, water—though I knew that was impossible.

A call slip beginning ★WB landed in the basket. "What's ★WB?" I asked Anjali.

"That's the Wells Bequest—next door to the Grimm Collection. Send it down to the Dungeon—Stack 1."

The Dungeon again. That was obviously where they kept the most interesting stuff. "What's in the Wells Bequest?" I asked.

Anjali took a deep breath and looked sideways. I could tell she was preparing to not answer my question, so I said quickly, "Dr. Rust told me the Grimm Collection is full of things the Brothers Grimm found when they were collecting fairy tales." I hoped Anjali would take that as permission to talk. "Is the Wells Bequest more fairy-tale stuff?"

It worked. "Sort of—it's science fiction," she said. "It's named after H. G. Wells, who wrote *The Time Machine*."

"Oh—so what's in the bequest? Is there, like, a time machine?" I joked.

Marc overheard me. He glared at Anjali from the desk. She got cagey.

"It's hard to say. I don't know anybody who's tried it," she said.

"Tried what?"

"The time machine."

"So there *is* a time machine?" That was crazy. "What else is in there?" I asked.

"Oh, I don't know, lots of things. That's really Aaron's department. You should ask him about it if you're interested. He's kind of a science-fiction expert."

Like Aaron would tell me anything! "Okay, but what's the collection all about? Is it stuff that inspired famous science-fiction books?"

"Yes, exactly! That kind of thing."

"Why's it called the Wells Bequest? Did the objects used to belong to H. G. Wells?"

"A few of them, but there are other things too."

"Like what?"

"Shrink rays and miniature rockets and so forth."

That had to be a joke. "Do they work?" I asked, playing along.

"Well, the rockets work. It's not hard to make a miniature rocket. I made one myself last year, for the science fair."

"What about the shrink rays?"

"What do *you* think?"

"What else is down there?"

"Where, the Dungeon? Well, there's the Garden of Seasons. And the Gibson Chrestomathy and the Lovecraft Corpus. They're both fairly recent additions."

Marc came over to our station. "You're telling her about that?" he said to Anjali. He sounded alarmed.

"It's okay, Merritt—Doc already told her about the Grimm Collection."

"Did she get her key yet?"

Anjali raised her eyebrows at me inquiringly.

"What key?" I asked.

"Anjali!" said Marc.

"It's okay," said Anjali. "She's one of the good ones. I have a sense for these things—I recognized *you,* didn't I?"

"If you say so," said Marc dubiously.

"What key?" I asked again.

"You'll find out soon enough, if Anjali's right," said Marc.

"So what's in the Gibson Crestothingy and the Lovecraft Corpus? And the Garden of Seasons?" I asked.

"The Gibson Chrestomathy is mostly software and computer technology," said Anjali.

"Really? I thought all that was on Stack 5, Tools."

"Most of it is. They keep the . . . special stuff downstairs."

"What kinds of things are in the Gibson thingy, then?"

"The Chrestomathy? Artificial intelligence, interesting computer viruses, that kind of thing."

"And the Garden of Seasons?"

"I'm not sure," said Marc. "I've never been in there. It's supposed to be as amazing as the Tiffany windows."

I made a mental note to check out the garden if I ever could. "And what about the Lovecraft Corpus, what's that?" I asked.

"Don't talk about that! You shouldn't even be thinking about it," Marc said. "Anjali shouldn't have mentioned it. Don't go down there."

"Why? What's in it?"

"I'm serious. Stay out of the Lovecraft Corpus! That place is bad news."

I really had to get down to the Dungeon soon, I decided. Even if Anjali and Marc were pulling my leg about some of these things, it sounded like all the really fascinating—and maybe dangerous—stuff was in the Special Collections, and I wanted to see it.

The next Saturday, Ms. Callender sent me down to Stack 2 with a hand truck of returns from the City Opera costume department. I had spent an hour packing sequined gowns in muslin dust bags and telling myself that at least it was more glamorous than putting away my own laundry, when a high, insistent voice interrupted me. I looked up and saw a little boy.

He looked like somebody, for a joke, had made an exact copy of Marc Merritt in miniature. He was dressed just like Marc, in jeans, a hooded sweatshirt, and bright white sneakers. He had the same big brown eyes and the same long, curly eyelashes. His cheeks were rounder, his skin a deeper brown, and his arms and legs proportionally shorter, but he had the same firm chin and the same determined frown.

"I gotta go," he said.

"Go where? Where'd you come from?" I asked.

A crazy thought crossed my mind. Maybe there really was a shrink ray in the Wells Bequest, and Marc had gotten caught in it. Maybe this *was* Marc.

"I gotta *go*," said mini-Marc again. "Gonna have a accident." He danced back and forth from one foot to the other.

"Oh! You mean the bathroom?"

He nodded vigorously.

"Okay, hang in there. This way." If finger acid was bad for the collection, I could only imagine what urine would do to it. I hurried him down the hall to the ladies' room.

Unfortunately, there was an icon of a person in a triangular skirt on the door. "That's the *girls'* room," he objected.

"Yeah, but I can't take you into the boys' room—I'm a girl. It's okay; they have toilets in here too. Come on." I held the door open.

He hesitated, then followed me in.

"You want me to help you?" I asked. He nodded. Feeling ridiculous for even entertaining the thought, I really, really hoped this wasn't Marc. How embarrassing would that be?

Of course, a shrink ray might make a guy smaller, but it wouldn't turn him into a three-year-old. I found that comforting at first, until it occurred to me that a time machine might.

Don't be silly, I told myself.

"All done," said mini-Marc.

I buttoned him up. "Let's wash your hands," I said, lifting him up so he could reach the faucet. Then he wanted to use the hand dryer for longer than seemed entirely necessary.

"Come on, buddy, I've got to get back to work, and your mom's going to wonder what happened to you," I told him.

He reluctantly let me lead him out into the hall. Once there, he started charging down it. I ran to catch up. "Hey! Where are you going?"

"I gotta find my butter."

"Okay, kid, hold your horses. Where's your mom? Maybe we should take you to Ms. Callender."

"I gotta find my *butter*! Butter! Butter!"

"Hey, calm down, sweetie. What is it? Are you hungry?" I knelt and took him by the shoulders. He shook me off and started stomping his feet.

"Where's my butter? I want my butter!"

"Andre? Andre, where are you?" Marc Merritt appeared as if by magic at the end of the hall. He was full size. I felt a wave of embarrassment for having imagined that he'd been tampered with by a shrink ray.

The kid—Andre—ran to him, his little feet thudding like pneums, and threw himself against Marc's legs, crying, "Butter!"

Marc knelt down and hugged him. "Brother yourself! Where'd you go to? Didn't I tell you to stay put? You scared me! Don't ever do that, okay?"

"Sorry, Butter. I hadda *go*," explained Andre. "The girl taked me."

Marc looked up as if noticing me for the first time. The look was not altogether friendly. He often looked arrogant, but this time I felt as if he was accusing me of something.

"I took him to the bathroom," I said. "He said he was going to have an accident. So he's your brother?"

"Yeah. Yeah, that's Andre. Thanks," he said, thawing a little. "Say thank you to Elizabeth, Andre."

"Thank you, Libbet," said Andre.

"Did you wash your hands?" asked Marc.

"Yeah, I like the wind thing. It goes *fffffffffff, fffffffffff, fffffffffff*. It's the girls' room. They have toilets there too."

Marc swung him to his shoulder as lightly as if he were lifting a kitten, not a solidly built three-year-old. "Okay, bro, let's get you to day care. Say bye to Elizabeth."

"Bye-bye, Libbet," said Andre, waving at me.

"Bye, Andre."

"Thanks, Elizabeth," said Marc, more warmly this time. "Thanks for taking care of him. Sorry for the trouble."

It felt good to have Marc Merritt thanking me. I watched as he carried Andre off down the hallway.

I noticed he was wearing the brown work boots again. Were they his? I found myself wondering. Or were they the mysteriously misshelved ones? Stop it, I told myself. If I wanted to make friends, I needed to be more trusting.

I finished putting away the opera gowns and trundled my hand truck back to the staging area. Aaron was sitting at his usual desk. He was mending something under a bright lamp, which cast the usual sharp shadows across his cheekbones.

"Anjali?" he said, looking up.

"No, just Elizabeth," I answered, slightly testily.

His face fell. "Oh. Hi, Elizabeth." I could hear the disappointment in his voice. How flattering.

"What are you doing?" I asked.

"I'm darning a sock," he said, holding it up to show me.

"What's that lump inside it?"

"A sock egg."

"A sock egg? I didn't know socks hatched from eggs."

"Only the best ones do. I can't wear the cheap kind, the ones that grow on trees. They give me blisters."

"Riiiiight, okay. Is that from the Grimm Collection?" I asked.

"Of course not. It's just an ordinary sock egg," he said shortly.

"I meant the sock."

"Why would it be? And why do you keep asking about the Grimm Collection?"

"Because it makes you mad, and you look so funny when you snarl," I said. "Is it? The sock, I mean. From the Grimm Collection."

"No, it's from my sock drawer. It got a hole. My toe was poking through—it was very uncomfortable."

"Oh." I was kind of impressed, despite myself. How many guys would bother to sew up a hole in their sock? "Seriously, what's a sock egg?" I asked.

He reached into the sock and pulled it out. It looked like an ordinary chicken's egg made of wood. "You put it in the sock to stretch it out where the hole is so you can sew it up more evenly," he said.

"I see," I said. "That's kind of a clever idea. I wonder who thought of it. Do you think the first sock eggs were real eggs?"

"No way. Too fragile. That would be pretty gross, if you broke an egg in your sock."

"So what do you think the first ones were?"

He shrugged. "Round stones, probably. If you're really curious, you could take a look at the egg collection."

"The Egg Collection? Is that like the Grimm Collection?"

He snorted. "Of course not. I just meant the various eggs in the repository."

"There are eggs here?"

"Sure, lots of different kinds."

"Hard boiled? Over easy?"

"Ukrainian Easter eggs. China eggs for tricking hens into laying. Ostrich eggs with scenes painted on them. Even a few fossilized dinosaur eggs."

"Wow, what do those look like?"

"Big and round."

"Could you use them to darn socks?"

"If you had giant feet." He looked at my feet and grinned.

I'm a little sensitive about the size of my feet, and I felt myself begin to blush.

To cover my embarrassment, I said, "How do you know they're dinosaur eggs and not giant eggs from the giant bird?"

"What giant bird?" Aaron sounded alarmed.

"The one that's supposedly following people around and stealing their objects."

His eyes narrowed with suspicion. "Who told you about that? Marc?"

"No, Anjali."

"Oh. Well, she shouldn't be talking about that. And you certainly shouldn't be joking about it!"

"Why not? Do you honestly believe there's a giant bird stealing things?"

"Maybe. But it's nothing to joke about, anyway."

"Elizabeth?" said someone behind me. This time it *was* Anjali.

"Anjali!" Aaron said again, his voice full of pleasure like a kid who hears the ice-cream truck. He hadn't sounded like that when he was talking to *me*. I decided I hated him.

"Hi, Aaron, mind if I borrow Elizabeth for a minute?" Anjali asked.

"What do you need her for? Maybe I could help you instead," said Aaron hopefully.

"It's girl stuff," said Anjali. She drew me into a dark corner near the ★V room. "I need your help with something . . . personal," she said.

"Of course! What is it?"

"It's those boots again. I need you to help me get them downstairs to the GC before someone requests them. Ms. Minnian is expecting me up on Stack 6 right now. She sent me down here to pick up that hand truck."

"Okay," I said, though I didn't understand why Anjali couldn't just put the boots on the return truck with the rest of the stuff for reshelving. "Wouldn't it be better to have Aaron do it, though? He knows his way around the Dungeon, and he's obviously dying to help you."

"No—don't tell him! He'd decide it was his duty to tell a librarian. He hates Merritt, for some reason. You'll keep it a secret, won't you? Promise?" She sounded terribly alarmed.

"Of course," I said. I didn't exactly see what Marc had to do with it, but returning the boots didn't seem like such a big deal to me. After all, putting something back in the right place wasn't like stealing it. Besides, I was flattered that Anjali wanted me to help her—and even more flattered that she trusted me to keep her secret.

"Thank you, Elizabeth! I really owe you." She handed me a plastic shopping bag. I peeked in and saw the familiar boots. "Take these down to Stack 1," she continued. "They go in the Grimm Collection, I ★GC 391.413 S94. Can you remember that? Here, I'll write it down. There's another pair that look just like them where these are supposed to go. Switch the boots and bring the other pair up here, Stack 2. They go in that aisle with the rest of the boots, call number II T&G 391.413 S23, like it says on this tag. Remember to switch the tags too."

"Okay. So I can just walk into the Grimm Collection? It's not locked?"

"No, you need a key. A key and a password."

"Is that the key you were talking about in the MER? The one I don't have yet?"

"Yes, the Grimm Collection key. It's irreplaceable, and I'm not supposed to give it to anyone. You'll take really good care of it, won't you?"

"I promise."

"Then here."

Anjali took a barrette out of her hair and handed it to me.

"What's this for?"

"That's the key."

"This is a key?" I turned it over. It still looked like a barrette.

"It's . . . disguised. For security. When you get to the Grimm Collection, hold it against the door and sing this:

> *Out is out and shut is shut,*
> *Turn the key and crack the nut.*
> *Push the door and break the shell:*
> *Let me in and all is well."*

Anjali had a sweet, high singing voice.

"What's that, some kind of voice recognition thing?" I asked.

"Something like that. Sing it back so I know you know it. You have to get the tune right."

"Maybe you'd better write it down, so I don't forget," I said.

She scribbled hastily. "Don't lose this! I could get in big trouble if the wrong person finds it."

I sang the rhyme until I got it right, feeling pretty silly. No surprise Mr. Theodorus never picked me to do solos in chorus. "Will the door know my voice?" I asked.

"It responds to the words and the tune, not the voice. It only works when you have the key, though."

"Anjali," called Aaron from the front of the stack.

"Boy, that's some sophisticated security! How does it work?" I asked.

"Anjali!" called Aaron again. "You still back there?"

"Just a moment, I'll be right there!" she yelled back. She looked worried and impatient. "I can't explain now," she told me. "Listen, though, this is important. Don't touch anything! That stuff looks harmless, but a lot of it's seriously dangerous."

"I'll be careful," I promised.

"Good. Now hurry. But don't get caught! If you do, blame me—say I told you Doc wanted you to do it. I'll back you up, and there's a chance they'll believe us. But please, don't get caught."

"Anjali?" Aaron loomed toward us through the gloom. "Ms. Minnian needs that hand truck. I can help you bring it up if you want."

"I'm coming," she said. "Thanks a million, Elizabeth, I owe you," she whispered, and followed Aaron down the hallway.

Then I was left alone with the mysterious boots. Clipping

the barrette in my hair for safekeeping, I twisted one of the timers that controlled the lights. To the sound of its buzzy ticking, I took the boots out of their bag to get a better look. There was nothing much to see: a pair of plain brown leather boots, old-fashioned, a little scuffed, the heels worn. Much too big for me, probably, if Marc could wear them—I have big feet for a girl, to my sorrow, but nowhere near as big as a basketball player's. But when I held the boots up to my feet, they looked as if they might fit. Weird. I was tempted to try them on to see, but the ticking of the light timer reminded me that Anjali had said to hurry. On an impulse, I brought the boots up to my nose the way the patron had done upstairs, scolding myself as I did it: Eww, Elizabeth, what's the matter with you, sniffing old boots?

To my surprise, I smelled something.

Well, I had expected to smell *something*—old leather, old wool, maybe old feet—but not this. The smell was faint, but the sensation was powerful, flooding over me like a memory of . . . of what, though? Summer rain on cement? Rye toast at my grandmother's? Something floral and fragile, like individual soap bubbles . . . no, something thick, like milk . . . but briny . . . no, lemony . . . I took deeper and deeper sniffs, chasing the smell farther and farther out of my mind's reach like a splinter you pursue hopelessly through the sole of your foot with a needle and tweezers. The sensation was almost as painful. Raw oysters? Marjoram? Jet exhaust? Wood?

The timer ticked its way to the end and the light snapped off, startling me with darkness. I stuffed the boots in their bag and hurried down to Stack 1, the Dungeon.

I expected something spooky, but despite its sinister name,

Stack 1 looked bright and ordinary—far less dungeony than Stack 2. Fluorescent tubes lit the aisles, humming slightly, as if bored. The usual metal cabinets stretched out to the right and left, interspersed with the usual file drawers and oak desks. The dumbwaiters whirred at the staging area, just as they did on all the other stacks, and the occasional pneum thumped through the tubes. The only difference I could see between the Dungeon and the rest of the library stacks was a number of areas fenced off with metal gratings, like the bicycle storage locker in the basement of my old school, and some closed doors.

A coat hung on a hook in the staging area, but there was nobody in sight. I'd better put the boots away before whoever it was came back, I thought. But which way was the Grimm Collection? I checked the wall map. There were several rooms marked off at the ends of the stack, like the ★Vs on the other floors: ★GChr, ★LC, ★GoS . . . There, that must be it, ★GC, at the far west end. I hurried down the aisle.

I half expected to find a spectacular entrance in the spirit of the Tiffany windows and the carved front desk, but the door to the Grimm Collection was as unremarkable as the rest of the stack. Just a plain metal door like all the others, rather scuffed, with ★*GC Grimm Coll* stenciled on it in shiny black paint.

I pressed down on the handle—it was the standard bar type, the kind they use to make doors easier to open for people with disabilities—but it wouldn't budge. Feeling foolish, I took the barrette out of my hair and pressed it against the door. *"Out is out and shut is shut, turn the key and break the nut. Push the door and crack the shell: let me in and all is well,"* I sang under my breath.

I tried the handle again. Nothing happened.

I sang it again, louder. Still nothing.

Was Anjali playing some kind of mean trick on me? But she had sounded so sincere, so genuinely panicked. Hearing footsteps in the aisle, I started to panic myself.

I was pretty sure I'd gotten the tune right. Maybe I'd gotten the rhyme mixed up? I got out the slip of paper to check.

*"Out is out and shut is shut,"* I sang, my hand on the handle. *"Turn the key and crack the nut. Push the door and break the shell: let me in and all is well."*

This time I felt a tiny click. When I pressed the handle, the door opened, just as it was supposed to. I slipped in and pulled the door shut behind me.

The room looked ordinary, with the same standard-issue metal shelves and cabinets as the rest of the library, the same fluorescent lights. And yet something was different here. Behind the usual buzz of the fluorescent lights and the pneumatic tubes, I heard another, deeper hum.

Then I noticed the smell. It was the same smell I'd noticed in the boots. Or was it? I stood just inside the door sniffing the air, mesmerized. Raw pumpkin? Mineral oil? Blood?

A pneum whizzed through a pipe in the ceiling, startling me. I remembered what I was doing there. I had boots to shelve and no time to lose.

The shoe section—*GC 391.413–391.413099—filled a whole aisle. Those Grimm brothers, or whoever had continued their collection, apparently had quite a thing for footwear. Most of it was in pretty rough shape. On a low shelf I counted twelve pairs of fancy little slippers with holes in their soles, like the ones in my favorite story about the twelve dancing princesses.

Could they be *those* shoes, the ones that had inspired the story? Could the dancing princesses have been real, like Marie Antoinette?

I felt a shiver run through me, like the one I'd felt looking at Marie Antoinette's wig. Not that their story made factual sense as the Grimm brothers told it, of course—it couldn't actually be true, with its cloak of invisibility and its magical forests with gold and silver trees. But why couldn't the princesses themselves have once been girls like me, living girls who loved to dance? Somebody with real feet had worn holes in those shoes—they looked as battered as my last year's ballet slippers. I wished I could show these to my mother. She'd be as amazed as I was.

Nearby was a series of worn-out shoes with iron soles, all gaping at the heel. Above them, glass slippers. Hadn't Dr. Rust told me they didn't have Cinderella's? These looked as though they could have been hers. They were far, far too small for *me,* anyway. Was there a real girl who inspired the Cinderella story too? A real Cinderella! Was I dreaming this?

More metal shoes, including some awful-looking iron ones, stained with what looked like old blood. Ugh! Just rust, I hoped. Pair after pair of boots. Wooden clogs carved like little boats, with dragons for figureheads. A pair of sandals with worn straps and tired-looking wings on the heels, folded like a sleeping pigeon's. When I reached out to touch the wings, to see if the feathers were real, they fluttered, startling me. I pulled my hand back, remembering Anjali's warning—though surely it was just a draft of air.

The decoy boots were right where Anjali said they'd be, in the second cabinet under call number I ⋆GC 391.413 S94.

Except for the number on the tag, they looked just like the ones in the plastic bag I was carrying. If I got the tags confused, I would never be able to tell them apart.

Maybe by smell? I sniffed the boots I'd taken from the cabinet. They smelled of leather and dust, with cheesy undertones of feet. I put them down and sniffed the pair Anjali had given me. Now the mysterious smell was so strong my eyes watered.

I switched the tags and put Anjali's boots in the cabinet. It felt right, like a puzzle piece clicking into place. That made me feel better about what I was doing. My promise to Mr. Mauskopf and his warning about the thefts had been eating at me; switching the boots seemed so sneaky. But clearly the boots with the strong smell were the right ones, the valuable ones—and I was helping return them, not steal them. That couldn't be so wrong, could it?

I heard a slight noise. Footsteps! Someone was coming!

As quietly as I could, I shut the cabinet and looked around for somewhere to hide.

Against the wall were some metal mesh sliding walls, like the ones that held the paintings on Stack 7. I slipped behind them and stood as flat and still as possible, trying to look like a painting.

I was only just in time. Peering around a picture frame and through the mesh, I saw Ms. Minnian, the skinny, bespectacled librarian, come striding down the aisle in her flat, pointy shoes. She stopped right in front of the cabinet where I'd just put the boots.

She opened the cabinet and took out the boots. She stroked them with her fingertips, frowning, then brought them to her nose for a sniff. Still frowning, she lifted her head and sniffed the air.

I had a horrible feeling she was sniffing for *me.*

I froze and held my breath.

To my relief, Ms. Minnian shut the cabinet and walked back up the aisle. She paused again at another cabinet, then continued on toward the door. I heard it click shut as she left.

I let out my breath but stayed behind the picture wall for a minute, just to make sure she wouldn't come back.

When I reached the door, though, I found my relief had been premature. I was locked in.

Chapter 7:
*A disagreement with a mirror*

I rattled the door handle as I sang the rhyme and tried the barrette at different angles, but nothing worked. Had I gotten the rhyme wrong again? I didn't think so—I was using the same one that had opened the door before.

Maybe that was the problem. I wasn't out this time; I was in. Maybe I needed to tell that to the door.

*"In is in and shut is shut, turn the key and crack the nut. Pull the door and break the shell: let me out and all is well,"* I sang hopefully. I took a deep breath and tried the handle.

Still nothing.

Forget secrecy. Now it was time to panic.

I banged on the door. It hurt my hands, but it barely made a noise. I banged again harder and hurt my toes kicking, but I couldn't hear anything except the hum of the lights and that strange hum behind the hum.

My cell phone had no signal. I walked up and down the aisles looking for a phone to call for help, but I didn't see one anywhere, just metal shelves and cabinets laden with sinister objects. No other doors, and no windows, either.

What if there were a fire? What if the ceiling collapsed? What if I were stuck here forever?

I sat down and leaned against the door, telling myself to calm down. I took stock of my supplies. I had a granola bar and half a bottle of water in my jacket pocket; at least I wouldn't die of starvation and thirst even if I had to stay overnight. Someone was bound to come, I told myself. The worst I could expect would be a boring few hours, followed by getting caught and losing my job.

What if I needed to go to the bathroom, though?

As soon as I thought of it, my bladder started making itself noticed.

Well, there might not be a ladies' room in the Grimm Collection, but there was sure to be something I could use, like a witch's cauldron. I checked the card catalog for cauldrons and found three of them, call numbers I ★GC 133.44 H36, I ★GC 133.44 M33, and I ★GC 133.44 T47. They were shelved with bowls, cauldrons, and brooms in a row of cabinets facing the picture rack.

I was reaching for the smallest one—not to use it right away, just to make sure I could, if worse came to worst—when I remembered Anjali's warning. If the thought of me touching the stuff on the shelves was enough to make her frantic with worry, what would she say to my using one of the items as a Porta Potti?

On the other hand, maybe that wouldn't be so inappropriate after all, I thought bitterly. The urine of a terrified maiden sounded like exactly the sort of ingredient witches liked to put in their cauldrons.

A thud came from the front of the room, making me jump. When the thumping sound came again, I recognized it: a pneum falling into a basket in the front of the room where the GC had its staging area.

Of course! I kicked myself for not thinking of it sooner. I could send Anjali a pneum asking her to let me out.

*Anjali—help, I'm locked in,* I wrote on a blank call slip. I didn't put in any details in case the note fell into the wrong hands. I wrote *Anjali Rao, Main Exam Room,* tucked the slip into an empty carrier, pulled the tube door open, slid it in, and let go. The pneum vanished after a small struggle, like a mouse down the gullet of a snake.

Now that I had taken some action, I felt much calmer. I strolled around opening cabinets and looking in, careful not to touch anything. There were knives and combs, laces and walking sticks, lamps and bottles. All sorts of shells: eggshells, nutshells, seashells. A whole cabinet of balls, mostly golden, but some made of wood, or rubber, or red or black or blue stone. Dresses sewn from cloth of copper, silver, and gold; dresses spangled with sparkly stones; dresses made of fish scales or feathers or the skins of animals I couldn't identify. Lots of objects in sets of three— either one copper, one silver, and one gold, or one brass, one silver, and one gold, or one silver, one gold, and one spangled with diamonds. Boxes. Tiny cages. A sinister-looking oven the size of the largest dumbwaiter, big enough to hold a medium-size child.

If only there were a dumbwaiter down here—maybe I could fit inside if I scrunched up small. But the nearest dumbwaiter was out past the locked door.

At last, a pneum thumped into the basket. I ran to get it and pulled out the slip. *I can't believe I forgot to teach you the exit rhyme! I'm SOOOO sorry! It's just like the entry rhyme, only backwards. You have to sing the tune backwards too,* she had written.

"*Well is all and in me let: shell the break and door the push. Nut the crack and key the turn, shut is shut and out is out,*" I sang. But it was no use. No matter how I tried, I couldn't get the tune right.

I sent Anjali another pneum: *It's not working. I suck at music.*

*OK. Send up the key. I'll come down and get you as soon as I can,* she wrote back.

I wrapped the barrette carefully, taped it inside a pneum, and slipped it in the pipe. The vacuum sucked it away with a whoosh like a sigh of relief.

Anxious and bored, I distracted myself again by strolling around. Something moving behind me caught the corner of my eye. I spun around and froze.

Whatever it was spun and froze too.

To my relief, I saw it was just me—my reflection in a large mirror hanging on the picture rack. Did I really look that haggard and grim?

I made a face at myself. "Mirror, mirror, on the wall, who's the fairest of them all?" I said.

My own lips moved in the mirror and I heard a voice just like mine answering:

"*You have to ask, Eliza Rew?*

*Then listen up: it isn't you.*"

I think of myself as a pretty savvy person. I grew up in New York City; I've seen a thing or two. I'm not the sort of girl who confuses fairy tales with reality. But as soon as I heard the mirror speak, I knew I wasn't imagining things—it really was magic. I knew it the way you know which way is up, the way you recognize your mother's voice, the way you know to pull your hand away from a hot stove before your brain registers the pain. My heart began pounding with excitement—excitement, but not doubt.

As soon as I had accepted this, other things started dropping into place in my mind. I could almost hear them, a light, sparkling clatter like ice crystals falling in a frozen street. The moving freckles, the ensorcelled door—all magic. My heart beat hard with the thrill of it. The boots too. That must be why Marc had borrowed them, why it was so important that I get them put back. And the smell, that vivid, shifty smell: the smell of magic.

I stared around me. Everything—everything here must be magic! Boots, books, tables, telescopes—everything must have some special power! And the mirror itself . . . I turned back to it. My reflection was scary, a cold, cruel smirk. That couldn't really be what I looked like—could it? I might not be the fairest of them all, but at least I was sure I didn't look *evil*. Was it making me look like that on purpose?

"Don't call me Eliza. My name is Elizabeth," I snapped through my fear. I had always hated Eliza. That's what my stepsisters called me to tease, usually in a fake English accent.

The mirror didn't answer this time.

If the mirror really was the one from Snow White's stepmother, no wonder it was so unpleasant—it had the excuse of belonging to somebody wicked. My skin prickled. But the Grimm stories weren't all witches and poisoned apples. Some of them described good fairies and friendly magic, like Cinderella's godmother. Were there any benevolent objects here?

Now the sense of magic all around me began to feel frightening, oppressive. No wonder Dr. Rust had called the objects here "powerful"!

I looked around again. On the sliding wall near the opinionated mirror hung several other mirrors and a dozen or so pictures, including one of a ship, one of a dragon, one of a hideous, leering old man, and one so dark and murky that I couldn't make it out. None of the paintings looked particularly benign, and the dark one was positively threatening.

Anjali seemed to be taking her sweet time rescuing me. Was there anything here that could help me escape? A flying carpet, maybe? I couldn't quite believe that I was thinking seriously about a flying carpet. But even if I found one, I was still trapped— not much use in flying a carpet indoors.

I thought about other magical devices from fairy tales. What a lucky chance I'd written that paper about the Brothers Grimm— or was it just chance? Who would have guessed all those childhood hours I spent daydreaming over fairy-tale books would pay off!

There was the cloak of invisibility from "The Twelve Dancing Princesses"—if the repository had it, perhaps I could hide by the door and slip out next time a librarian came in. Mom and I loved that story, with the trapdoor in the floor of the princesses' bedroom that they snuck through every night to go dancing with twelve handsome princes. The girls danced until they wore holes in their slippers. I especially envied the youngest princess. She had an active social life, plenty of masculine attention, and big sisters who actually wanted to hang out with her—even if she did have to share her room with eleven of them.

Of course, there were other magical items that would be more efficient than an invisible cloak. There were tons of wish-granting objects in fairy tales. Usually they came loaded with three wishes; the trick was to formulate the wishes carefully. When I was little, I used to spend hours planning my wishes for just this day.

Which would be better: a cure for cancer? Universal happiness? Peace for all nations, forever? The people in the fairy tales always seemed to waste their wishes on ridiculous things like sausages or turning each other into donkeys and back into people again. Sometimes, though, the wishes would backfire. Someone would wish for a sack of gold and it would fall on their head and kill them.

So even if I could find a wishing ring, I wasn't sure I would have the courage to use it. What if I wished to leave the Grimm Collection, only to be carried out in a body bag?

The whole thing was too freaky! I wanted to get away from this magic-soaked room and think about it calmly somewhere safe and normal, somewhere that smelled of daily life—like dust and dinner—not the shifting reek of enchantment. And in real life if I had been granted three wishes, I knew exactly what I would change—I would wish my mother alive, my father himself again, my best friend, Nicole, still here instead of in California.

I glanced behind me at the mirror. It was still smirking.

Where on earth was Anjali? I sent that pneum at ten to three.

Hey, that rhymed. I said it out loud:

*"I sent that pneum at ten to three.*

*Where on earth is Anjali?"*

My reflection raised an eyebrow and answered,

*"Liz, are you addressing me?*

*She's right where she's supposed to be."*

"No, as a matter of fact, I wasn't addressing you, I was addressing the painting next to you," I lied. "And don't call me Liz either. I'm Elizabeth."

The mirror didn't respond, but I noticed some movement in the neighboring picture as the murky shapes inside the frame started to change form in a random, incomprehensible way. It was nothing like any video effects I'd ever seen on a movie or computer screen—more like the forms you see when you press your hands against your closed eyes or the images from a dream that fade as you try to remember it the next morning.

To my astonishment the shapes in the middle resolved themselves into a picture of Anjali, hard at work in the Main Examination Room. I felt almost dizzy watching her slide briskly on her stool, popping pneums into pipes. It looked very busy up there; no wonder she couldn't get away.

"Wow! Can you show me anything I ask for? Like, I don't know, my friend Nicole?" I said.

No response; still Anjali.

Rhyme, maybe? "Picture, picture, on the wall, please can you show me my friend Nicole?" I tried.

My reflection in the Snow White stepmother mirror rolled her eyes with bored scorn.

"Okay, sorry, that didn't really rhyme, did it?" I said. I thought about it for a while.

*"Picture, help me reach my goal*
*Of communing with Nicole."*

That worked. The picture did its dizzying thing again, dissolving Anjali into random geometric forms that shuffled themselves darkly, then brightened into a new scene: Nicole shopping with her new friends in California, trying on clothes and laughing silently—at least, *I* couldn't hear them. I could imagine the squeals and peals, though. It was like watching some horrible reality show with the sound off. It made me feel more lonely and helpless than ever.

*"Thanks, that's quite enough of them!*
*Show me Anjali again,"* I said.

Nothing happened. Bad rhyme, I guess.

*"Please, just show me Anjali.*
*She's the one I need to see."*

More swirling, then Anjali at the pneum station again. Then I heard a click and a creak: the door was finally opening. But it couldn't be Anjali coming to free me if she was upstairs in the MER.

*"Enough! Turn off,"* I muttered to the painting. Fortunately, it accepted the almost rhyme and quieted to murk as I hid behind the picture wall.

## Chapter 8:
## A multiple-choice test
## and a binder clip

"Elizabeth? You in there?" It was Marc's voice. I crept out from behind the picture wall. He was standing at the end of the room, holding the door open with one long leg. "Hurry up, we can't stay here," he urged.

I felt a shiver of relief as I heard the door click shut behind us.

Marc took the stairs two or three steps at a time while I ran panting behind. I used to be in better shape when I still took ballet.

Marc waited for me at the third landing. "Come on, you'll never make the team at that rate!"

"What team?"

He looked me over. "I don't know, Girls' JV Dawdling?"

"Where are we going?"

"Preservation."

"Where's that?"

"Top floor."

"Can't we take the elevator?"

"*You* can—Coach'd kill me if *I* do." He took off again.

At last we reached the top of the staircase, with the corridor that led to the MER on the right and parts unknown—at least to me—on the left. There we ran into Ms. Callender. There was a frown on her friendly face.

"Elizabeth! Where have you been? I've been looking all over for you; aren't you supposed to be on Stack 2?" she asked.

I didn't know what to say—and even if I *had* known, I was panting too hard to say it. Fortunately, Marc stepped in. "Didn't Ms. Minnian tell you? I'm supposed to take her to Preservation and get to work on the backlog of repairs," he said.

"Oh. No, she didn't mention that, but I'm afraid it'll have to wait. Dr. Rust wants to see Elizabeth. I'll send her up to help you when they're done." She made a note on her clipboard and said to me, "Go on down, honey, Dr. Rust is waiting."

I guess she must have seen my dismay. She smiled and added, "Why the long face?"

"Did I do something wrong?" I asked.

"No, no. Just the opposite. There's nothing to worry about. We thought you were ready for the next step, that's all. Or at least, the next step toward the next step—or . . . well, I'll let Dr. Rust explain. Go on downstairs, honey."

"Okay." I hurried away, still feeling uneasy.

Dr. Rust looked up when I tapped on the open door. "Ah, Elizabeth. Come on in. Sit down, sit down. Let's see, you've been with us since January, right?"

I nodded.

"Martha Callender tells me you're a good, hard worker, and Stan Mauskopf speaks highly of your character. I've heard good reports from one or two of the patrons as well. We think it may be time to give you a little more responsibility. Do you feel ready?"

Hardly. What I felt was guilty. Had Dr. Rust and Ms. Callender been discussing my noble character at the very moment I was sneaking around the Grimm Collection?

I cleared my throat. "That's so nice of Mr. Mauskopf and Ms. Callender. What kind of responsibility?"

"Let's discuss that after you take the test. That will give me the information I need to make a decision about what work would be right for you here."

"Okay. What kind of a test? Sorting buttons again?"

Doc smiled. "No, this is a standardized test—multiple choice. Let's find you a quiet place to work."

We walked down the hall to a small office with a desk by the window. "Here you go," said Dr. Rust, handing me a sheaf of papers held together with a binder clip. "You have forty-five minutes to complete the exam. Make sure you fill in each circle completely on the answer sheet. Do you have a number 2 pencil?"

"I think so." I fished around in my backpack and brought out the pencil the homeless woman had given me, the one I'd used to outline my social studies paper. I'd come to think of it as my lucky pencil.

"Excellent. I'll be back in exactly forty-five minutes."

The questions on the test were bizarre:

7.   A carpenter has three sons. The eldest builds a palace from
      alabaster and porphyry. The second builds a courthouse from
      granite and sandstone. The youngest builds a cottage from a

walnut shell and a corn husk. How many nails do the three sons use?

- ◯ A. π
- ◯ B. Infinity minus one
- ◯ C. One too many
- ◯ D. One too few

8. A child offers you a choice of two caskets, one gold and the other lead. Which do you take?

- ◯ A. The gold one
- ◯ B. The one in the child's left hand
- ◯ C. The one the moth lands on
- ◯ D. A river underground

I chewed my pencil and stared at the paper. I couldn't imagine which answers were correct. I couldn't even tell which were wrong, although on most multiple-choice tests I can usually cross out at least one or two right away. I had that terrible nervous feeling you get in nightmares, where you're taking a test in a class you never signed up for.

A minute or two ticked by.

Well, I decided, there was nothing for it but to try my best.

I went through the questions carefully, filling in circles. I read each question, then shut my eyes, imagined the choices as vividly as I could, and let my heart decide. When my heart didn't have an opinion, I left it up to my pencil.

At last I reached the end of the test, but there were still a couple of pages attached with the binder clip. The first one was a list of some sort: *Paper towels, dish soap, ~~laundry soap~~, pistachios, milk, ~~carrots~~, sardines, cayenne* . . . Doc's groceries?

I turned to the next page. On top of the sheet, in the same typeface as the exam, was written: *Repository Qualifying Exam Level Two, 209v04 Key.* Beneath was a list of answers. They seemed to correspond to the questions on the exam I'd just taken.

Doc must have accidentally given me the answer key!

I felt a wave of guilt. But really, I told myself, how was Dr. Rust's carelessness my fault?

Running my eye down my sheet, I saw with alarm that I hadn't gotten a single answer right. The key called for all the safest, dullest answers.

I started to erase my answer to the first question, to change it to the one on the answer sheet. My pencil didn't seem to like that. It made an ugly pink smear on the page, the color of an infected cut. The color, I thought, of cheating.

Feeling as if I'd had a narrow escape, I turned the pencil around and filled in the circle again next to my original answer: *D, With all her heart.* I was relieved by my decision, but I was disappointed too. Now that I knew I wouldn't get the promotion, I realized how much I wanted it.

The door opened. "Elizabeth? All done?"

I handed Doc my answer sheet, along with the other papers. "I think you gave me the answer key," I said.

Doc grunted. "Indeed I did . . . huh, so that's where my shopping list got to. Sardines! I knew I'd forgotten something important. Now, let's see how you did. CDD, ADC, BAB, CCB, ACB . . . Excellent. Almost a perfect score."

"What do you mean, almost perfect? I only got one right!"

Doc smiled, freckles drifting across one cheekbone. "Only one wrong, you mean. This key is a list of *wrong* answers. You passed with flying colors."

"I did?"

"Yes. Not only did you choose correct answers, but you did it without peeking at the key. Well done, Elizabeth Rew! And now, I'm pleased to present you with the key to the Grimm Collection. Guard it with care and use it with wisdom." Doc unclipped the binder clip from the exam and put it in my hand.

"This is the key? A *binder clip*?"

"Exactly."

"But . . ." Well, I thought, Anjali's key was a barrette. Why shouldn't mine be a binder clip? "How does it work?" I asked.

"Come downstairs and I'll show you."


". . . *Let me in and all is well*," I sang, pressing my binder clip against the door that had so frustrated me only an hour before. Doc was impressed by how quickly I'd memorized the rhyme— and by how calmly I'd taken the news that the room was full of genuine magic. Naturally, I didn't explain that I'd seen it already.

I had more trouble with the exit tune, but I got it right after six or seven tries. My music teacher, Mr. Theodorus, would have been proud of me.

"What if I forget the exit song? Will I get stuck here?" I asked, remembering my panic and hoping it wouldn't show. "Doesn't that violate all sorts of fire laws?"

"Technically, I suppose. But if there's a fire, the Grimm Collection is the place to be. As far as fires go, it's the safest room in the entire repository—besides the Garden of Seasons, of course, if you can call that a room. You'll see there are some pretty powerful objects down here, with powerful senses of self-preservation. And the guards we set on the door will keep out most natural threats."

As if on cue, the door opened from the outside. I jumped, but it was only Ms. Callender. She hugged me. "Congratulations, Elizabeth! See, I told you there was nothing to worry about, sweetie. Gumdrop? Go ahead, take two—you deserve it. Did Dr. Rust show you around?"

"Not yet," said Doc. "Want to help?"

"Of course! Where should we start? Let's see . . . Elizabeth, do you have a favorite fairy tale?"

"Sure, lots of them. If I had to pick just one, though . . . I love 'The Twelve Dancing Princesses.'"

"Then you're in luck. This way."

I followed Ms. Callender through the aisles to the shelves of shoes. I couldn't stop myself from glancing nervously at the boots I'd just shelved. They were sitting right where I put them, looking dull and harmless.

"There you go!" With a flourish of her hand, Ms. Callender pointed to the twelve pairs of shoes I'd wondered about, the ones with holes in their soles.

"Those are the princesses' shoes?"

She nodded. "Twenty-four of their shoes, anyway."

"Can I touch?"

"Go ahead." She picked up a purple silk pump and handed it to me. "Here's the twelfth princess's pair."

The smell of magic was so strong in this room, and my nerves were so fluttery from everything that had happened, I couldn't quite tell whether I was feeling my own excitement or actual magic. "Does it . . . I mean, is it . . ."

"Is it what?"

"Is it—you know—magical?"

"No, not the shoes."

"Oh." I was disappointed. Still, this wasn't just *any* dancing shoe—it was the shoe that the youngest princess had worn to dance with the smart soldier who figured out how the princesses were sneaking out at night. Magic or not, that was pretty amazing.

"You don't have the soldier's cloak here, do you?" I asked. "The cloak of invisibility that he used to follow the princesses to the dance?"

Doc and Ms. Callender exchanged glances. "We're not sure," said Doc at last. "It's supposed to be here, but nobody can find it."

"Did it get misshelved?"

"I don't know," said Ms. Callender. "It might just be invisible."

"Oh. But you have other magical things, right?"

"Yes, many."

"Could I see one?"

"Of course," said Doc. "Let's see, what should I show you? . . . Do you remember 'The Spirit in the Bottle'?"

"Is that the one where the student lets the spirit out of the bottle, and the spirit says he's going to cut his head off, so the student tricks the spirit back into the bottle by taunting him and saying he doesn't believe he'll fit?"

Doc nodded. "That's the one. Do you remember what the spirit gives the student in exchange for letting him out again?"

I shook my head.

"Come. I'll show you."

We walked down the aisles again, past rows of glass bottles, bowls of all shapes and sizes, dozens of spinning wheels, and on and on until we came to a chest full of cloths carefully folded and labeled. Doc took one out and shook it open. It was ragged and dirty.

"Wait, Lee! Test it first!" said Ms. Callender sharply.

"Don't worry, I'm going to! That's why I chose this bandage. I want to show her how very dangerous the objects in this room can be. Elizabeth, did you see the bottles we passed?"

I nodded.

"If you opened the wrong one without thinking, a spirit might come out and cut off your head."

"Why couldn't I trick him back into the bottle like in the story?"

"That only works once," said Doc. "Our bottled spirits know better—they would never fall for that again. So don't assume anything in here is harmless or manageable. Everything is dangerous in a different way, but everything is dangerous."

Ms. Callender was nodding her round face in agreement. "Even the stuff that sounds safe is dangerous," she said. "Like the pot in 'Sweet Porridge.' When you say, 'Cook, little pot, cook,' it makes sweet millet porridge. Sounds harmless, right?"

"Yes, I remember the story," I said. Nobody told the pot to stop cooking until it had filled half the houses in town with porridge. The householders had to eat their way out. The story didn't say whether anybody drowned.

"Okay, Lee. Show her the rag," said Ms. Callender.

Doc took out a pocketknife, unfolded it, and—to my horror—
made a deep cut across the base of one finger.

"Martha, will you do the honors?" Doc held out the rag. "I
don't want to drip blood over everything."

"Sure." Ms. Callender took the rag. "Elizabeth, do you have
some small object you could spare? A penny or a pen or something?"

I felt in my hoodie pocket and found an acorn I'd picked up
in the park a few weeks ago. "How's this?"

"Perfect." She rubbed it with the rag. Nothing happened.
She turned the rag over and rubbed it again, with the other
side. She held it up, smiled, and handed it to me.

It was heavy and cold, white-gray and shiny. It had turned to
silver.

"Wow!" I said, staring. "It's so—so cute! It's like a perfect
little silver acorn."

"It *is* a perfect little silver acorn," said Doc.

"Now give me your hand, Lee. Elizabeth? You watching?"

I had still been staring at the acorn, admiring the tiny silver scales on the cap, but I turned to watch the librarians. Ms.
Callender had taken Doc's hand and was rubbing it with the
cloth.

The cut closed up as if it had never been there.

"Wow! Can I see your finger?" Doc held it out. I inspected
it closely. I couldn't see any sign of the cut.

"I remember the rest of the story now," I said. "One side of
the bandage turns things into silver, and the other side heals
wounds."

"That's right," said Doc. "And if Martha had used the wrong side, I would now have a silver hand. Pretty, but useless."

"But that thing could save lives! Why is it here? Why don't you give it to a hospital or something?"

"Yes, it could save lives," said Doc. "But it would certainly also cost lives. Not just by turning people into silver, but by starting more wars than it could ever heal the wounds from."

"I would say that's the most important lesson of the day," said Ms. Callender, folding up the cloth and putting it back in the chest. "Not only are the objects here extremely dangerous, but so is the knowledge of them."

"That's right," said Doc. "Remember, Elizabeth: tell no one about the magic here. At best they won't believe you. At worst, they will."

"Don't worry, I won't tell a soul. But *lots* of people must know about the magic. You do, and now I do. And I've seen people take objects out of the Grimm Collection when I was up in the Main Exam Room. Who are they? Do they know about the magic?"

"Yes," said Doc. "There's a far-flung, exclusive community of people like us—now, people like you. People who recognize magic and wield it."

"Do they borrow things from the collection? Magical items?"

"Yes, members of the community can earn borrowing privileges."

"Even the pages?" Maybe I would be allowed to borrow magical items myself!

"Some of them."

"Wow!" Imagine having a magic cloth that could change things to silver in your own home! Or a cloak of invisibility. "Can I take things out too?"

"Eventually, I hope. But that's another step for another day. Give yourself a chance to digest what you've learned first."

"All right," I said. Thinking about everything that could go wrong, I wasn't sure I was ready for that kind of responsibility, anyway.

"Aren't you going to tell her about . . . you know?" said Ms. Callender.

"The thefts. Yes." Doc turned to me. "Elizabeth, unfortunately there have been some thefts of Grimm objects recently. And now we've been hearing about items that sound like ours turning up on the open market or in private collections."

"Somebody's robbing the collection?" I said. "That's terrible!"

"It is," said Doc. "And they seem to be replacing the stolen items with fakes—some of them, anyway."

"Oh, no!" I said. Fakes, I thought, like the unmagical boots Marc had me trade the real ones for! Was Marc . . . ? I shuddered away from the thought. "But what can *I* do?"

"We need trustworthy eyes down here. We need to be able to rely on everyone who's working here. If you see anything out of place, please let us know."

"Of course I will," I said. "And how do you decide which pages to give the test to?"

"It's a combination of things. Watching how you do your work in the repository. Recommendations from former pages and other members of our community, like Stan Mauskopf."

"Although the page we had to fire recently did have a

recommendation from Wallace Stone, one of our patrons," put in Ms. Callender.

"I don't want to blame Wallace," said Doc. "He was devastated when I told him we had to fire Zandra. He took it hard. He's one of our most generous donors."

"What did Zandra do?" I asked.

"Besides spreading chaos, we caught her substituting a new vase for a valuable old one," said Doc.

"A magic vase?"

"No, just a Ming dynasty vase on Stack 7. But that's quite bad enough," said Ms. Callender.

"Wallace Stone felt so bad about the whole thing that he donated a group of related porcelain to the repository. He's an art and antiques dealer, and he's done a great job helping us round out our collections," said Doc. "He was especially generous after the Zandra incident. I told him we didn't blame him, but he still wanted to make amends."

"So Zandra's gone now and things are still disappearing," I said. "She couldn't still be stealing, could she?"

"No, I don't think so. But it's unlikely she was working alone. A kid like Zandra wouldn't have the resources to dispose of a Ming vase. Whoever was behind it must have found some other way in—into the Grimm Collection, which is even worse."

"Anjali said there was another page who vanished. What happened to her?" I asked.

"Mona Chen. She was one of our best workers," Doc said. "She passed all the tests with flying colors, and she had some really good ideas about how to keep the Grimm Collection call slips safer. We're trying to locate her."

"Where do you think she went? Did she return the key?"

"Yes," said Ms. Callender. "She dropped it off with Lucy Minnian. She said her family was moving, but she didn't say where, and it's surprising not to hear from her at all. Most of our alumni, especially Special Collection pages, keep in touch."

"Do you think she's okay?"

"I hope so," said Ms. Callender. "We're putting out the word and hoping someone in the community will hear from her soon."

"What do you mean, 'the community'?"

"We're a close group," explained Dr. Rust. "Most of us librarians are alumni—former pages—and other alumni end up working in related areas. In other repositories, or academia, or research. Most of us"—Doc waved a hand at the shelves—"most people don't want to give up their connection to all this."

I could certainly understand that. And I didn't want to do anything to jeopardize my chance of being part of it. But all this talk of disappearing objects in this unnerving room was freaking me out, given Marc's—what to call it?—*irregularity* with those boots. Marc's irregularity, and the way I'd helped him.

"Well, Elizabeth, we are happy to have you here," Doc said. "And please remember to keep your eyes open and let me know if you notice anything suspicious. Can you do that?"

I swallowed. "I'll try."

"Thank you. And congratulations on your excellent test results."

"Yes, congratulations again, Elizabeth," echoed Ms. Callender. "Now let's get you upstairs to give Marc a hand in Preservation."

As we walked past the wall of pictures, I saw something

move out of the corner of my eye. I turned to look. It was my own reflection in the Snow White mirror.

I didn't move my hands, but my reflection in the mirror lifted her finger to her lips, gave me a wicked smile, and shut her right eye in a wink.

scissors

The Preservation Room was a long, airy attic, lit by a northern skylight. It was bright and chilly; drafts seeped around the edges of the window, and high white clouds flew by above. Objects from the stacks lay in heaps and clusters, neatly labeled. It was the sort of place where you could imagine the thirteenth fairy with her poison spindle, lying in wait for Sleeping Beauty.

Marc looked up when I came in. "Thanks, Elizabeth," he said seriously, meeting my eye. "You really had my back. Sorry you got stuck down there."

"That's okay," I said—and it was. Being thanked by Marc Merritt was worth any number of conversations with rude mirrors and dismal thoughts about the sanitary uses of witches' cauldrons. And being let in on the secret of this magical place was worth more than all of it combined. "If you'd only waited an hour or two," I said proudly, "I could have gone in there on my own—Doc just gave me the key."

"Really? That's awesome! Congratulations, Elizabeth! Welcome to the inner circle." He held out his hand.

He had a beautiful, firm handshake.

"Listen, though," I began, then hesitated. Should I say something about how uncomfortable I felt helping him break the rules? I didn't want to jeopardize my friendship with Marc Merritt, no less. It wasn't like I had friends to spare. But even before I'd been given the key, I'd felt a kinship to this place. Mr. Mauskopf and Doc trusted me, and I felt like I owed them—not just them, but the repository. Now that I'd seen the magic in the Grimm Collection and been entrusted with the key, I felt I owed it to this magical place to take the best care I could of it.

I went on, "Doc told me there'd been some thefts here recently. So did Mr. Mauskopf, the one who got me the job. They both told me to keep an eye out and tell them if I saw anything suspicious. You're not—you don't—?" I didn't know how to put it diplomatically.

"Not what? Stealing things?" said Marc. He had that haughty look of his, like a prince being accused of something far beneath him.

"Well, I didn't mean to accuse you, but . . . I don't know, they trust me, and I helped you, and I just want to make sure . . ."

"I'm sorry—you're right," he said. "It does look bad. But I wouldn't do anything to hurt this place. I belong here. It's like it's, I don't know, part of me."

He looked so sincere I put my doubts aside. "Okay," I said. "I'm sorry. But you still need to tell me what's going on. You pulled me into this and got me locked up in a pretty scary place! That was a big deal. You can't just not tell me why."

"Yeah, all right. I've been borrowing the seven-league boots. I have to pick up Andre from my aunt's in the Bronx and drop him off at day care in Harlem, in between basketball practice and work. That would take hours on the subway. If I use the boots, I can do it in no time."

"You're kidding me—real seven-league boots! So you take them instead of the A train!"

Marc smiled. "Yeah—it's a lot more fun than the A train. And like I said, way faster. You never get stuck in between stations."

"But it's—you know—*magic*!"

"Yeah," he said. "Magic. You'll get used to it."

Okay, so it was silly of me to expect Mr. Cool himself, Marc Merritt, to express astonishment, even at real magic. I told myself to be cool too. "How long is a league?" I asked.

"About three miles."

"So that's twenty-one miles per step? Even the Bronx isn't that far away."

"Yeah, the tricky part is making my steps small enough."

It did sound tricky, but if anybody had control over where his feet went, it was Marc.

"Aren't you worried Andre will tell somebody?"

He shrugged. "Who's going to believe a three-year-old when he says his big brother can fly?"

"But I don't get it—why not just borrow the boots officially? You have borrowing privileges."

He nodded. "I tried that at first, but they keep crazy tabs on the stuff in the GC. You can't take it out more than once a month. Plus you have to leave a serious deposit, not to mention the late fines."

"But why do you have to drop Andre off anyway? Why can't your parents do it?"

"They're both busy," he said shortly.

"Sorry, I didn't mean . . . ," I trailed off.

"That's okay . . . I shouldn't have snapped at you. We better get to work. You know how to sew?" He led me to a table piled with cloth.

I shook my head. "That's really not the kind of thing I'm good at," I said.

"Okay, then. I guess you'll be learning today. We've got to get through all this so it can go back on the shelves."

"Is this from the Grimm Collection?"

"Nah. Just normal, everyday priceless treasures."

Marc was a surprisingly good sewer. His hands could handle a needle almost as well as a basketball. Not mine, that was for sure—especially not when I was distracted by thoughts of magic and Marc Merritt. The sky was starting to darken and my fingers were riddled with jabs by the time I managed to tack together the sides of a torn tunic.

I thought of all the fairy-tale girls who ran afoul of needle-work: Snow White's mother, who wished for a daughter with lips as red as the blood from her pricked finger. Sleeping Beauty, with that fateful spindle, and Rumpelstiltskin's victim, locked up with the impossible task of spinning straw into gold. I had more sympathy for them than ever.

"Let me see that," said Marc. I handed him the tunic. He laughed. "You really weren't kidding, were you? Well, practice makes perfect."

"Where did *you* learn to sew so well, anyway?" I asked.

"Same place you will. All the pages have to."

"Who taught you, then?"

He got a dreamy half smile on his face. "Anjali."

As if he'd conjured her, the door opened and in she walked.

"It's dead quiet on Stack 2," she said. "Ms. Callender sent me up here to see if you need help—unless you're done already?"

"Ha," said Marc. "With Ms. Thumbs here? You're dreaming." He winked at me.

Anjali laughed. "How gracious! You should be extra polite—you owe her. Don't worry, Elizabeth, I remember not so long ago when Merritt had five big toes on each hand. Just call him Toe Jam and see how he likes it."

They grinned at each other.

Anjali picked up an embroidered silk garment—I couldn't tell if it was some lord's ceremonial cloak or just a fancy bathrobe—and selected a spool of thread in a matching shade of teal. She threaded a needle and began sewing with quick, tiny stitches. It looked so easy when she did it.

"Hey, Elizabeth," she said seriously, her eyes on her sewing, "I'm really sorry I forgot to tell you how to get out. I feel like such a lamebrain."

"That's okay. It all worked out."

"I know. But I'm still sorry."

"Well, if you'd just waited a little while, I could have used my own key—Doc just gave me one."

"Wow, congratulations!" Anjali put down her sewing and gave me a hug. "Let's see! Oh, a binder clip? Cool!"

"Hey, that reminds me. I better give you yours back," said Marc, handing her the barrette. She clipped her hair up with it.

"So what was Zandra like—the page who got fired?" I asked. "Doc and Ms. Callender were talking about her."

"I didn't like her," said Anjali. "All she cared about were *things*—clothes and vacations and music players. She always wanted the newest, most expensive stuff. I wasn't that surprised when they caught her stealing."

"But why a vase?" I said. "That doesn't make sense."

"I know," said Anjali. "Why would she care about a Ming vase? You can't wear it. She must have been planning to sell it."

"She's too dumb to think of that herself," said Marc. "I bet she was working for someone."

"Who?" I said.

"That's the big question," said Marc.

"What about the other page, the one who disappeared?"

"Mona? I really liked her," said Anjali. "But something was freaking her out. Before she left, she started getting really jumpy, but she wouldn't talk about it. Then one day she turned in her key and just . . . disappeared."

"What was she scared of? Was it really that gigantic bird? That sounds so unbelievable. At least—it did before I saw the Grimm Collection."

"I know, that's why I wasn't sure I should tell you at first," said Anjali. "I thought you'd think I was crazy. But now you've seen some magic firsthand. And if you think about it, there are plenty of gigantic birds and fantastic creatures in fairy tales."

I remembered how scary the Snow White mirror was, and it didn't even have claws. "All right, so where did you hear this rumor about the bird?"

"I overheard some of the patrons talking about it," said Anjali. "Then that creepy little art dealer said something to me."

"The one who keeps staring at you?" I asked.

Anjali nodded. "He told me to keep an eye out for an enormous bird and to make sure I didn't carry anything valuable around alone. He even offered to walk me home."

"Eeewww!" I said. "Are you sure he wasn't just trying to . . . I don't know, get close to you?"

"I can walk you home anytime you want," said Marc. "You don't need any slimy patrons to take care of you. I hope you told him that."

"I told him no thanks," said Anjali. "But he sounded like he meant it about the bird, and the other patrons seemed to believe it. Those Russian guys who play chess all the time—they said they stopped playing in Washington Square Park because the bird tried to attack them. And right before Mona disappeared, I thought I saw something hovering in the sky."

"Where? Did you tell Doc?"

Anjali shook her head. "Outside the repository. But it was gone too soon. I wasn't sure what I saw." She finished her robe and snipped off the thread with scissors. "Enough about all this. It's too creepy. Hey, is there any fun stuff to work on?" she said with determined cheerfulness.

"Check the cabinet," said Marc.

"Fun stuff?" I asked.

"Magic." Anjali walked over to a large gray cabinet with double doors at the end of the room. "This is where they keep items from the Grimm Collection that need repair." She unclipped her barrette, letting down a cascade of black hair, and pressed the barrette to the handle. *"Open, friend, so I can mend,"* she intoned. The door swung open. "Oh, we're in luck! Table-Be-Set! Anybody hungry?"

"The French version or the German?" asked Marc.

"German. The French one's out on loan, as usual."

"Too bad. Well, better than nothing. I'm starving—I didn't have time to eat after practice."

"What's Table-Be-Set?" I asked.

Anjali reached into the cabinet and pulled out a little wooden table. "Don't you remember in the Grimm story 'Table-Be-Set, Gold-Donkey, and Cudgel-in-the-Sack'? The table sets itself with food when you tell it to."

"Why's it in the repair cabinet? Is it broken?"

"I doubt it—it probably just needs a good cleaning, as usual." Anjali consulted a piece of paper tied to one leg. "Yup. Somebody spilled beer or *blutwurst* or something. We're going to have to scrub it, so we might as well have a snack first. Table, be set!"

In the twinkling of an eye, the table was covered with steaming dishes, so many of them that it bowed slightly in the middle and gave a little creak.

"Wow, that looks good! But isn't this—I mean, should we be doing this?" I objected. "Aren't we not supposed to touch anything magic?"

"It's like milking a cow. The table gets antsy if it goes too long without feeding people. And we'll have to touch it anyway, to clean it." Anjali lifted the lid of a dish. A savory smell, heavy on cabbage, filled the room. "Want to start with the sausages or the potatoes?"

"Sausages, definitely," said Marc.

"Okay . . ." She lifted more lids and poked around with a fork. "You can have *blutwurst, zervelatwurst, bockwurst, plockwurst, leberwurst, knackwurst,* and, of course, *bratwurst.* And what's this? *Weisswurst,* I think."

"Some of each, please," said Marc.

Anjali handed him a plate piled with wursts. "What about you, Elizabeth?"

"Um, I'm not crazy about sausage—maybe just some potatoes?"

"Okay," said Anjali. "*Kartoffelbällchen, kartoffeltopf, kartoffel-kroketten, kartoffelbrei, kartoffelknödel, kartoffelkrusteln, kartoffelnocken, kartoffelpuffer, kartoffelklösse,* or *kartoffelschnitz?* Or maybe some *schmorkartoffeln?* Or just plain fries?"

"I don't know—surprise me."

"Here. *Überbackene käsekartoffeln,* my favorite. It has cheese."

"Thanks." It was delicious and very rich—tender potato slices, with a creamy cheese sauce. "How do you know all those names?" I asked.

"I looked them up. I wanted to know what we were eating." Anjali peered under more lids.

"You know Anjali—she loves to look things up. Any *spätzle?*" asked Marc.

"What's *spätzle?*"

"Sort of a cross between homemade pasta and dumplings," said Anjali. "Oh, here's *hasenpfeffer!* I love *hasenpfeffer!*"

"What's *hasenpfeffer?*"

"Stewed rabbit with black pepper." She dished herself a plate. "Mmmm! Don't tell my parents—we're vegetarians at home."

"Can I have some of that too?" Marc handed her his plate.

"One thing I don't get," I said, taking another bite of cheesy potatoes. "If these magic objects are so strong and powerful, how come you don't have people using them to take over the world? Or do you? Is that what the thieves are after?"

"I wondered that too, when I first got here," said Anjali. "But a lot of them aren't as powerful as they sound, to begin with, and we have modern technology now."

"Yeah," said Marc. "There's magic swords and sticks that can beat people up, but that's nothing compared to guns and bombs."

"Or like the enchanted ram's horn that lets you speak to someone miles away," said Anjali. "Hello? Cell phone, anybody? Or the flying carpet. It's nice, but it's not like we don't have airplanes. These things are amazing, collectors love them, but they wouldn't be that much help conquering the world."

"Yes, but surely there are some things in the collection that haven't been invented yet. Like invisibility cloaks. Or what about the lamp in that Grimm story 'The Blue Light,' where the dwarf appears and grants wishes whenever the soldier lights his pipe with the magic light? That would be pretty useful for taking over the world."

"Yeah, that's true. But most powerful objects have minds of their own—I wouldn't count on being able to control them."

"I guess," I said.

"Time for dessert?" asked Marc.

"Maybe we should do a little, you know, *work* first," said Anjali, looking in the cabinet again. "Here's a pair of flying sandals; it looks like they need a buckle replaced."

"Flying sandals?" I said. "Like, actual *flying sandals*?"

"Flying sandals," said Anjali, holding them up. They had wings on their heels. They looked like the ones that had fluttered at me. I wondered how they'd gotten here so quickly.

"I can do that," said Marc. He opened a cabinet drawer and sorted through buckles.

"And here's the brimming bowl," said Anjali, holding a stone bowl full of water, which was dripping from the bottom. "I need caulk."

"Try the plumbing supply cabinet," suggested Marc.

"Got it. Elizabeth, can you give me a hand?"

"Sure," I said. I held the bowl over the sink while she worked on it. It seemed pretty incredible that we were using ordinary, everyday silicone gel to caulk an endlessly brimming magic basin.

"Thanks, Elizabeth, I think that's good now . . . Merritt! What are you doing?"

Marc had taken off his shoes and was buckling on the winged sandals. "I have to make sure the buckle holds, don't I?" He jumped up into the air and glided forward like an airborne ice skater. He made it look so easy. "Need anything from up here?" he said. I stared, my eyes wide. Bits of dust came raining down. I sneezed, rubbing the dust out of my eyes. "Sorry, Elizabeth," he said. He did a loop de loop and landed with a flourish.

"Flying sandals!" I said. "Flying. *Sandals.*"

"Want to try?"

"Really? Me?"

"Of course."

"But—but don't you need some special—I don't know . . ."

Marc laughed. "You'll get the hang of it; it's not that hard. I'll show you." He unbuckled the sandals and handed them to me.

His feet were much bigger than mine, but the sandals still fit me. Magic, I thought. "How do I get them to work?" I said.

"Jump as high as you can and start the wings. You have to sort of flutter your heels."

I tried it. I had gotten about six inches off the ground when my feet shot straight out from under me. I landed hard on my rear.

Marc started to laugh, but Anjali frowned at him and he straightened his face. "That was a good start, Elizabeth, but you have to sort of follow your feet with your body," he said. "Keep your weight centered right above your feet."

"You better spot her," said Anjali, hauling me to my feet.

I tried again, this time with Marc standing behind me, his hands under my upper arms. His closeness was as strangely thrilling as the winged sandals on my feet.

He pushed me forward over the sandals. I lurched forward, then back; I almost fell again, but he lunged and caught me, pushing me straight.

After a couple more falls, I started to get the hang of it. It was a little like skating, only slipperier—there were more directions for my feet to fly off in. I had to sort of teeter and glide, teeter and glide.

"What are you doing?" The voice came from the door, startling me so that I fell over.

Fortunately, I was high enough off the ground that I didn't hit my head. I just hung upside down from my feet, the wings at my heels beating furiously.

Aaron snorted. He was standing in the doorway.

"Oh, hi, Aaron! You startled us," said Anjali.

"Why's Elizabeth hanging upside down? Why are you showing her this stuff?"

"It's okay, Aaron. I know about the magic. I passed the test and Doc gave me the key." I fished it out of my pocket and held it up—that is, down.

"They gave you a key? And the first thing you do is play with the magic?" He sounded as stern as Mr. Mauskopf giving back exams.

"I'm not *playing*," I said with as much dignity as I could muster while hanging upside down. "Marc fixed these sandals, and I was testing them."

Aaron bent over so that he was looking at me right-side up. "Oh, you were 'testing' them, were you? I have to say it's a little hard to take you seriously with your hair standing straight up. Though you do look kind of cute that way," he said. "Like a broom with a face."

"Thanks—your hair's pretty funny too," I said, feeling as witty as an eight-year-old. I put my arms down and lowered myself onto the worktable. I had a little trouble getting my right foot to come too. Aaron guffawed.

Anjali distracted him. "Want some dessert?" she offered. "We were just about to have some."

"Well . . . maybe just a little."

*"Table, be cleared!"* said Anjali. All the *kartoffel*-this and *kartoffel*-that and something-wurst and something-else-schnitz vanished in a twinkling, leaving drips and crumbs in their wake. She gave the table a perfunctory wipe with a sponge and said, "Dessert now, please. *Table, be set!*"

The table groaned again. Even in my wildest childhood dreams, I had never seen so many cakes and tarts and puddings.

Marc and Aaron helped themselves.

"What would you like, Elizabeth?" asked Anjali.

"It all looks so good. Maybe that chocolate cake in the corner, the one with the cherries and cream?"

"One slice of *Schwarzwälder kirschtorte,* coming up." She handed me my plate and helped herself to apple strudel. "So, Aaron," she said, "what's up? Were you looking for something?"

"Just you," he said. "I mean, I wondered where you disappeared to," he added, a little stiffly. "It's after closing time. Doc will be locking up soon."

Anjali looked at her watch. "Oh, you're right. Time flies. *Table, be cleared!* Sorry, little thing, I'll give you a thorough cleaning next time." She patted it.

I helped her put the table back in the cabinet and we all gathered our things to get ready to go.

Then suddenly Anjali screamed.

"What? What is it?"

"Anjali!"

Both boys ran over to her. She was pointing to the skylight, her other hand at her neck. "There! It's really there, the bird!"

sewing box

Anjali was right—something was outside the skylight. The shape was dark and hard to make out against the evening sky, but we could clearly see a hooked beak and huge yellow eyes. Then, with the beat of what looked like a giant wing, it was gone.

I found I was trembling.

"Wow, that really was a giant bird!" Marc sounded freaked out. "Are you okay, Anjali?"

"I'm fine. Just scared," said Anjali.

"You're not walking home alone. You've got to let me take you," said Marc.

"Marc—you know you don't have time!"

"Let me, then," said Aaron.

I noticed nobody was offering to walk *me* anywhere. "You think the bird's after Anjali?" I asked.

"She saw it once before," said Marc. "It could be following her."

"We'd better tell the librarians," said Aaron.

Marc and Anjali looked at each other. "He's right," said Anjali. "They should know."

Doc was already gone, but we found Ms. Callender on Stack

6. "Oh, how scary!" she said. "What was it doing, just looking through the window? Or did it try to get in?"

"It was looking through the skylight," said Anjali. "It flew away as soon as I saw it, like it noticed me noticing it. What do you think it wanted?"

"Were you working on any Special Collection objects?"

"Yes, the winged sandals and Table-Be-Set—the German one."

"Well, this is very troubling. We'll have to talk to Dr. Rust tomorrow. You better all be extra careful. Are you going home together?" Ms. Callender asked.

"Good idea," I said. "Let's go together."

"Yes, honey," said Ms. Callender. "Stick together and stay safe."

The four of us put our heads down and hurried through the cold. Anjali's building wasn't far, just a few blocks away. As we reached her corner, a sharp, icy wind caught us and shook us. I pulled my collar up around my neck and wound my scarf around it, but the wind came in anyway.

"Why don't you replace that top button?" asked Anjali.

"You saw how I sew."

"You should have told me upstairs; I would have done it for you."

"Thanks, maybe I'll take you up on that next week."

"You know what? Come upstairs and I'll sew it now," she said.

"Oh, that would be great. Are you sure?"

"Of course. It's easy."

"Thanks, Anjali!"

We said good-bye to the guys at Anjali's door. She lived in one of the grand apartment buildings on Park Avenue. I often walked past them and peeked in at their gilded, marble-lined lobbies, but I'd never been inside. A doorman in a uniform, with brass buttons and a peaked cap, hurried forward to open the door. "Good evening, Miss Anjali," he said.

"Thank you, Harold," she answered without a trace of embarrassment, as if men in uniform opened the door for her and called her Miss Anjali every day of her life. Well, I guess they did.

The elevator had satinwood paneling and leather upholstered benches. We got off on the fourteenth floor. There were oil paintings hanging on the walls and a vase of fresh flowers standing on a little table. Anjali opened the door on the right. A delicious, spicy smell spilled out onto the landing. I followed her in.

"Anjali? Is that you?" someone called from deep within the apartment.

"Hi, Mom! I brought a friend home," Anjali answered. She hung up her coat in a closet by the door and took mine over her arm. I followed her down a hallway to a large living room. Her mother jumped up when she saw us and walked quickly across the carpet with the same springy pace as her daughter. She had on a conservative skirt and sweater, with expensive-looking shoes and rubies in her ears. She was about six times as beautiful as any mom I'd ever seen. I would have felt very intimidated if she hadn't been smiling so warmly.

"Mom, this is Elizabeth," said Anjali.

"Elizabeth Rew, yes? I'm Krishna Rao," said Mrs. Rao, holding out her hand. "I'm so very glad to meet you at last. Anjali has told me so much about you."

"She has?"

"Oh yes!" She had a high voice like her daughter's, with a melodic accent. "You work in the repository with Anjali and you go to Fisher High School and you are a great fan of basketball. Did I remember everything? It was so very kind of you to invite Anjali to the basketball game. I know how much she has been looking forward to it." She gave my hand a last squeeze and let go.

I glanced at Anjali, who seemed tense. "Our games are nothing compared to Fisher's," she said. "Fisher is so much bigger than Wharton, and of course Wharton is all girls, so Fisher's literally out of our league."

"That's right, and we have some amazing guys on the team. Like our star forward," I said, a little pointedly. "I think you know—" Anjali shook her head slightly with a panicky look, so I changed course. "You know what a blast the games are," I said instead.

Mrs. Rao beamed at me. "You are staying for dinner, of course? Do you like spicy food?"

"Oh, I . . . I don't know." I looked at Anjali, trying to get a sense of whether I was really welcome. She nodded almost imperceptibly. "I mean, yes, I love spicy food."

"Why don't you call your parents, then?" suggested Mrs. Rao.

As if they'd care, I thought, but I called home and got Cathy. "You were supposed to clean the bathroom tonight, but I guess you can leave it for tomorrow," she said.

"My stepmother says it's fine," I told Mrs. Rao. "Thank you so much."

"Lovely," she said. "Anjali, tell Aarti not too spicy. We don't want to scare away Elizabeth on her first visit."

Anjali's bedroom was vast for Manhattan, big enough for a queen-size bed, a desk, a small sofa, an armchair, and two floor-to-ceiling bookcases.

"So," I said, "we're going to the basketball game."

Anjali sat in the armchair opening a sewing box. It was made of dark wood, elaborately carved and inlaid with contrasting materials—ivory and mother-of-pearl. She bent over it so I couldn't see her face.

"I hope you don't mind. I wanted to meet Merritt and watch him play," she said. "But my parents . . . my parents think I should date Indian boys. Or nobody. Preferably nobody."

"Well, you can certainly come to the game with me. It'll be nice to have someone to go with."

Anjali looked up. "Thanks," she said. "Really, thanks. Do you have that button?"

I handed it to Anjali. As soon as she touched it, she looked startled. "This is from your coat?" she said. "Where did you get your coat?"

"Hand-me-down from my stepsister. But I lost the original top button. Dr. Rust gave me this one when I passed the sorting test."

"Oh! Should I sew on an ordinary button, then? I think I can find one that would fit." She handed it back.

Holding it up to my face, I knew at once it was no ordinary

button: I caught a faint whiff of smell that reminded me of the Grimm Collection. Where had Dr. Rust gotten it? What do magic buttons do?

"No, let's use this one. Dr. Rust must have meant it for my coat—it matches the rest of my buttons," I said.

Anjali pulled the head of her gooseneck reading lamp closer and threaded a needle.

As I watched, something caught at the edge of my vision, something out the window. How many floors up were we? Fourteen? A noise came from my throat, half gasp, half scream.

"What? What is it?"

I pointed to the window.

Anjali jumped out of her chair and snapped down the shade. She pulled the silk curtains shut. "What did you see?" she asked.

"I'm not sure. I think it was the gigantic bird again. Was Marc right—is it following you?"

"There's nothing there now."

"You're right. I could be imagining it. We're both jumpy."

From behind the door I heard a little shuffle. I gasped again. Anjali spun around. "Jaya!" she cried.

She leapt across the room to slam the door shut, but it was too late. There was a foot in the way—a biggish, sneakered foot on a skinny leg. Anjali seemed to grow bigger, like a great, glaring, black-feathered hawk herself. "Out!" she shrilled.

The sneaker didn't move.

"Jaya! I said *out!*"

"Anjali!" wailed the voice behind the sneaker. "What's following you?"

"You are, obviously. Get out of my room."

"I'm not in your room."

"Your foot is." Anjali kicked at it.

"Don't stomp! I'll tell Mom!"

"Go on, tell her. Run along and tell her and get your foot out of my door."

The foot didn't budge. "Come on, Anj, let me in. I want to meet your friend. I promise I'll sit very quietly in the corner; you won't even know I'm there. If something scary is following you around, I have a right to know. I could help. Or I might even be the one it's after."

"Yeah, right. It's a pest eater."

"Come on, Anjali! Please?"

"Oh, let her in," I said. "What's the harm?"

Anjali paused and looked pained. "This is a mistake," she said, slowly opening the door. A bundle of knees and elbows, topped with eyebrows, liquid black eyes, and a spiky dark cloud of hair flounced in and threw itself on the bed.

"Jaya! Get your sneakers off my quilt!"

Jaya shifted slightly so that the sneakered part of her legs was sticking out over the edge of the bed. She turned the eyebrows my way. "You're Elizabeth, right? You go to the school with the good basketball games. Can I come too?"

"No," said Anjali.

"But I want to see Merritt play!"

"Jaya! You disgusting little spy!"

"Oh, don't worry, I won't tell Mom and Dad. Who's Merritt, anyway? Your boyfriend?"

"Get off my bed! I mean it, get off!" Anjali lunged. I was

amused to see she was so bad at sister-wrangling. Was this the poised, unflappable Anjali I'd been admiring ever since I started work at the repository?

"Anji has a boyfriend! Anji has a boyfriend!" Jaya singsonged, kicking her feet in the air. Anjali looked ready to tear her to pieces.

I stepped in hastily. "Do you play basketball, Jaya? You look like you'd be good at it," I said.

"Really?" She sat up and looked at me. "Why?"

"You're tall for your age, and you have those long arms and legs. Get up, let me see you."

Jaya jumped up, leaving the quilt crumpled behind her.

"Catch!" I tossed a little lace pillow from the sofa. She snatched it out of the air and threw it back.

"Gently," I said, throwing it again. "You want to go for precision and control. Yeah, you'd definitely be good. You're not just tall for your age, you're quick too."

"How do you know I'm tall for my age? Do you know how old I am?"

"Ten," I said.

She looked disappointed. "Did Anjali tell you?"

"No, you look like a ten-year-old."

"If I look like a ten-year-old and I *am* a ten-year-old, how can I be tall for my age? If I'm tall, I should look like a twelve-year-old."

"You look like a tall ten-year-old."

Anjali was starting to look impatient. Still, at least Jaya wasn't talking about Marc anymore.

Now that she was no longer lying on Anjali's bed, Jaya threw herself around the room pretending to shoot baskets with the pillow. "Put that down, you're going to break something," said Anjali.

"Here," I said. I held my arms in a circle. Jaya made the layup, and I kept the pillow. I kicked off my shoes, stretched out on the sofa, and tucked the pillow under my cheek. Jaya pouted, then walked around the room, picking things up.

"Put that down, Jaya! It's fragile."

Jaya was holding a sandalwood fan. "Is this the fan from Auntie Shanti?" She inspected both sides. It was elaborately carved with what looked like stylized feathers.

"Yes. Put it down."

Jaya flounced carelessly over to the sofa where I was lying and fanned me. The air coming off the fan had a faint, disturbing, familiar smell. Sandalwood, yes, but what else? That fresh smell in the air after a thunderstorm? Vinyl? Toast? "Can I see that a sec?" I held out my hand.

Jaya looked at me suspiciously. "Why?"

"I want to check something out."

"Promise you'll give it back."

"We'll see." I kept my hand out.

Curiosity won over contrariness. She handed it over. I fanned my face and sniffed; I sniffed at the back, the front, the handle. Definitely magic. I looked at Anjali. "What is it?" I asked.

She shrugged. "Sandalwood?" Was she just being discreet in front of her sister, or did she really not know? I handed the fan back to Jaya. "Put it back on the shelf," I said. "Carefully."

A little to my surprise, Jaya obeyed, sniffing it herself on the way over. She reached for an inlaid box next to it on the shelf, but Anjali said, "No!" in a new, quiet voice.

It was clear she meant it; even Jaya paused. "Leave that," Anjali said.

"But I just want to see inside," said Jaya.

"Leave it alone. I mean it. Auntie Shanti said it's bottomless, and so will you be if you touch it."

Was she kidding, or did she mean it literally? And what was Anjali's family doing with these magical objects?

In a way, I thought, it wasn't any weirder for Anjali's family to have magic than for magic to exist at all. And after all, they had lots of things most families didn't have, like carved tables and inlaid chests and fancy flower arrangements. I wondered again what magical properties the fan had.

Jaya shrugged and threw herself on the sofa next to me. "So, what's the scary thing that's after you?" she asked conversationally.

"Oh, Jaya, go away," said Anjali. "Don't you have homework or something?"

"Already did it. What's the scary thing?"

"Nothing."

"Then why was Elizabeth screaming?"

"She wasn't screaming."

Jaya turned to me. "Is something scary after you? Because I know a good protection spell."

"You do?"

"I need a piece of string. Or thread or ribbon or something." She flung herself up off the sofa like a fountain of sticks, pounced on Anjali's sewing box, extracted some fuchsia yarn, and snapped off a length with her teeth.

"Jaya, that's disgusting," said Anjali automatically. She knotted off the thread she had been using to sew on the button and snipped it neatly with little bird-beaked scissors.

Jaya ignored her. "Hold out your arm," she ordered. She wrapped the yarn around my wrist twice and began working on a knot, biting her lower lip, tucking the ends under and over, making loops around her fingers.

At last she took an end in each hand—pinching me slightly—and declaimed, *"By this charm, be safe from harm!"* With that she pulled the knot tight and grinned at me proudly.

I looked at my wrist. It had a bracelet of hot-pink yarn with a lumpy knot and slightly frayed, spit-wet ends. "Thank you, Jaya," I said.

"Don't take that off. As long as it stays on your arm, you should be safe—from bad magic, anyway. I don't think it works for muggers or car crashes."

"Where did you learn that? Auntie Shanti?" asked Anjali.

"No, Miss Bender."

"Who's Miss Bender?" I asked.

"Sewing teacher."

"You guys take sewing?"

"Of course. All Wharton girls learn how to sew. It's an important part of a young lady's education," said Jaya. She sounded like she was quoting a teacher.

"Miss Bender's the one who got me the job at the repository," said Anjali.

"Oh. I see." Anjali's equivalent of Mr. Mauskopf.

If their sewing teacher—Anjali's connection to the Grimm

Collection—was teaching the Rao girls magical spells to ward off evil, perhaps Mr. Mauskopf would have some that would help me, I wondered. Should I ask him? What a difference this job was making in my life! On the plus side: magic! And maybe even more important: friends. On the minus side: also magic. The dark, scary kind—the kind that makes you worry about warding off evil.

We heard a knock on the door. "Anjali? Jaya? Dinner is ready."

Anjali's parents ate with their fingers. It sounds messy, but it wasn't, not at all—they had elegant table manners, delicately scooping and pinching morsels with bits of thin flat bread or clumps of rice. Mr. Rao saw me looking nervously at my plate. "Didn't Aarti give you a fork?" he asked me. "I'm sorry, I should have told her; that was thoughtless of me. Aarti! Silverware for our guest, please," he called. He was a portly man, genial and commanding. He looked a lot like his younger daughter, despite her skinny spikiness. "Do you need something else to drink, Elizabeth? Some ginger ale?"

"Yes, please, I'd love some."

"Ginger ale, please, Aarti."

"I want some too," said Jaya, jumping up.

"Sit still, Jaya. Aarti will bring it," said her mother.

We ate a sort of bean stew and a puffy thing and a vegetable I didn't recognize. It was all delicious; I happily accepted second helpings. I was sorry when the meal ended and a little scared too—scared to walk out into the cold, dark streets where the bird might be lurking. Anjali offered to walk me to the subway, but of course I said no.

I fingered the yarn around my wrist nervously and buttoned the top button of my coat tightly around my throat. But the sky was empty all the way home. Whatever the bird was after, evidently it wasn't me.

# Chapter 11:
## A feather and a key

I went looking for Mr. Mauskopf on Monday. Evidently he'd been looking for me too. "Elizabeth," he said. "When do you next work at the repository?"

"Tomorrow."

"Good. Will you give this to Dr. Rust for me?" He handed me a largish package wrapped in brown paper and tied with string. "Put it in Lee's own hands. It's very important. Do not entrust it to anyone else. Can you do that?"

"Sure."

"And don't open it."

"Of course not!" As if I would open someone else's mail!

"Thank you, Elizabeth. How are you getting on at the repository?"

"It's fantastic—I love it. They gave me a key to the Grimm Collection."

"Yes, Lee told me. Congratulations! They don't give out those keys lightly, you know. If things go well, you'll have borrowing privileges soon too."

"Really, you think so? That would be so awesome! I can't believe the things they have in the collection!"

Mr. Mauskopf smiled. "No, I couldn't believe it at first either.

You understand what an honor it is to be asked to take care of them, don't you? An honor and a responsibility. It's not always easy."

"Yes, I know. Mr. Mauskopf, a strange thing has happened. Remember how you said you'd heard the rumors about an enormous bird? I think we saw it—me and the other pages, Marc and Anjali and Aaron. It was hovering near the skylight at the repository, and then when I went over to Anjali's apartment, I thought I saw it again."

"You saw the bird! Tell me, how big was it?"

"Bigger than me. It was definitely no ordinary bird."

Mr. Mauskopf looked worried. "I'm glad you told me. If it makes you feel better, I'll have a word with Griffin. I'll tell him to keep an eye on you."

"Griffin? Your dog?" I wanted to ask what good that would do, but it seemed too rude.

"That's right. And I think you'd better take this." From his shirt pocket, with two long, bony fingers, Mr. Mauskopf plucked something small, brown, and smudgy, which he held out to me. It was a feather.

"Thank you. What—what do I—?"

"Keep it safe, and when your need is great, give it to the wind. And remember to take care with that package."

I wanted to ask him more, but the second bell rang and I had to run or be late for French.

Mr. Mauskopf's package was too wide for my backpack, so I carried it under my arm, clutching the string with my gloved fingers.

A faint smell rose from it, like swimming pools, reminding me of summer. Swimming pools and bananas . . . no, something else. Tire swings, maybe? I walked downtown along Fifth Avenue beside the park, trying to tease apart the shifting components of the magic smell and watching the sinking sun paint the snow with purple shadows. It felt good to be walking; the cold pinched life into my cheeks. A flock of crows passed overhead, silhouetted against the sunset. Something odd about the birds caught my eye, and I stopped and looked up. One seemed too big to be a crow. A hawk? I couldn't see it any longer, but I had a bad feeling, like at Anjali's. I picked up my pace, craning my head behind me.

Then the enormous bird appeared again. It spun and swooped, coming right at me. I started to run.

Something even bigger than the bird appeared from behind a clump of trees, crossing the sky. It didn't look like the bird—it was the wrong shape, more rectangular, like a horse or a lion. They were both coming at me fast. I panicked, running faster while looking at them over my shoulder instead of where I was going. I crashed straight into someone, hard, and my package went flying. I landed facedown in the snow, but at least I was alive and had only been hit by a human.

"Are you all right?" A man stood over me, holding out his hand. He pulled me to my feet.

"I'm so sorry!" I said, brushing off snow. "I'm okay—did I hurt *you*?"

He smiled, a crooked smile amid a neatly trimmed little beard. "No, no, I'm fine. You were in quite a hurry." He bent over to pick up the envelopes and packages we had dropped, and I recognized him—he was the creepy little man from the Main Exam Room who liked to stare at Anjali.

"Yes, I—" I looked around for the bird, or birds. No sign of either one. "I'm sorry, I wasn't looking where I was going."

"No harm done."

"Is that my package?" I asked. He was carrying several largish packages like the one Mr. Mauskopf had given me, wrapped in brown paper.

"No, I don't think so—but I do seem to have one or two too many."

"Mine was addressed to Dr. Rust at the New-York Circulating Material Repository," I said.

"Well! Isn't that a strange coincidence! I was just on my way there myself." He showed me one of his packages, addressed to Dr. Rust. "I thought you looked familiar. You're one of the pages, aren't you? I've seen you in the repository. I can take your package along to Dr. Rust with mine."

"No!" It came out panicky and rude. "No, thank you, that's okay. I need to take it to Dr. Rust myself."

"It's no trouble, and it'll get there faster. I'm on my way to the repository right now. I assure you, it will be safer with me." He hesitated. "Tell me, do you work in the Grimm Collection?"

"What? Why do you want to know that?"

"Ah, you do. Don't worry, you're not spilling any secrets. I know all about the collection," he said reassuringly.

"I still need my package," I said.

"Yes. Well. About that . . . I don't mean to frighten you, but there have been some thefts of Grimm items. Some members have reported a—well, a large flying *creature*—menacing them or even snatching items out of their hands. And I think we both saw what was following you."

"You saw the bird!" I said, shivering. "Is it gone now?"

"For now, yes. But I really think you'll be safer if you let me take charge of your package. You may have something that the creature is after."

"Why wouldn't it just follow *you* then?"

He smiled. "It might. But I'm older and more experienced with . . . well, with these sorts of situations. I can take care of myself. And I would feel really terrible if anything happened to you."

"Thank you," I said. "It's nice of you. But I just can't. I promised I would take the package to Dr. Rust himself. Can I have it back, please?"

He shrugged. "Here you go, then." He handed me one of the packages. Like the one Mr. Mauskopf had given me, it had Dr. Rust's name in brown ink on the wrapping and was tied with string. But something wasn't quite right. I sniffed it. It smelled like wet brown paper . . . and firecrackers . . . and skunk cabbage . . . Like magic, but the wrong magic.

"This isn't it," I said.

"Of course it is."

"No, you must have gotten them mixed up. Mine is that one." I pointed to the package under his arm.

"No, this one's mine," he insisted.

"Let me see it." I took hold of it with both hands. He hung

on as I pulled it toward my chest. The top button of my coat, the button Anjali had sewn on for me, pressed against his hand as he grabbed for the package.

The man's fingers uncurled slowly, trembling a little, as if against his will. He snarled. For a moment I had the awful feeling he was about to . . . I don't know, *attack* me somehow.

Then he pulled himself together. He picked up the package he'd tried to give me. "I'm sorry," he said. "I was just trying to protect you. But I can see you're a stubborn young lady. Brave too. Be careful. I hope you can keep yourself safe." And he strode away through the snow.

I locked my bedroom door when I got home and put the package on my desk. I couldn't shake the creepy feeling the encounter had given me. I looked the package over. The snow had smudged the brown ink on the brown paper wrapper, but I could still recognize Mr. Mauskopf's handwriting. It *was* his, wasn't it? I hadn't been mistaken and taken the wrong package? I sniffed at it. It smelled magical to me, with summery magic: a little piney, a little salty, carnations. But the other package had clearly been magical too. Maybe I should open it and see what is inside, I thought.

No sooner had the thought occurred to me than a passionate desire to do it swept over me. I knew it was foolish. What would be the point? I had no idea what was in Mr. Mauskopf's package, so opening this one wouldn't tell me if this was the right one. I would break my promise for nothing. But my curiosity was so strong I could hardly bear it. What if I just opened a corner and peeked in? Almost against my will, my fingers crept toward it.

"Stop it, Elizabeth!" I said out loud. I locked the package in my desk drawer, slammed my mind shut, and concentrated on French irregular verbs.

The next day at the repository I tapped on Dr. Rust's open door.

"Do you have a moment? Mr. Mauskopf asked me to bring you this."

"Excellent, thank you." Doc turned it over and looked at the blurred address and the wrinkled wrapping. "You didn't open it, did you?"

"No," I said, feeling obscurely guilty, as if I had. "I dropped it, though. In the snow. I hope it didn't get damaged. I had a hard time getting it here—I wanted to talk to you about that."

"That's to be expected." Doc took out a paper knife—it looked like a small dagger—and slit the wrappings. Inside was a plain wooden box. "Let's take a look first, shall we?"

I craned forward. Doc lifted the lid, revealing a stack of paper dolls. Before my startled eyes, layer after layer sprang to life, puffing into three dimensions and leaping out of the box. They threw themselves into the most beguiling acrobatics, dancing around the room like Doc's freckles on fast-forward.

A pair of the acrobats balanced a pencil across the stapler and used it as a seesaw, catapulting each other into the air. Another pair shimmied up the desk lamp and cannonballed into the water carafe below. A third pair unrolled tape from the tape dispenser and stuck the other end to the desk lamp. They held both ends of the tape tight while half a dozen of their friends took turns cavorting across in a series of leaps, flips, and cartwheels, like gymnasts on a balance beam.

"I see you were telling the truth," said Doc.

"I was. But how can you tell?"

Doc smiled. "Try to get them back in the box."

"All right." I turned to the little people. "Enough, now. Back in the box with you," I told them.

Ignoring me, they lined up to dance the Virginia reel.

"Come on, now. Back in the box!" I held it open near them, as invitingly as I could.

Still ignoring me, they began prancing up and down the desk.

Quickly, before they could get away, I picked up the head couple and put them gently in the box. But the lid wouldn't close—their heads were too thick. I had to let go and try to pick up another pair. But they wouldn't let me catch them at all. They joined hands and skipped just out of my reach.

"I give up," I said at last.

"Feisty little critters, aren't they?" Doc took a thin stick out of a drawer and tapped the dancers with it one by one. As soon as the stick touched them, they lost their girth and fluttered down to the desk, paper thin again. Doc stacked them in the box and snapped the catch shut.

What a good thing I hadn't opened the box! Or let the man with the beard take it. "Dr. Rust? Did a man bring you a package yesterday that looked just like this one?" I asked.

"I was out yesterday, but I did get some packages—I often do. One or two of them might have been wrapped like this one. Why?"

"I ran into a man on the way home from school yesterday when I was carrying this package. Literally ran into him. I dropped the package, and he tried to take it. He said he was on his way to give you some other packages just like this. When I told him to give it back, he said he was a repository member and it would be safer for me to let him give you the package. He tried to switch them, but I wouldn't let him."

"That was the right decision."

"But there actually *was* a flying creature following me. We saw it a few days ago too—me and Anjali and Marc and Aaron. Did Ms. Callender tell you?"

Doc nodded. "Yes, she did. That's very serious! Did the man tell you his name?"

I shook my head.

"What did he look like?"

"Short, with a beard. I've seen him in the Main Exam Room."

"Will you come and find me if you see him again?"

"Of course. Why do you think he wanted my package so badly? Do you think he's the guy who's stealing things from the Grimm Collection?"

"I wish I knew. But right now I'm more concerned about the creature. Can you describe it?"

"It definitely looked like an enormous bird. It was bigger than me and it came flying right at me. But then another huge bird—or something, I couldn't see too clearly—showed up and then I bumped into the guy with the beard, and then the bird or birds were both gone. Do you think the man was right—were they after the package? Would they have hurt me?"

"I'm very glad they didn't, at any rate. Probably the man was right and they were after the package."

"But what *were* they?"

"The bird sounds like the one we've heard about before. This is the first I've heard of the other creature, though. Was this the first time you saw them?"

"I'm pretty sure I've seen the bird before—through the sky-light in Preservation and through Anjali's window."

"What did Stan Mauskopf have to say—did you tell him?"

"Just that I thought I had seen the bird—but that was before it chased me and I got a better look and the stuff happened with the package."

"Did Stan give you a charm or a ward or anything?"

"No . . . well, yes, I almost forgot; he gave me a feather."

Doc's face brightened. "Good—that's just the thing. Make sure you keep it with you. I'm sorry about all this. I knew it would be challenging for you to bring me the acrobats, but I had no idea it would be dangerous too. You can be proud of yourself. You've passed a harder test than we intended."

"What do you mean? What test?"

"For borrowing privileges."

"You don't mean—the Grimm Collection?"

Doc nodded. "Stan asked you to bring me the dancers to see whether you're responsible enough to be trusted to take care of Grimm items outside the repository. Clearly the answer is yes."

"You mean it? I can borrow things now? *Magic* things?"

"Yes. Whenever you feel ready."

"Can I take out anything I like? Even, like, I don't know—a genie bottle?"

Doc smiled. "I wouldn't go straight for the genie bottles

right away. The Grimm objects can be pretty tricky. Best to start with something small."

"All right. Thank you!" This was so exciting!

"Meanwhile," said Doc, "given the recent thefts and that bird, I'll be changing the door codes and the procedures. Librarians have master keys, but you pages will need two keys to get in, yours and another page's—Anjali, Aaron, or Marc—as well as the key song. You'll have to go down there in pairs so you can keep an eye on each other. Never lend your key to anyone, and let me know if anyone asks to borrow it."

"I will. I'll do everything I can to keep the collection safe," I said fervently.

I hoped I could keep myself safe too.

*Chapter 12:*
*An invisible armchair*

I was excited the next day when Ms. Callender sent me to work in the Grimm Collection with Aaron.

"What will we be doing there?" I asked. "Running slips?"

"Yes, if you get any. I mostly just want someone down there keeping an eye on things. Until we catch the thief, at least we can try to make things harder for them by guarding the collection."

Aaron was at the door when I arrived. He looked different in the bright, fluorescent light. I realized I had only spent time with him in the half darkness on Stack 2. He was surprisingly normal-looking without all the dramatic shadows. Handsome, even—I made myself do him the justice of admitting it. He had pro-nounced, chiseled features, like a prince in a fairy tale. High cheekbones, a single dark curl tumbling gracefully over an up-right forehead, and a cleft chin. "There you are," he said. "Where've you been? I can't get in without both keys."

"Sorry I kept you waiting!" I held my binder clip against the door and sang, as softly as I could. I didn't want to risk any sar-castic comments about my singing voice.

"Louder," said Aaron. "They'll never hear you in the back of the house."

The lock didn't mind; it clicked open.

"That was the point," I said. "I was trying not to hurt everybody's ears."

"Why? You didn't sound so bad, at least the part I could hear."

"Um, thanks."

I held the door for Aaron and followed him into the Grimm Collection. There were two chairs by the pneum station: an armchair carved elaborately from dark wood with a velvet seat and back and a standard-issue gray metal folding chair. I hesitated. The armchair looked more comfortable, but it also looked old enough to be part of the collection. Perhaps the folding chair was safer?

While I was deliberating, Aaron sat down in the armchair.

I unfolded the folding chair and sat down myself. I took off my sweater too and draped it over the back.

Aaron took out a book.

"What are you reading?" I asked.

"H. G. Wells. *The War of the Worlds.*"

"Any good?"

"So far." He leaned back in the chair and stretched out his legs.

"You look comfy. What is that chair? Is it part of the collection?" I asked.

Aaron looked up from his book and grinned. "Naturally. It's in here, isn't it?"

"So it's magic? What does it do?"

"It's amazing. When I lower my weight onto it, it magically causes my butt not to hit the ground."

"Uh-huh. Unlike every other chair in the universe."

"Yes, but this one does it so much better," he said. "Even better than that one over there." He pointed to the blank wall on the other side of the pneum station.

"Where? I don't see any chair," I said.

"Well, you wouldn't, would you? It's invisible," said Aaron. He got up and walked over to the wall where he'd been pointing, then lowered himself until his knees were bent at a right angle.

"You're faking it," I said.

"Whatever you say." He crossed his legs and opened his book. If he really was miming, he must have very strong legs.

I walked over and inspected him. His legs seemed steady. "How long can you go on sitting that way?" I asked.

"As long as you want, unless we have to run a call slip or something. It's a comfortable chair," said Aaron. "Want to try it?" He got up and stepped aside, as if he were offering me his chair.

"Ha! You can't fool me. You just got up because your legs were tired," I said.

"My legs, tired? From sitting in this comfortable chair? Don't be silly. Try it, you'll see," he said.

"Okay, I will." I lowered myself slowly along the wall.

A little past the point where the chair seat should have been I lost my balance and slid to the floor.

Aaron held out his hand, laughing. "I'm so sorry, Elizabeth! I tried to stop that elf from pulling the chair out from under you at the last minute, but I didn't catch him in time. Bad elf!"

"Pig!" I said, laughing myself and letting Aaron pull me to my feet. "I don't really feel like sitting anyway," I said. It seemed like such a waste to be sitting still in a room full of magic. I strolled over to the cabinets.

"What are you doing?" asked Aaron.

"Just looking around."

"Don't touch anything."

"I'm not. Don't touch anything yourself," I said.

"No, really. All kidding aside, this stuff is dangerous. Don't touch."

"Don't worry, I won't."

Instead of sitting back down with his book, Aaron strolled beside me.

"What's the matter, you don't trust me? *You're* the one who tricked *me* into falling all over the floor," I said, but I didn't actually mind having him there. On my last visit down here, I remembered, the very air had seemed to be holding its breath with a threatening buzz. The place felt less threatening with Aaron there.

"You're saying I made you weak in the knees? Well, I do tend to have that effect on girls," said Aaron.

"You mean they trip all over their feet trying to get away from you?"

"Ooh, harsh," he said.

I sniffed as I strolled, enjoying the shifting smells. Faint jasmine. Or was it honeysuckle? No, fresh-caught fish when you fillet it on the dock before putting it in the cooler. No, a wet feather pillow. No, plastic bags. Cough syrup.

We passed the bowls and cauldrons, the bottles, the shoes.

"Hey, Aaron. How come there are so many shoes down here?"

He shrugged. "They show up in a lot of fairy tales. 'Puss in Boots.' 'Cinderella.' 'The Elves and the Shoemaker.' Those stupid dancing princesses."

"Stupid? That's my favorite story! What's stupid about them?"

"They were too busy thinking about dancing to notice a great big soldier in their boat, for one thing."

"But he was invisible!"

"Like that would stop *you* from noticing. He was following them the whole time."

"Well, the youngest princess did notice. She heard him breaking twigs in the forests of silver and gold and diamonds."

"Okay, so maybe she was less stupid than her sisters. But she still had that dancing obsession like the rest of them. She wore out her shoes dancing every night. You wouldn't waste all your nights like that, would you?"

"I couldn't afford to," I said, thinking of how much I'd enjoyed my dance classes with Nicole and my friends at my old school. But no more dance classes and no more old school, with Dad spending our money putting my stepsisters through college. "Which brings us back to the shoes in this collection. Why so many?"

"I don't know. There weren't any cars back when the Brothers Grimm were collecting stuff. Maybe they thought about shoes a whole lot because they had to walk everywhere and their feet hurt."

"That's an interesting theory. You think maybe other stuff was just as important, but the Grimm guys only noticed the shoe aspect? Like, they missed whole stories about hats and scarves because their feet hurt?"

Aaron laughed. "Yeah, I bet you're right. There are a few hats here, but not nearly as many as the shoes."

"So how did you get this job, anyway?" I asked.

"My science teacher."

"Why'd he pick you?"

"For my brains and good looks, obviously."

"Yeah, right. My social studies teacher picked me, but I can't really figure out why."

"For your brains and good looks, obviously."

"Um, thanks." Had Aaron just complimented me? Wow. "Seriously, though," I said. "Why *us*? I can't believe my luck to be in a place like this. You know how when you were a little kid reading fairy tales, you always dreamed that the magic was true? Why are we the ones who get to find out it is?"

Aaron nodded slowly. "I know," he said. "For me it was science fiction, but yeah, that's exactly how I feel too. How can we be so lucky? Is it really just affinities, like Doc says?"

"What do you mean?"

"You know, the things you're drawn to. The things you find compelling. Like the way I'm always trying to figure out how stuff works. Or with you, you always seem to be looking closely at everything. You see how objects relate to each other. It's as if, for you, the whole world is alive." He paused, then added with a little smile, "Except maybe invisible chairs."

Wow, had he noticed that about me? That was pretty observant. "You know, you're right," I said. "I think I got that from my mother. She cared about objects, but not in a material way. She was always looking for the souls in things. She had this great antique doll collection—she treated them as if they were alive. Like she knew they had a past."

We reached the end of the room and turned back toward the door. As we passed the rack of paintings, I felt eyes on my back, as if the figures in the paintings were looking at me.

Even with Aaron there, I felt spooked.

We heard a noise up front. The door was rattling, as if someone—or something—was trying to get in. I froze, then told myself not to be so silly. But I noticed Aaron looked alarmed too.

"Who's there?" he asked loudly.

"It's just me." Anjali's voice came through the door faint and muffled. "For some reason my key's not working."

"Hang on, we've got another one. You need two now," I said. I held my clip to the door, sang the opening chant as softly and quickly and in key as I could, and pushed the door open.

"Thanks, Elizabeth," said Anjali.

"Are you running a slip? What's the item?" Aaron asked. He had that eager sound in his voice again, the way he always did around Anjali, and I remembered that I hated him.

"No, I—I think I forgot something last week. My . . . sweater. I think I left it in the back."

It sounded like an excuse she'd made up on the spot. "I think I saw it back near the paintings. I'll show you," I said. Aaron got up to follow us. "You better stay here and keep an eye on the pneums," I told him.

"If one comes, I'll hear it thump."

Boy, was he persistent! He just couldn't keep away from her.

"No, really, I—I need to talk to Anjali about something. Girl stuff again," I said.

"Fine." He sat back down.

Anjali and I walked back toward the wall of paintings. I stopped in front of the shoe section. "I know you didn't actually forget your sweater. Is it the boots again?" I whispered.

Anjali nodded. She took the real boots out of her book bag and swapped them for the fakes, switching the tag. This time I found I could tell them apart easily. They might look exactly the same, but they gave off a different atmosphere. It was obvious—I didn't even have to sniff. I wondered how I could ever have missed it.

"Can't you make Marc stop taking them? He's going to get in trouble. He's going to get *you* in trouble—us." I kept my voice down. I doubted Aaron could hear, all the way up in the front of the collection, but I had the feeling there were other ears listening all around us.

"Marc says it's the last time."

"Didn't he say that before?"

"He has to pick up Andre. His mother's working late."

"He always has to pick up Andre."

"I know. He says he'll find some other solution."

"Well, he'd better do it fast. Come on, you better get out of here."

"Hey, you're still wearing that!" Anjali touched the hot-pink yarn Jaya had knotted around my wrist. It was getting grubby, but it had lasted through quite a few showers. I nodded. Anjali said, "Jaya will be pleased."

The door was opening as we got back to the front of the room. Ms. Callender came into the collection.

"Anjali? What are you doing here, honey? Didn't I put you on Stack 9? Did I get mixed up?" said Ms. Callender. She consulted her clipboard.

"She came back for her sweater," said Aaron helpfully.

Ms. Callender turned to Anjali. "Did you find it, honey?"

"Here," I said, grabbing my sweater from the back of the folding chair and handing it to Anjali. Aaron frowned at me, but he didn't say anything.

"Oh, so that's where I left it," said Anjali, a little too loudly. You'd think she would be better at lying, with a nosy little sister like Jaya. "Thanks, Elizabeth," she said, putting on the sweater.

It looked ten thousand times better on her than on me. She had the right kind of figure for a sweater like that. Of course, I reflected, if she were wearing a paper bag, I would probably think she had the right kind of figure for paper bags. She had the right kind of figure, period.

Ms. Callender waved something at the lock—must be the master key, I thought—causing it to click open, and held the door for Anjali, who left with my sweater.

I was right to trust Anjali and Marc, wasn't I? The suspicious look on Aaron's face made me feel less certain than ever.

*Chapter 13:*
*I lose a*
*thumb-wrestling match*

When Anjali was gone, Ms. Callender put a sheaf of papers on Aaron's desk. "Aaron, Elizabeth, I have a big job for you. I need you to pull these objects off the shelves for me," she said.

"What are they for?" I asked.

"These are items we're . . . concerned about. I told you about the reports of objects like ours turning up in auctions and other collections? Some of these match those descriptions, or raised a red flag somehow. Dr. Rust and I want to examine them more closely. Send a pneum up when you're done, okay? If something's missing, make a note of it."

"All right," said Aaron.

"Thanks, hon." Ms. Callender waved her key at the door again and left.

"So much for *The War of the Worlds*," I said.

Aaron shrugged. "I wasn't getting that much reading done anyway. What was that all about with Anjali?"

"I told you, girl stuff. You really want me to spell it out?"

"Actually, yes."

"Fine. Feel free to stop me whenever you like. When a girl gets to be a certain age, she experiences certain changes caused by something called hormones. These are chemicals that signal to the reproductive organs, causing the blood—"

"Okay, okay, enough! I get it—you're not going to tell me what it was really about. Which half do you want?" He held out a clump of pages in each hand.

I took the ones in his right hand, and we each set off in opposite directions, pushing our carts down the rows of cabinets.

My half of Ms. Callender's list was heavy on clothing: cloaks, helmets, dresses, buckles, veils, and the inevitable shoes. I found them all in their proper spots except one bracelet—when I went to look for it, all I found was a wooden bracelet-shaped placeholder tagged with a form saying the original had been missing since 1929. I made a note of it.

Nevertheless, I noticed something was odd about the items when I pulled them off the shelves. What was it? It nagged at me as I piled my first truckload on the table by the door and started on the paperwork. I filled out a slip for each of them, naming Ms. Callender as the requester. The paperwork took longer than gathering the objects had.

Aaron came back with a load—mostly musical instruments—and sat down to fill out slips.

"What should I put for *Purpose of Loan*?" I asked.

"I'm putting *Internal*. They're not actually leaving the repository."

I picked up the next one, little metal binoculars. Something felt off about them too. "What's wrong with these things?" I asked.

"What do you mean?"

"I don't know—they don't feel right to me." I put down my

pencil and walked over to Aaron's cart. "What about yours, are they wrong too?" I picked up a wooden flute and blew it. It made a raspy, woody note, like a cheap recorder.

"Stop!" Aaron shouted.

I lowered the flute. "What? What's the matter?"

He looked terrified and puzzled. "That's a dancing flute. It's from the same section as the Pied Piper's pipes. People can't stop dancing when you play it. In some of the stories they dance themselves to death."

"Really? I don't see you dancing."

"Thankfully! Maybe it takes a few bars to warm up? Or maybe you're not a good enough musician?"

I lifted the flute again.

"Stop!" Aaron grabbed my hand. "Weren't you listening? Are you trying to kill me?"

His hand was cold. I shook it off. "Let go, I'm not going to play it." I brought the flute to my nose and sniffed. It smelled like old, slightly dusty wood. "Does that smell right to you?" I held it out.

He sniffed it and shrugged.

I sniffed it again. "I think that's what's wrong with these things—they don't smell right." I sniffed a cymbal; it smelled like brass. A bellows smelled like dusty leather. On my own cart, a coat smelled like wool, a linen shift like fabric softener, and a gold pin like nothing at all.

"What's this supposed to do?" I asked, holding up a glove that smelled a little musty.

Aaron checked the list. "It makes your hand strong."

I put it on.

"Don't do that! You could get in big trouble. You know we're not supposed to use the stuff!"

"Doesn't matter—I have a feeling it's not going to work anyway," I said. "Thumb wrestle?" I held out my gloved hand. He took it and pinned my thumb immediately. I wiggled and struggled, but I couldn't get it free.

"Quit waving your elbow around, that's cheating," he said.

"Okay, okay, let go. Clearly this glove isn't working. I think these things are fakes."

"Let me try it."

I handed him the glove, and he put it on. He pinched the corner of the metal desk, trying to dent it; nothing happened. He punched the wall. "Ow!" he said, shaking his hand. The wall appeared undamaged.

I sniffed my way through my cart. A few of the objects gave off that mysterious, shifting scent, but most smelled of nothing much.

"What are you doing?" asked Aaron.

"Sorting out the fakes. Those are okay, but these smell wrong—I mean, they smell normal. There's no magic in them."

"You can smell magic?"

"Can't you?"

"I don't know. I don't think so. I've never tried."

I handed him a comb that smelled like oyster shells—no, wet marble. "Try this one; it's pretty strong. Can you smell it?"

He sniffed and shook his head. "I don't smell anything. I think you're right, though. It has that shimmer."

"What shimmer?"

"It's—you know—the color. It's sort of . . . It's hard to

describe. It's like the colors are sort of buzzing. Like there are more colors than just the ones you see."

I squinted at the comb, but I couldn't see anything funny about the color—it looked like a plain mother-of-pearl comb to me. I held out my hand. "Here, give, I'm going to try it."

He held it out of my reach. "Bad idea! Combs can be deadly! Remember Snow White?"

"Oh, is this Snow White's?" Snow White's stepmother, I recalled, paralyzed the princess with a poisoned comb. I didn't want anything more to do with that family, especially after my recent chat with the mirror. "Where's it from?"

Aaron consulted Ms. Callender's list. "It says it's a mermaid's comb," he said. "Mediterranean. Abalone."

"Oh. Well, that's all right, then. Mermaids just sit on rocks combing their hair and enticing sailors to their doom. It should be safe—there's no water for you to drown in. Hand it over." I held out my hand again.

"Shouldn't you do a little more research first?"

"I'm feeling lucky. What's the worst that can happen? You'll act all lovesick puppy about *me* instead of Anjali?"

Was he blushing? "Yeah, right." He gave me the comb. "Go wild. But don't blame me if your hair turns into seaweed."

I ran the comb through my hair. It felt great, like a tingling herbal massage. I combed for a while, practically purring with pleasure. I shook my head out and combed from one side and then the other. I bent over and combed from the nape of my neck to the top of my head.

"Having fun?" said Aaron.

"Mm, it's great! Are you in love with me yet?"

He snorted. "In your dreams."

"Seriously, has anything happened? Does my hair look any different?"

He shrugged. "Still looks like hair to me."

I brought a fistful around to my eyes, but it didn't look particularly different. It felt different, though. Thicker, silkier, somehow floatier, the way your hair feels on the perfect hair day, just after you've washed it and before it's quite dry. Like a slow-motion shampoo commercial.

"You don't have a mirror, do you?"

Aaron snorted again. "In what, my handbag? I'm a guy, remember?"

I thought about looking for a mirror in the collection, but I dropped the idea immediately. Even if I found one that wasn't evil, how would I know whether any apparent changes in my appearance were the result of the comb's magic or the mirror's?

"I don't know," I said. "I can't tell for sure, but I think it worked."

"Yeah," said Aaron, "I think so too." To my surprise, he reached out and ran his fingers through my hair. "It's nice . . . It's a nice . . . color." Then he quickly pulled his hand back and turned away.

After a pause, I cleared my throat. "So, um, what do you think this means?"

"Means?" He blushed beet red.

"I mean," I said quickly, "are all these dead objects substitutes for ones that got stolen? But if so, then why do some of them smell like magic?"

"Oh. Oh . . . I don't know. Maybe you're right—maybe the dead ones are fakes. Or maybe someone took the magic out of them somehow?" He started going through my piles, picking up the objects one by one and holding them to the side of his face, tilting them this way and that way to inspect them. He held out a silk coin purse. "This one's shimmering. You had it in the fakes pile."

I sniffed it. "Oh. You're right. It's very faint, though. What is it?"

He consulted the list. "Silk purse. English Midlands. Sow's ear."

"I wonder what it does?" I turned it upside down and shook it. Nothing came out.

"I don't think it does anything. I think it's just an impossible object—haven't you heard that expression, 'You can't make a silk purse from a sow's ear'?"

I nodded and put the purse in the pile of magical items. I hadn't, in fact, heard that expression, but I didn't feel like giving Aaron yet another thing to tease me about.

"What's the difference between the ones that work and the ones that don't?" I said.

Aaron looked at me like I was an idiot. "Um, the ones that work work, and the ones that don't don't?"

I felt my cheeks redden again. "I meant, is there any other difference? Do the useless ones have anything in common? Is there a pattern in the paperwork?"

"I don't see any, do you?"

I shook my head.

Aaron finished filling out slips and went back for another

cartload. I continued to write, sniffing the sow's ear purse absently. No, it really didn't smell like much. I squinted at it sideways, imitating Aaron, but the color—a fleshy pink, like the inside of a shell—still looked perfectly normal. On an impulse, I held the purse to my ear. I heard waves and whispers, like when you listen to a shell, but nothing definite.

I took my half of the list and went for another load. This time two objects were missing, a perfume flask and a ring.

I was starting to fill out my third slip when Aaron came back, his face grim. He was holding the boots Anjali had just returned. "Where have I seen these before?" he said. The teasing Aaron was gone. He sounded mean.

I shrugged.

"Don't play dumb! I thought you were just a sucker for Marc, like Anjali, but now I'm starting to think maybe you're actually in on it. Maybe I should warn Doc."

My heart started pounding, as if I'd done something wrong. But really, I thought, what had I done? Just helped a friend. "What are you talking about?" I said, trying to sound angry and puzzled and innocent.

"These boots," said Aaron, thumping them on the desk. They made a hollow, booming thud. "Marc was wearing them last week. And the week before, and the week before that too. Anjali's been running around with them, looking all secretive. She was just up here carrying something bulky that she didn't want me to see. You were helping her. You lied to Ms. Callender about your sweater. You lied to *me,* about 'girl stuff.' And now these same boots are on Ms. Callender's list of suspicious articles"—he thumped them again—"and you're going to pretend you don't know anything about it?"

"So what?" I said. "So Marc borrowed the boots. We're allowed to borrow stuff."

"Well, I don't see call slips for these boots, do you?" Aaron waved at the record box.

I took a breath and decided to tell him. "Okay, Aaron, you're right. Marc didn't fill out call slips for the boots. But that's all he took, and he's only borrowing them. He has to take his little brother to day care. He always brings them back. Ask Anjali."

"I can't believe you girls! You fall for that crap? Marc's been taking those boots for weeks, and now they show up on a list of suspicious objects, and you pretend like there's nothing going on. Just because he plays some stupid ball game! You girls let him get away with anything—you help him! And the librarians are no better! Would you let *me* go around stealing priceless magical objects if I were a basketball star too?"

"What are you talking about, stealing? Who stole anything? The boots are *here,* aren't they?" I pointed out. "And they're perfectly fine—they're still magic."

"The boots are, sure. But dozens of other things are gone or, at least, their magic is. Look at all this! It's trash! Useless trash!" He hit the pile of unmagical items with the back of his hand. A golden egg wobbled to the edge of the desk, but I caught it before it fell.

"You can't seriously believe Marc is responsible!"

"You can't seriously believe he isn't!"

"What about that page that got fired, the one right before me?"

"Who, Zandra? That ditz? She couldn't steal candy from a baby, she doesn't have the brains, and she hasn't been here for months. Marc, on the other hand . . ."

"Why aren't you accusing Anjali, while you're at it? You just said you saw her with the boots too."

"I *know* Anjali. She's not a thief. She just has bad judgment, like the rest of you moronettes. What do you see in that arrogant egomaniac, anyway? Just because he's tall? Just because he can throw a ball through a ring?"

"You're just jealous," I said.

"You can believe what you want," Aaron said. "But somebody's stealing from the Grimm Collection. They're either taking the objects or somehow sucking out their magic. Doc and the librarians are going to find out who, and if Marc is in on it, you're going to be sorry you were helping him."

"Marc isn't in on it. And I love this place too! We're all on the same side!"

"I hope that's true," Aaron said.

armchair

I found Marc and Anjali in the Preservation Room, sitting rather close together. They didn't look all that pleased to be interrupted, but they greeted me politely.

"Did you cut your hair?" asked Anjali.

I shook my head.

"Well, whatever you did, it looks great."

"Yeah, it does," said Marc, scrutinizing me like he'd just noticed I was an actual female girl—the kind guys look at. The comb must really be magic, I thought.

"Thanks . . . Listen, I'm sorry to barge in, but I thought you guys should know. Ms. Callender had me down in the GC with Aaron, and she gave us a whole list of objects to pull off the shelves for her. She said she wanted to check them because some stuff's been stolen. It was really weird—I think a lot of the objects on the list are fakes. Half of them smell wrong, and they don't work."

"What do you mean, smell wrong?" asked Marc.

"Smell normal, like they're not magical. You know what I mean?"

"I do," said Anjali. "Marc's better with touch."

"Oh, you mean like how magic objects *feel* magic," said Marc.

I nodded. "Aaron couldn't tell about the magic from the smell either," I continued, "but he said the objects *looked* wrong to him. I guess we all have different ways of sensing magic? Anyway, the ones that smelled wrong to me didn't work. We tested a few of them."

"That's weird," said Marc.

"Yeah, but here's the really bad part. One of the things on the list was those boots you're always borrowing. Now Aaron thinks you stole the missing objects—the ones that don't work, I mean—and replaced them with fakes."

"Oh. That's really bad," said Marc. He rubbed his face with his hand.

"How does Aaron know Marc's been taking the boots?" asked Anjali. Did I hear a hint of an accusation in her voice?

"I don't know how he found out."

"I obviously didn't tell him, and neither did Anjali, so who did?" said Marc.

"Why would anyone have to?" I asked. "He saw you. You've both been running around with the boots for weeks. He's not blind, and he's not stupid. And he does have a reason not to like you."

"What reason would that be?" asked Anjali.

"He's jealous of Marc, because he likes you."

"What an unpleasant thought," said Anjali. "But what are we going to do?"

Marc curled his lip in that haughty, contemptuous way of his.

"Aaron's fair," I said. "I'm sure he won't tell on you unless he really thinks you're the thief. You just have to convince him you didn't take the objects."

"How am I supposed to do that?" snapped Marc.

I hated this. I'd finally managed to make friends, and now they were mad at me. "I'm sorry," I said. "I just want to help."

"The best thing to do," said Anjali, "is to find out who really took them."

"That's what Ms. Callender and Doc are trying to do," I said.

"We have to help, before Aaron decides to tell them about Marc. Otherwise they'll just assume he's the thief and stop looking."

"Okay, but how?" I asked.

"Do you have that list?" asked Anjali.

I shook my head. "Ms. Callender didn't leave us a copy, but I bet she has it on her desk."

"I'll take care of it," said Anjali. "Can you guys meet me at the coffee shop on Lexington after school tomorrow?"

When I got to the coffee shop the next day, Marc and Anjali were already there, waiting for me. "Okay, let me show you," said Anjali, taking her expensive laptop out of her expensive knapsack. She opened a spreadsheet program. "These are all the items on the list, along with the info from the last ten times each one was requested or checked out. I included everything I could think of, in case it helped. Like the other objects the patron took out at the same time, with their recent history. Or the patrons' affiliations and contact info. Stuff like that."

"Wow," said Marc, "you looked up all that info about all those objects in the card file and typed it into your computer? That must have been a ton of work."

Anjali shook her head. She looked proud of herself. "Copiers and scanners aren't really good for handwritten card catalogs and call slips—it would have taken all week to do it that way. I used a dereifier from the Chresto. It's point-and-click. It works instantly."

"Smart," said Marc. He sounded impressed.

"What's a dereifier?" I asked. "What's the Chresto?"

"The Gibson Chrestomathy, remember? One of the other special collections in the Dungeon," said Anjali. "A dereifier transforms things from reality-based to virtual. It outputs representations of the input."

The waitress came by and refilled Anjali and Marc's coffee cups.

"What does that mean? What kind of input?" I asked.

"Anything," said Anjali. "An apple. A mouse. An armchair. In this case, a huge pile of call slips, catalog cards, and Ms. Callender's notes."

"And what happens to the armchair and the notes?"

"It depends on the settings. I set the dereifier to *computer database*. But you could use it for all kinds of things. Like, for example, you could make a picture of the apple or a poetic description of the armchair."

"What happens to the original armchair? Or apple, or whatever?"

"That depends on the settings too. I left the dereifier on

*duplicate* instead of *replace,* so it just made electronic copies of the paperwork. The originals are still on Stack 6."

"Isn't that dangerous?" I objected. "What if somebody used it on people—what if they put it on *replace* and turned us all into fictional characters?"

"How do you know they haven't?" asked Marc.

"Wow, that sounds like a seriously powerful object! How did you get your hands on it? Did they just, like, let you borrow it?"

"No, it was more like . . . an unofficial loan. I have the key to the Gibson Chrestomathy, like Aaron has the key to the Wells Bequest. I'm good with computers—it's kind of my special domain. I just went in and took the dereifier. I put it right back afterward."

"How big is a dereifier? What does it look like?"

"Like a cross between a quill pen and a remote control."

"And it's just sitting there in the Chresto? Why couldn't someone borrow it and make perfect identical copies of the *Mona Lisa,* or duplicate diamonds, or make a vast robot army and conquer the planet?"

"I don't think a dereifier can make exact copies of anything," said Marc. "It makes *virtual* representations—pictures and sculptures and descriptions, stuff like that."

"But what's the difference between the *Mona Lisa* and a picture of the *Mona Lisa,* if it was good enough? They're both pictures."

He thought about that. "Okay, maybe you could duplicate the *Mona Lisa.* But that would only work for stuff that was already a representation of something—art and that kind of thing. It wouldn't work for things that are, you know, *real*."

"I'm not sure you're right—I think you *can* make copies," said Anjali. "There's an *identity* setting. I think that makes the object represent itself. If you set the dereifier to *duplicate* and *identity,* you might be able to make identical duplicates. But you would have to be a pretty serious computer geek to do that, or anything else really dangerous. You can't use the advanced settings without tons of passwords and access codes. I played around with it a little, and the worst I could get it to do was change my French textbook cover into a cartoon of the Eiffel Tower. My little sister draws better than that, and *she* couldn't draw her way out of a paper bag."

I sympathized. I couldn't draw my way out of a paper bag either.

"Plus the dereifier is supposed to be incredibly buggy," Anjali continued. "I seriously doubt you could get it to make a perfect *Mona Lisa*. It's just not good enough."

"Still—wow," I said.

"Hey, guys? I have to be at basketball practice in forty-five minutes," said Marc. "Can we talk about that list?"

"Oh, sorry! Right. Here, these are all the objects Ms. Callender wanted, with all the info I could think of that might help. Elizabeth, do you remember which ones are duds?"

"I think so," I said. I went through the spreadsheet, clicking on boxes next to the items that had smelled wrong.

"Great. Is there anything that jumps out at you as different about those items?" Anjali asked.

Marc and I studied the screen. Some of the objects had been borrowed as recently as last week; some hadn't been requested for over a year. With one or two exceptions, the latest patrons for each object were all different. A few names repeated here and there, but those patrons also seemed to have taken out many of the objects that smelled magical.

Marc shook his head. "I don't see a pattern."

"Me neither. What about you, Anjali?" I said.

"Not yet. But I have a strong feeling . . . Give me a few days."

We paid our check and went our various ways, Marc back to school for basketball practice and Anjali toward home. I walked to the subway half worried about the magic items but more than half relieved that the two of them were treating me like a friend again.

Friday was the big game, the one I had promised to go to with Anjali. I'd loved all the compliments on my "haircut." Even my stepmother had noticed; she accused me of using her good shampoo. But the effect had died down disappointingly soon. What if I borrowed the mermaid's comb from the GC to use it again before the game? I wanted to use my new borrowing priv- ileges, and Doc had warned me to start with something small. There was no harm in looking my best for the occasion, I told myself—perhaps some of the kids at school would notice I existed.

I found Ms. Callender at her desk. "Excuse me, Ms. Callender, do you have a minute?" I asked. "Doc told me I could borrow things from the Grimm Collection now, so I wondered—can I take this out?" I handed her the call slip I'd filled out.

"Your first Grimm loan! How exciting! . . . What's this? A mermaid's comb? Hot date tonight?" asked Ms. Callender with her dimpled smile.

I felt myself blush. "Not a date, exactly. There's a big basketball game at my school Friday."

"Oh, wait a minute." Ms. Callender looked at the call number more closely. "This is one of the objects I have out for study."

"I know. That's why I'm asking you. I . . . noticed it when Aaron and I were pulling the objects for you. Have you figured out what's going on with them yet?"

"No, we're just getting started," said Ms. Callender. "You and Aaron were really helpful, the way you sorted out the questionable ones. You have a great nose!"

"Thank you. So can I borrow the comb, or should I find something else?"

"No, it's okay, I guess—I don't really need it right away. There are plenty of others to keep me busy. You're sure it actually works, though, right? This isn't one of the questionable objects?"

"No, it's fine. I . . ." Should I tell her I tried it? "It smelled right."

"That's all right, then. Let's see . . . Grimm objects usually circulate for three days, but I'll let you keep this until Saturday so you can look your best for the big game." She scribbled a revised due date on the slip and handed it back to me. "Dr. Rust has the deposit *kuduo*. You'll have to go downstairs to leave your deposit. Come back when you're done, and I'll give you the comb, okay, hon?"

"Great. Thanks so much, Ms. Callender."

She winked at me. "I was your age once."

She must have been fun to hang out with back then, I thought. I hurried downstairs to Doc's office and knocked on the door, feeling nervous but excited about my first magic loan.

"Come in? Ah, Elizabeth. What can I do for you?"

"Ms. Callender says I need to give you a deposit before I can borrow a comb from the Grimm Collection."

"A comb? As your first loan—are you sure? Some of those are rather dangerous . . . Sit down, sit down. Let's have a look."

I handed Doc the call slip.

"Oh, a *mermaid's* comb. Heady stuff, but safe enough as long as you don't use it around water. Or a busy highway. You're not planning to lure any young men to their doom, are you?"

How embarrassing! I shook my head, blushing. "I just want to look nice for the big basketball game."

"I see. You know there's a three-hour limit on this?"

"Three hours? But Ms. Callender said I could bring it back on Saturday!"

"No, I mean a limit on the effects. They taper off, and everything goes back to normal after three hours. Most of the Grimm Collection objects have a time limit—some of them last three days, or a fortnight, or a year and a day. This one's just three hours. If you're looking for a permanent love potion, this isn't it."

A freckle was floating up Doc's nose like the shadow of an airplane skimming across the grass. It fascinated me. I made an effort and tore my eyes away. "Really? Is there a permanent love potion in the Grimm Collection?"

"Interesting question. There's a great deal of scholarly debate in the community over whether any artificially induced love can ever be permanent. Or any natural love, for that matter. Any so-called natural love, assuming any love is natural."

I noticed that wasn't really an answer. I also noticed Doc didn't seem to be signing the slip. "So, the deposit," I said nervously.

"Mmm." Doc didn't seem to be in any hurry. "Let me explain how this works. Here in the repository we keep the objects safe under lock and key. Out in the world, the borrower is responsible for them. When you sign the slip, you're pledging not to use the object for ill. You're also pledging to return it whole and potent by the appointed hour. Otherwise your deposit is forfeit. You understand?"

"Of course."

"I just want to make sure you understand how serious this is. It's not always easy to keep the objects safe. Not everyone who's part of our knowledge community is well intentioned, unfortunately. There's a thief out there, not to mention that bird. It's possible someone could try to take the comb. It might make you a target, and you're responsible for keeping it safe."

That sounded serious. Was it worth it, I wondered, just for pretty hair? But Doc had said to start with something small. If I didn't have the guts to borrow a mere mermaid comb, how would I ever work my way up to something really big, like flying shoes or an invisibility cloak?

"Are you saying I shouldn't do this?"

"Not at all. We trust you. You passed the test, and I believe you're ready. And you've chosen something appropriately small to start with. I just need to make sure you're going into this with your eyes open."

"I see. Yes, I'm ready."

"All right. Now, where did I put that *kuduo?*" Doc opened and shut desk drawers, stood up, scanned the bookshelves, walked over to a closet and peered in. "Do you see it behind your chair?"

"I don't know. What does it look like?"

"It's rather ornate. It has a puff adder and a hornbill on the lid."

I didn't know what a puff adder or a hornbill looked like, but there was nothing behind the chair. "I don't think so," I said.

"Oh, there it is!" Doc pointed to the top of a bookcase. "Drag over that chair, would you?" I held the chair while Doc handed down a heavy bronzy-black object, roughly cylindrical, about the size of a cantaloupe.

A puff adder is a snake and a hornbill is a bird, evidently.

I put the object on the desk. "Thanks," said Doc, scrambling down from the chair and lifting the lid.

I peered inside. There seemed to be things in it, but I couldn't make out what. Looking at them made me dizzy. "What *is* this thing?" I asked.

"It's a *kuduo,* a ceremonial vessel from the Akan people. They're traditionally used to hold a chief's gold and spiritual treasure."

"Is it from the Grimm Collection?" I asked.

"No—it's on loan to the repository from one of our close families."

"Like the way Anjali's family has magic?" I asked. Thinking of my own family, I felt faintly jealous. "Do all the other pages have magic families—the Grimm pages, I mean?"

"Not all of them, but some do, yes."

"Who does the *kuduo* belong to, then?" I asked.

Looking a little uncomfortable, Doc answered, "Marc Merritt's uncle. He loaned it to the repository to use for keeping the deposits. Now, what deposit would you like to leave?"

"I don't know," I said doubtfully. "How much is it supposed to be? I have about two hundred dollars saved up." It didn't sound as if it could possibly be enough. A mere two hundred dollars—for real magic?

"Money?" Doc sounded shocked. "No, no, Grimm deposits are never money. You'll have to leave something else."

"Oh. Like what?"

"You have plenty of choices. We're quite flexible. The most traditional forfeit, of course, is your firstborn child. Or your skill with your right hand, but that could be inconvenient. Your beauty, your courage, your eyesight, your sense of gravity, your free will, your luck. Those are some of the more common deposits. But most of them are a little heavy for a mere mermaid's comb, and giving up your beauty would defeat the purpose, I imagine. Your sense of smell, maybe?"

I shook my head, horrified by all these options, especially smell. How would I do my work in the Grimm Collection if I couldn't smell magic?

"No? Many people don't mind giving that up for a few days, but of course it's a matter of individual preference. Your sense of humor, then?"

"Are you joking?"

"Your ear for music? Skill at games? Ability to take tests? Childhood memories? Sense of direction?"

"Sense of direction," I said quickly. It seemed like the least important of all the possibilities Doc had mentioned. My sense of direction wasn't all that great to begin with, and it was only for a few days.

"You're right-handed, right? Give me your right hand."

I hesitated. "You want my right hand? Didn't you just say my sense of direction?"

Doc smiled reassuringly. "Not as the deposit. Just as a conduit."

"Oh. Okay." I laid my hand in Doc's cool, dry one.

*"Orientation,*

*Spatial relation,*

*Out of this body and to your new station!"* Doc intoned impressively.

Nothing happened.

I cleared my throat.

"My, my," said Doc mildly. "I wonder why that didn't . . . Ah, what's this?"

"This" was the matted remains of the yarn Jaya had tied around my wrist.

"Just a knot Anjali's little sister tied."

"Clever girl. What's her name?"

"Jaya."

"Jaya Rao. One of Abigail Bender's students, isn't she? Hm . . . Would you mind taking that off?"

"Not at all," I said.

I pulled on the yarn, but it wouldn't break. I sawed at it with my teeth; no good. I picked at the knot, but I couldn't tease it loose.

"Do you have scissors?"

Doc reached into a drawer and handed me a pair. It looked sharp, but like the cheap, blunt baby scissors they give kids in grade school, it just gagged uselessly on the yarn.

"You might try saying a word or two of encouragement," suggested Doc. "Tell it you forgo the protection and so on. In rhyme, if you can."

I thought for a minute.

"*I forgo*

*Protection, knot.*

*Please let go,*

*And . . . thanks a lot,*" I said, feeling very silly. But it worked: the knot collapsed as soon as I touched it.

I brushed the yarn off my wrist. So it really had some magic power, then! I'd assumed Jaya was just playing around. Did that mean it was actually protecting me? Maybe I should have thought harder before giving it up. Well, too late now.

"Very good," said Doc, taking my hand and intoning once again.

This time the incantation worked. Something poured out of me, flowing weightily, like when you give blood. It had a complicated, patterned structure that seemed to take up more space than just the part I saw, as if it had extra dimensions. It flowed out and out—could *that* have been inside me?

Doc carefully balanced it on the edge of the desk. I worried that all the internal motion would make it fall, but it didn't. It smelled appallingly intimate, like my own breath.

"Sign here," said Doc.

I signed.

"Now the vow. Repeat after me:

*Forfeit fair and given free,*
*I resign a part of me.*
*In exchange I'll keep with care*
*What is given free and fair:*
*Potent, uncorrupt, and whole.*
*Else the bargain shall be null—*
*My pledge forfeit, or my soul.*"

I looked at the intricate, throbbing blob balanced on the edge of the desk and hesitated. What a grim vow! But if this was what it took to borrow items from the Grimm Collection, so be it. "Can you say that again, slowly?"

"Sure. We can take it line by line," said Doc.

Piece by piece I repeated the rhyme, as firmly as I could.

"Great! That's it," said Doc, scooping up my sense of direction, tucking it in the *kuduo,* and signing the call slip.

I felt strangely shaken. I guess it must have showed. "What you're feeling is normal, Elizabeth," Doc said, putting a hand on my shoulder. "It's hard to give something up, something that's a part of you. I know a mermaid's comb is a small thing, but this is a big step. I remember my first Grimm loan—I started small, like you, with a magic darning needle. I left my singing voice. I remember how I felt when I watched it go."

"Did you get it back?"

"Of course, the very next day. And even if I hadn't—because there have been things I've been asked to give up for good . . . Well, over the years here I've learned that sometimes a great loss is also a great gain." Under the slowly swirling freckles, Doc's face looked infinitely sad. Somehow I didn't find that reassuring.

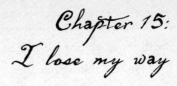

doorknob

I had trouble getting back to Stack 6 to claim the mermaid's comb. Somehow I got turned around on my way to the elevator, and then I got turned around again on my way out. I had to look at the fire evacuation map on the wall, and even then I took a wrong turn.

I was late to social studies on Wednesday—I went to the wrong floor first. Mr. Mauskopf squinted at me and frowned as I slipped into my seat, but he didn't mark me late in his book.

I was late to my next class too. I started to wish I'd pledged my sense of humor instead of my sense of direction. Getting lost all the time was so annoying, I was starting to lose it anyway.

My phone rang that evening while I was doing my trigonometry.

"Elizabeth? It's Aaron. Aaron Rosendorn."

"Hi, Aaron. How—where did you get my number?"

"From Sarah, at the repository."

Did he always have such a deep voice? He sounded different—older, but less sure of himself.

I waited for him to tell me what he wanted. He hadn't been all that nice the last time we'd spoken, as I recalled.

He cleared his throat. "Did you figure out what's going on with those objects from the Grimm Collection?" he asked.

He was calling me about the Grimm Collection? At home? How weird!

"No, I still have no idea what's up with them," I said. "Ms. Callender said she was just getting started looking into it. Do you know?"

"No, but . . . Do you think we should talk to Anjali? Maybe she could help figure it out."

Oh. Of course. Of course that was why he was calling. He just wanted to talk about Anjali.

"I already talked to Anjali about it," I said. "She input the objects into a spreadsheet and she's working on finding a pattern."

Aaron laughed. "That's so like her! Maybe I should call her and see if there's anything I might know that could help. What do you think?"

A wave of irritation swept over me. Why was he asking *me*? "I don't know. I don't know what more you could tell her, but you can call her if you want. Or you could just talk to her next time you see her. I don't think it matters."

"Oh. Okay. Thanks."

His voice disappeared. I was about to hang up when he spoke again. "Um, so how are you?"

"How am I?"

"Yeah. How are you?"

"Uh . . . fine?"

"Good." I heard him swallow.

"How are *you*?" I asked.

"I'm fine too."

"Good. We're both fine."

Another pause.

"What are you up to?" he asked.

"Up to?"

"Yeah, what are you doing?"

"My trig homework. Why? What are *you* doing?"

"Nothing. Calling you."

"Oh. Okay."

Neither of us said anything for a while. "I guess I should get back to my homework," I said eventually.

"Yeah. Well, thanks, Elizabeth. Call me if you figure anything out, okay? Or if . . . or if you just want to talk."

Talk? About what? "Okay, I will," I said.

"Okay, thanks. Bye."

"Bye." I pressed the off button on my phone and stared at the screen for a while. Then I stared at the wall for a while.

That was one weird conversation.

Well, it was a weird week, and he was a weird guy. I shrugged and went back to cosines and tangents.

Half an hour later he called back.

"Hi, Elizabeth, me again."

"Hi, Aaron."

"Listen, I was thinking. What if we asked some of the objects in the Grimm Collection to tell us what's wrong with the other ones?"

"You mean ask the objects themselves? You think that would work?"

"It might. Some of them are pretty talkative. At least, they are if you talk to them in rhyme."

"Tell me about it. But aren't you the guy who thinks we shouldn't touch anything or use anything?"

"Yeah. But what if . . . I don't know, we could borrow them officially. That would be legit."

"Hm. That's not a bad idea, actually," I said. "Which objects did you have in mind?"

"I'm not sure. I haven't really thought it through yet."

"Okay. Well, maybe we should go through the card catalog and see if there's anything useful."

"Okay . . . Well, bye."

"Bye."

I had just finished a tricky math problem and was feeling proud of myself when the phone rang again.

"Elizabeth? It's Aaron again."

What on earth was going on with him?

"You don't say," I said.

He laughed uncomfortably. "Actually, I was wondering. What are you doing Friday?"

"I'm going to the basketball game," I said. "There's a big home game at my school. Why?"

"Oh." His voice fell. "I just thought . . . never mind."

Before he could hang up again, I said, "Well, maybe—you could come to the game if you want."

What on earth was I doing? Was I asking him out? Why was I doing that? He was kind of awful, and he liked Anjali—*Anjali,* not me. I was making a complete fool of myself.

"It'll probably be an exciting game," I went on. "We're play-ing the World Peace Academy. They're a charter school, they have a dumb name but a killer team, and they keep winning. But we're doing great too this season." I was babbling, but I couldn't stop. "We have a lot of talent on our team. Especially Marc. I think this time we might actually have a chance of winning. You should see Marc play. He's been amazing lately."

Aaron finally spoke. When he did, nice, nervous Aaron was gone. He had turned into cold, sarcastic Aaron, the Aaron who hated Marc. "Yeah, I bet he has. I just *bet* he has," he said.

"What's that supposed to mean?"

"There's more to sports than just speed and strength, you know. There's also honesty and fair play."

"What are you talking about? Are you implying Marc cheats?"

"I know what I've seen at the repository."

"You know what you think you've seen, but you're wrong. Marc is just as worried as you are about the suspicious objects. He's helping me and Anjali figure it out and get them back."

"What? You *told* him about them?"

"Of course I did. Why shouldn't I?"

"I can't believe you! I can't believe *myself*. What was I thinking, deciding I could trust you?"

"What's the matter with you, Aaron? I didn't do anything to you, and you call me up out of the blue and start yelling at me!"

"Fine. I'll get off the phone now." He hung up.

"Bye," I said to the dead phone. I went back to my math, wondering why I felt like I was about to cry.

I didn't see Aaron at the repository on Thursday. Ms. Callender sent me to the MER to handle the pneum traffic, and it was so busy I didn't have a moment free to look for helpful GC objects in the catalog, even if I'd had the heart to.

Friday after school I made my way to Anjali's house. I managed to get there by keeping careful track of the building numbers as I walked up Park Avenue. I gave my name to the doorman, who gave it to whoever answered the buzzer at the Raos'.

"Fourteenth floor," he told me.

I found the elevator okay. It was in plain sight, right in front of me.

"Elizabeth! So nice to see you again, dear," said Mrs. Rao, opening the door. "Are you excited about the basketball game tonight?"

"Totally," I said. "We're playing World Peace Academy. They have a cutthroat team, but we're doing great this year, so it should be a close one."

"It sounds exciting. Anjali is in her room—you remember the way?"

"I think so."

"No, the other way—to the left," said Mrs. Rao.

I opened the door to a linen closet and what must have been Jaya's room, judging by the sparkly clothes strewn all around, before I came to a door marked *Anjali* in careful calligraphy. I knocked and tried the handle. It was locked.

Anjali's voice came through the door, muffled but firm: "Go away."

"Anjali? It's me, Elizabeth."

"Oh, sorry!" The door opened. Anjali was wearing pink sweats with clouds on them, and even in sweats she looked great.

"Sorry, I thought it was Jaya." She stood aside to let me in, then locked the door again.

"Well? Did you figure out who took those objects?" I asked.

"I think so. Maybe. Marc wants us to meet him in your school library after the game so the three of us can go over it together. But why don't you take a look now and see if there's anything I missed?" She got out her laptop and patted the sofa pillow next to her. I sat down and tilted the screen so that I could see it better.

"What am I looking at?"

"This is everyone who checked out any of the objects on Ms. Callender's list. These are their affiliations—their business or school or whatever. Here are pairs of people who checked out at least one object in common. Do you see the pattern?"

I shook my head.

"Yeah, I didn't get it either at first. All right, let me show you one more list." Anjali opened a new window on her computer. "This has all the objects you pulled for Ms. Callender on the $y$-axis, with all the patrons who took them out in chronological order along the $x$-axis. The objects that still smell like magic are highlighted in red. Okay, now I'm going to highlight the patrons who work for a place called Benign Designs." She touched a key, and a bunch of spreadsheet cells lit up in blue. "Get it now?"

I shook my head. "I don't really understand what all the boxes mean. How do you know this stuff? Is this what they teach you at Miss Wharton's—like, AP Spreadsheets or something?"

Anjali laughed. "Sorry, I forgot not everybody has to live

with my dad. He had Jaya and me using these programs the minute we were born. Look." She pointed to the screen. "These seven patrons are from some business called Benign Designs. Notice how somebody from Benign Designs took out every one of the objects that you said doesn't smell magical?"

She was right. At least one of the seven names appeared on every row. "Yes, but they also took out most of the ones that do smell magical," I said. "Maybe they're just heavy library users. And they're not the only ones who took out the messed-up objects. Look, two or three other people did too, including Ms. Minnian."

"Maybe. But look at *when*. With the ones that don't smell right, someone from Benign Designs took them out at least three patrons ago. The ones that still smell magical have been checked out only once or twice since the Benign Designs patron."

"Except for the ones that haven't ever been checked out by Benign Designs. Like the seven-league boots," I pointed out.

She waved her hand. "I'm not counting those. They're clearly mistakes."

"You can't just decide anything that doesn't fit your theory is a mistake! And what actually is your theory, anyway?"

"That the people at Benign Designs are doing something to the objects."

"What kind of something?"

"I don't know. Stealing their magic, maybe."

"Can you do that? Can you take the magic out of something magical?"

"I don't know. *I* can't, obviously, but maybe *somebody* can."

"But then why do the objects still work for the next three patrons?"

"I'm not sure. It has to be some kind of delayed action. Maybe the magic fades slowly."

"Or maybe they put a spell on them so the third person to take them out has to give them to Benign Designs, and they replace it with a fake, like you and Marc do with the seven-league boots."

"Maybe—that's another possible theory. We could test it, by borrowing one of the objects."

"Oh, wait!" I remembered the comb. "I already did!" I took it out of my bag. "This was on the list."

"What is it?" Anjali turned it over in her hands.

"It's a . . . comb," I mumbled, suddenly embarrassed.

She looked at me intensely. Under her scrutiny, I felt mortifyingly vain. I couldn't believe I had borrowed a mermaid's comb so I could look nice while watching someone else's boyfriend play basketball.

"What kind of comb?" she asked.

"A mermaid's comb. I wanted . . . I thought . . . ," I trailed off.

"Okay." She sounded embarrassed by my embarrassment. "Does it still work?" She lifted the comb to her hair.

I wanted to stop her, but I couldn't. I sat paralyzed.

She combed. At each stroke, her hair shone with the rainbow darkness of a starling's feathers. It waved like a midnight river, smooth and cold and singing with ripples, stars dancing on its surface and death in its depths. If it *had* been a river, I would have thrown myself in and let the torrent dash me against the sunken rocks.

She raised a questioning eyebrow at me. "Well?"

"Your hair looks fantastic," I said. "But then, it always looks fantastic."

"Here, you try it." She tossed me the comb. I sniffed it and nodded in recognition. That smell—that wild, shifting, unmistakable smell of magic, overlaid with the floral musk of Anjali's hair.

"Aren't you going to use the comb?" she said.

I shrugged. There didn't seem to be any point.

"Go on, I want to see what it does."

I shrugged again and lifted the comb.

The door gave a great rattling shudder. "AANNjaliiiiiiii!"

Jaya.

"Open up, Anjali! You've got Elizabeth in there, I heard you! And you're doing your *hair*! I want to heeeeelp!" she wailed.

"Oh, brother," said Anjali, but she opened the door. "Go away, Jaya," she said.

Jaya ignored her. "Hi, Elizabeth," she said. "Want me to do your hair?"

I handed her the comb.

I expected painful tugs, but Jaya was surprisingly gentle, or maybe it was the comb. My scalp tingled with delight. I closed my eyes and murmured, "Mmmmm."

"You have nice hair, Elizabeth. Want me to make you a French braid?"

"Sure."

Her quick fingers parted and pulled and tightened my hair,

combing each section as she joined it into the braid. When she reached the end of the braid, she fastened it with a scrunchy that she took out of her own hair. "Go look," she said, pointing to the mirror on Anjali's dresser.

Usually my hair wisps out of braids and updos, but this time it lay gleaming and orderly. It flattered the shape of my face. For once I actually had cheekbones.

"Nice," I said. "Thanks, Jaya. I guess the comb still works."

Anjali glanced at Jaya and frowned at me.

"Don't worry, Anji, I already know all about it," announced Jaya. "I was listening at the door. This is a magic comb, and some magic objects aren't magic anymore, and you're trying to catch the bad guys. Let me help! You know I'm good with spreadsheets— Daddy says so." She started to comb her hair.

"Jaya, you are such a pest," said Anjali wearily.

"Is that a good idea, Jaya?" I said.

"Of course it is! I could help you find the bad guys, and I could tie them up for you," Jaya said.

"No, I mean using that comb." Her hair still looked like a cloud of spikes, but an increasingly attractive cloud of spikes. "You're kind of young for that kind of thing."

Jaya looked insulted. "I borrow Anjali's makeup all the time!"

"You *what*?" The clouds gathered on Anjali's exquisite brow.

"Don't worry, I always put everything back." She found a knot in her hair and tugged at it with the comb.

"Be careful with that, Jaya!"

"Give Elizabeth the comb, Jaya," said Anjali. The thought of her sister meddling with her makeup must have been what gave her voice such a cold edge. She could be surprisingly scary some-times, I thought.

"Fine. I'm done with it anyway." Jaya handed me the comb with dignity.

"Thanks, Jaya," I said, putting it away in my bag. "Okay, so the comb still works. What does that prove?"

"Nothing yet," said Anjali. "Maybe it doesn't lose its magic until after you return it. Maybe somebody's planning to take it away from you. What about that bird? Maybe they're going to send it to get the comb. Or do you have an uncontrollable urge to give the comb to someone from Benign Designs?"

"What's Benign Designs?" asked Jaya. Anjali ignored her.

"Not as far as I know," I said. "The only people I've given it to so far are girls in the Rao family. You don't work for Benign Designs, do you?"

"What's Benign Designs?" said Jaya again.

"We don't know yet," I said. "We need to find out."

Anjali said, "Let's do a search." She went back to typing on the computer.

"Let me help, I'm good at finding things," said Jaya, inserting herself between my shoulder and Anjali's legs to peer at the screen.

Anjali batted her away. "If you break my computer, Dad will be very angry," she said.

"I'm not breaking anything," said Jaya, but she subsided next to me on the floor. She glanced at my wrist, then pushed up both my sleeves. "Hey, what happened to the knot I made you?" she said accusingly.

"I . . . It came off," I said. "I'm sorry."

"It's not supposed to. Maybe I didn't do it right. I better make you another one—you're not safe out there, with monsters and Benign Designs and everything."

"Leave her alone, Jaya," said Anjali. "Elizabeth doesn't want to wear some ugly piece of yarn to the basketball game."

"Why are you so mean to me? All I'm doing is trying to help! I hate you!" Tears hung in Jaya's enormous dark eyes. The contrast between her pouting face and her glamorous hair was comical but heartbreaking.

"You can make me a new knot, okay?" I said quickly.

Jaya turned the pout on me. "Don't pretend to be nice! You're just as bad as my sister."

"Please? I really would feel much safer."

"Oh, all right. I'll do your ankle so the *ugly knot* won't show. Which foot?"

I held out my left. Or was it my right? Without my sense of direction, it was hard to tell.

Jaya got a piece of yarn and began the lengthy ritual. "But I'm not making *you* one, stinkhead," she said to Anjali. "The monsters can eat you for all I care. If they do, you'll probably poison them."

wineglass

We got to the Fisher gym in plenty of time and claimed seats in the third row, far enough from the band not to blow out our eardrums. Anjali insisted on wearing the Fisher colors: white and an unflattering shade of purple. She achieved this by borrowing an old blazer of her mother's that would have made anyone else look like a Halloween version of a newscaster, but this was Anjali—Anjali aglow with the mermaid glamour. All the girls raked her with appraising glances. All the guys raked her with the other kind of appraising glances and held out their hands to help her over the bleachers.

Anjali took it in stride. I don't think she even really noticed. She focused completely on Marc, grabbing my arm so tightly it hurt when he missed a layup, roaring "Mer-RITT! Mer-RITT!" with the rest of the crowd when he stole the ball back and nailed a three-pointer from the top of the key.

The distraction didn't seem to bother Marc. In fact, I've never seen him play better. Once, he turned our way and gave a little bow before leaping onto an escalator in the air and allowing himself to be borne gracefully aloft within inches of the basket. He sank the ball like a lump of leaden butter over the fingertips of the snarling World Peace center and winked at Anjali as he landed. The gym went wild.

Friends, ones I didn't know I had, clustered around us at the end of the third quarter.

"Are you guys coming to Jake's Joint afterward?" Sadie Cane asked Anjali.

"Jake's Joint?"

"The hamburger place on Ninety-first Street. We always go there after the games. Marc didn't tell you?" She was clearly fishing for info about Anjali's relationship to Marc.

"No, Marc and I have plans with Elizabeth," said Anjali.

"I hope we're not dragging Merritt away from a fun tradition," she whispered to me. "He would have told us if he minded missing it, wouldn't he?"

"I'm sure the plans he makes with you are the ones he wants to keep," I said.

Somebody behind me snorted quietly. Swiveling to see who, I found myself looking up at Aaron Rosendorn. Despite the heat in the gym, he was wearing a black leather jacket and a blue-and-green-striped scarf, the World Peace Academy colors.

"Aaron! You came after all!"

"Yeah, I found out my favorite pages would be here," he said. "I figured I'd better show up and keep an eye on you."

"Well, anyway, I'm glad you're here," I said, then immediately blushed and wished I hadn't said it. It's not like he came for *me*, I told myself. Unless that's what he meant by "keep an eye on you"?

Evidently not. "Hi, Anjali," he said.

Anjali turned around. "Oh, hi, Aaron. What are you doing here? I didn't know you were a basketball fan."

"Didn't Elizabeth tell you? I'm a humanitarian. I'm praying for World Peace," he said.

Anjali laughed. "Good—they can use all the help they can get." She turned back to the game.

Instead of leaning back again, Aaron whispered in my ear. It tickled. "So, Elizabeth," he said. "Did you see Marc's air ball at the buzzer?"

I lost my temper. "Aaron, you're the most annoying person I've ever met in my life," I snapped.

Aaron flinched as if I'd hit him. "That's quite a superlative, considering how many annoying people you must have met," he said. "I imagine you run in very annoying circles."

"Not if I can help it," I said, turning my back. The ref blew his whistle and the last quarter began. I concentrated on the game with all my might.

Marc scored the winning points. After we'd finished screaming ourselves hoarse, Anjali told me she was going to the bathroom. "I'll meet you at"—she noticed Aaron leaning closer, hesitated, and said—"where Marc said."

"Okay. You know where it is?"

"I'm sure I can find it."

She picked up her things and glided away among the bleachers. I put my coat over my arm and scrambled after her toward the door.

Aaron scrambled after me.

"Why are you following me, Aaron?"

"You invited me here in the first place."

"And you insulted me and insulted Marc and hung up on me, so why did you come?"

"I told you. I'm worried about the Grimm Collection. No way I'm going to miss the meeting of the Pages' Conspiracy, Fisher Branch. I'm sorry if you find that insulting."

"Don't be ridiculous. There is no conspiracy. You're just trying to horn in on Anjali's date with Marc."

"Is that what you think? I could say the same thing about you."

"You could say it, but you would be wrong." I headed for the girls' room, figuring he couldn't actually follow me in there.

Well, I *tried* to head to the girls' room; in my excitement, I'd forgotten about my little sense-of-direction problem. I managed to stop myself before going into the boys' room. I found the girls' room after only two trips around the third floor.

By then Aaron had regained his cool. "Are you trying to shake me? You're not very good at it," he said companionably, striding along beside me.

I gave him the most sarcastic smile I could muster.

"I was right," he said. "You do run in extremely annoying circles." He chuckled at his own joke.

I liked him much better before, I thought, when he was making me sit on imaginary chairs and fall down. I went into the girls' room and let the door swing shut in his face.

Anjali wasn't there. I took my time, reading the graffiti in the stall, then touching up my lip gloss. I noticed I was looking good: confident, a little fierce, with very nice hair. Mermaid magic?

I gave my hair a few extra strokes with the comb.

Aaron was waiting for me outside the bathroom, leaning against the wall. He tilted his head to one side and made a show of inspecting my face. "You really didn't need to spend all that time on your makeup just for me," he said. "Not that you don't look nice, of course—but you overdid the mascara. I prefer the natural look."

"I'm not wearing mascara."

"No? Hm. So where are we meeting Anjali?"

"*You're* not meeting her anywhere."

"Sure I am. I'm pretty stubborn, in case you haven't noticed."

"I don't get it, Aaron. Do you really think there's a conspiracy? Because if we wanted to conspire, we could perfectly well do it sometime when you're not around to watch. So tell me. Why are you really following me?"

"I don't know, Elizabeth—maybe because I can't stand to be parted from you?" His smile, which was exquisitely balanced between sarcasm and sincerity, revealed beautiful white teeth.

"If that were true, you would never say so."

"Maybe you're right. Or maybe I think it's perfectly safe to say so because I know you'd never believe I would admit a thing like that if it were true."

"Or maybe you're talking in circles to confuse me so you won't have to answer my question."

"Talking in circles is no worse than walking in circles."

"If you don't like the way I walk, you don't have to follow me."

"Oh, but I do like the way you walk. Very much. I'll happily watch you walk all evening."

I gave up. Anjali and Marc would have to get rid of him themselves. I headed toward the school library—or at least, I tried. But the library seemed to recede before me, wiggling away like a clam when you don't dig fast enough, and I found myself instead standing in front of the social studies department office.

"Oh, the door's shut. I guess they left without me," I said.

"Nice try," Aaron said.

"See—it's locked." I rattled the door to show him. My coat brushed against it, and the buttons made a scraping noise.

To my surprise, the doorknob turned. Aaron pushed the door open and snapped on the light. A cold wind blew in our faces from the window, which was open a crack, blowing papers off the desks. I shut the window. Should I pick up the papers too?

Aaron sat down.

"What are you doing? That's Mr. Mauskopf's chair!"

"Who's Mr. Mauskopf?"

"My social studies teacher. He's not going to like you sitting there."

"That's okay. He's not *my* social studies teacher."

"Come on, Aaron, you're going to get me in trouble. Let's get out of here before someone shows up."

"Like who—Anjali and Marc? . . . Hey, Elizabeth?" Aaron's voice changed, the bantering tone dropping away. "What is your social studies teacher doing with *Art Murk*?"

"With what?"

He pointed. Hanging over Mr. Mauskopf's desk was the muddy, shifting painting from the Grimm Collection.

"I have no idea. Are you sure that's what it is?"

Aaron turned back to the painting and said, *"Well? Don't keep us in the dark—show us Anjali and Marc."*

The dim, sinister forms in the painting began to ooze like nightmare lava.

The picture showed Anjali and Marc, standing in one of the Fisher hallways. They were in the middle of a slow kiss.

Aaron stared at them, his face an unsettling greenish color. The kiss seemed to go on forever. So did Aaron's stare.

"Stop it, Aaron!"

He didn't seem to hear me. He went on staring with an expression like someone watching his house burn down. In the painting Marc and Anjali came up for breath and he began kissing her neck.

"Don't watch that!" I shook his shoulder, but he ignored me, so I covered his eyes with my hands and yelled at the painting, *"Much too frank! Please go blank!"*

It obeyed slowly—so slowly it seemed to be taunting me. Marc's lips melted into Anjali's throat; her hair blended with his hands.

Aaron gripped my wrists tightly as if to pull away my hands, but instead he held them still against his face. I felt his eyeballs roll beneath my hands under their thin lids, the lashes tickling my palms; it was disturbing, embarrassing, almost like the amorphous shapes in the painting. His hands felt hot on my wrists. I thought I felt his pulse race, but maybe it was mine.

He let go of my hands and pointed at the picture. "What is your social studies teacher doing with this?"

"I have no idea. He must have borrowed it from the GC. I'm

sure he has some good reason. He's the one who got me a job at the repository. He's a friend of Dr. Rust's."

"Oh, is he the one who got Marc the job too? Maybe he's the real thief, and Marc's just working for him!"

I lost my temper again. "You don't know what you're talking about! Look, I'm sorry. I'm sorry Anjali doesn't like you. I'm sorry she likes Marc instead. I'm sorry he's tall and handsome and popular and a fantastic athlete, and I'm sorry you're not. But why do you have to be a jerk about it? It's not like I'm all that pretty or popular either, and you don't see me taking it out on Anjali, do you? I'm nice to people. Why can't you just be nice?"

"Nice!" he said. He made it sound like a curse. "You, nice— not pretty but *nice*? You don't know the first thing about yourself. You think it's *nice* to make me like you and trust you, over and over again, and then every time you turn out to be lying and covering for that—that liar? You think it's *nice* to break Doc's trust and help people ruin the one true place of magic we know? Is your teacher behind it? Is that who you're working for?"

"I'm not working for anybody!" I protested. "I want to catch the thief. That's what Anjali wants too. So does Marc. So does Mr. Mauskopf, I'm sure."

Aaron snorted. "We'll see about that." He turned to the painting. *"Masterpiece beyond belief, show the Grimm Collection thief."*

I didn't think it would work. Otherwise, Dr. Rust could have just asked the painting who was stealing the objects weeks ago. Sure enough, the painting had a mind of its own. The shapes flowed and the murk paled into a brightly lit art gallery crowded with people. They clustered around gesturing at paintings or stood in groups with their mouths moving, nodding and sipping from glasses. There were dozens of them. If the thief was there, it was impossible to tell who he or she was—the room was too crowded to see most of the faces.

"Oh, that's helpful!" said Aaron.

"It is, actually," I pointed out. "Marc and Anjali aren't there. We just saw them hooking up in the hallway."

"So maybe Marc's not the actual thief. Maybe he's just working with him."

"Can't you ever admit you're wrong? Maybe instead of accusing our friends, we should try to figure out who the crooks really are."

But the painting gave us no clue, so after watching people mill around and sip wine for a while, Aaron told it to shut down. He waited while I texted Anjali that I'd gone home and put the scattered papers back on the desks.

"Look," he said when I was done. "I . . . I'm sorry I said all that. I have my suspicions about Marc, but I don't actually think *you* . . . you and Anjali, you're just so . . ."

"That's okay," I said quickly, before he could say something terrible and make me lose my temper again. "I'm sorry too. I shouldn't have said all those things either. I don't actually . . . I don't really believe those things about you."

"Peace, then?" Aaron held out his hand. "Or," he said wryly, "maybe I should say World Peace?"

"Peace," I agreed.

We put on our coats, turned out the light, and locked the door behind us. Aaron followed me as I followed the exit signs out. They took us to the back door behind the cafeteria, but at least we weren't stuck wandering endlessly around the building.

"See you next week," he said as the big school door swung shut behind us.

"Wait—would you mind—can you walk me to the subway?" I asked. With my lost sense of direction I was afraid it would take me all night to get home on my own.

Aaron looked surprised, but he didn't object, even when I took his arm.

He didn't say much on the way to the subway station. He watched me go down the stairs; I saw him still standing at the top until the wall blocked my view.

There was a message from Anjali waiting in my voice mail when I got off the train. I listened to it as I turned toward my building (after walking half a block in the wrong direction first). *Sorry! I didn't mean to ditch you. Marc and I just got a little . . . caught up in stuff, and then when we got to the library, I guess you'd gone home. I hope you're not mad! Wasn't that a great game? I like your friends. Thank you SOOOOO much for inviting me, I really owe you. Well, see you next week.*

That night I dreamed about the scene in the painting, the scene with the kiss. The dream had the same sickening intensity as the shifting picture, the same over-intimate embarrassment when the kiss moved from mouth to neck, and even the same sense of dissolution when the image blurred into darkness. Only instead of Marc, the guy in the dream was Aaron.

And even more disturbing, instead of Anjali, the girl was me.

# Chapter 17:
## Anjali vanishes

When I got to work at the repository the next morning, I went to Doc's office to return the mermaid's comb.

The door was open. I knocked on the door frame and stuck my head in.

"Hello, Elizabeth. Come in, come in—what can I do for you?"

"I brought that comb back, from the GC."

"Oh, good. I hope everything went well? Now, where did I put the *kuduo*?" Doc rummaged around and found it in the corner of the room behind a rather sad-looking ficus tree. "Let's see—what was your deposit again? Your sense of humor?"

"No, direction."

"Yes, of course." Doc lifted the *kuduo* lid, and I got the comb out of my bag.

As soon as I touched it, I knew something was wrong. It felt different. I lifted it to my nose and sniffed. A faint smell of scalp but nothing else. No magic. Just a comb.

"What's the matter, Elizabeth?"

"I don't know. The comb's weird. I mean, it's not weird. It smells wrong."

"Let me take a look."

I handed it to Doc, who sniffed it, held it to first one ear and then the other, plucked each tooth, and finally, shockingly, delicately licked the back.

I watched Doc's freckles. They seemed to be moving faster than usual. A butterfly shape floated by quickly, followed by a triangle.

I waited anxiously.

"Are you sure this is the right comb?" said Doc at last.

"Yes. I've had it in my bag the whole time, except when I was using it." I had a sick, sinking feeling.

"This doesn't look good. Well, we'll see what happens." Doc fished around in the *kuduo* and pulled out my sense of direction, which swirled alarmingly, shuffling its angles.

"All right," said Doc, lifting it. It glittered. "Hold out your hands. Faceup, that's right. *The loan returned, the debt is quit. Seek then the heart wherein you fit.*"

My sense of direction fell clattering from Doc's hands into mine. It sat there. I felt it jitter and tingle. It felt wrong, wrong, wrong.

"Well? How do I get it back inside me?"

"I don't understand—it should already have . . . Wait, you're not by any chance wearing one of young Miss Rao's charms again?"

"Yes!" I said with relief. "Could that be it? Should I take it off?"

"Let me take a look."

"It's on my foot." Clutching the sense of direction, which was hard to hold and put me off balance, I held out my ankle.

Doc bent over my foot and inspected the string carefully,

twirling it. "Lovely work, but no—this wouldn't stop you from reenveloping what's rightfully yours. I'm sorry, Elizabeth. This looks very, very bad. I'm afraid you're a victim of whoever's been messing with the Grimm Collection objects."

"Oh, no! What do you mean?"

"There's something the matter with that comb—whether it's a different one or someone's damaged it somehow and drained the magic, I don't know. But the vow specifies that the object must be returned 'potent, uncorrupt, and whole,' which this comb clearly isn't."

"But I didn't do anything to it, I swear!"

"I believe you. Unfortunately, the vow doesn't care who damaged it, only whether it's damaged."

"So what happens? I don't get my sense of direction back?"

"I'm afraid not—at least, not now."

My feelings must have shown on my face, because Doc went on, "I hope we can catch the thief—we'll try our best. In the meantime I'll keep your sense of direction safe here. Don't worry, it's in good hands. Nobody can take the *kuduo* out of the repository except its rightful owners. As the Akan proverb says, when a string of beads snaps in the presence of the elders, none are lost."

"Will I just go on getting lost?" This was a disaster.

"Oh, yes. I'm afraid so." Doc took my sense of direction out of my hands and carefully poured it into the *kuduo*. I watched it vanish into darkness.

I checked in with Ms. Callender, who sent me up to work in the Main Exam Room. To my surprise I saw Jaya there, pacing back and forth under the west Tiffany window, the fall scene. Sunlight poured through the glass foliage, turning her hair a dark auburn and giving her skin a reddish cast. She looked like a worried leopard.

She hurried over to me. "Elizabeth! Where's my sister?"

"I don't know—I haven't seen her since last night, at the basketball game. She's not working here today. Why?"

"She's gone! She disappeared! The magical monster must have gotten her!"

"What?"

"The monster! The one that's after you! It got Anjali and it's all my faaault!" Jaya was starting to wail. The patrons—the usual collection of art students sketching, appraisers making notes in their laptops, and elderly Russians playing chess—looked around at us.

"Shh, Jaya. This is a library; you don't want to get thrown out. Tell me what happened. Did you see the monster—the gigantic bird?"

She lowered her voice, but not her panic. "No, but if it got Anjali, it's my fault!"

"How is it your fault?"

"Because I didn't make her a protection spell."

"Oh, Jaya! She didn't let you. Remember?"

"I should have done it anyway. I should have sneaked into her room in the middle of the night and made a protection spell and then the monster wouldn't have gotten her and now she's gooooone!" Jaya was wailing in whispers.

I put my arm around her and sat her down on one of the carved wood benches against the wall. "Shh . . . it's okay, Jaya . . .

Don't cry. It's okay, we'll find her. Hey hey hey, Jaya, it's not your fault. We'll find your sister."

I didn't know if that was true. I hoped so. But how was I going to find Anjali, or anything else, without my sense of direction?

I found a mostly clean tissue in my pocket and gave it to Jaya, who blew her nose loudly. The chess players glanced over at us, then went back to their game.

"Where was the last place you saw her?" The question sounded absurd, even to me—as if Anjali were some toy Jaya had misplaced, a favorite doll.

"This morning at breakfast. She was supposed to help me with my science project. She promised!"

"Maybe she just forgot. Maybe she's shopping or something."

"Anjali doesn't forget things. Anyway, I would know if she was shopping. I'm good at knowing where she is."

I bet you are, I thought. "And did she say anything before she disappeared?"

"Anything about what?"

"I don't know. Where she was going? Or anything weird or unusual?"

"No, she complained because I finished the cornflakes. That's not weird or unusual. The last unusual thing was when you were over before the basketball game, with the missing magic and Benign Designs. Do you think that's where she went? Benign Designs?"

"Maybe."

"Where is it? I'm going to go get her back!" Jaya jumped up off the bench, as if she were about to run off right that minute.

"Jaya, wait! We don't even know for sure if that's where Anjali went. Or if she's even missing at all."

The door opened and Marc hurried over to our bench. "Are you Jaya? Anjali's little sister?"

Jaya frowned at the word *little*. "Who are *you*?"

"I'm Marc. Where's Anjali? Is she okay? She hasn't been answering my messages."

"You're Marc Merritt? Anjali's boyfriend? How did you know I was here?" Jaya looked at him with interest.

"Sarah said you were here talking to Elizabeth. Is Anjali okay? Where is she?"

"You're the basketball star?"

"Yes, yes, yes. Where's Anjali?"

"I don't know. I think the monster, or maybe Benign Designs, kidnapped her."

"No!" He hit his leg with his fist. It looked like it hurt. "I told her not to go there without me!"

"Where? Benign Designs?" I asked.

"She told me last night she thought they took the objects," he said. "She thinks they replaced them with copies that only work for a few days. She wanted to go investigate. I told her to wait until I could come with her."

"Oh!" That would explain why the comb stopped working suddenly. "I'll bet she's right!"

"Where is it? Where's Benign Designs? I'm going to go rescue her," said Jaya.

Marc glanced at her with that carelessly haughty look of his, as if he'd just remembered she was there. "You can't—you're only ten."

I could have told him that was exactly the wrong thing to say. "She's my sister! You can't stop me."

Marc turned and faced her this time. "Anjali would never forgive me if anything happened to you," he said.

"She's *my* sister! I'm coming with you. If you don't let me come, I'll go alone."

"All right, Jaya," I said. "Go get Anjali's laptop. Bring it here. We'll go through it and see if we can figure out where she went. It'll be safer if we all go together."

The three of us went to the coffee shop on Lexington and turned on the laptop.

"Here's the address for Benign Designs, down on Twenty-third Street. I also found the address for the owner—somebody named Wallace Stone. He had it registered under a business name, but Anjali looked up his actual name on a state database."

"Wallace Stone," I said. "I've heard that name before."

"Where?" asked Jaya.

I thought about it. "Something about the page that got fired for stealing stuff. I think they said he recommended her."

"Great! So we're on the right track, at least," said Jaya.

"I guess the best thing to do is just to go down to Twenty-third Street and look for him," Marc said.

"I don't know—that's probably what Anjali did, and she's missing," I said.

"Got any better ideas?"

"Shouldn't we ask Doc for help? Or the other librarians, or Mr. Mauskopf?"

"No! We don't know who Doc will tell about it, and any one of the librarians could be involved with the thief. They all have access to the Grimm Collection. The fewer people we trust, the better."

"You think the *librarians* are involved?" That sounded crazy.

"I don't know who to trust," said Marc.

"I think he's right," said Jaya. "Anjali disappeared because of the repository. I don't trust anyone there—except you, of course, because you're nice, and Marc, because he's Anjali's boyfriend."

But the Twenty-third Street address was a dead end. There was no Benign Designs listed on any of the buzzers, and when we rang them anyway, nobody'd heard of the place—at least, that's what they said.

"What do we do next?" I asked.

"We go see the owner—Wallace Stone," said Jaya. "I got his address and phone number. It's on Otters Alley, downtown. Let me see your ankle."

"What?"

"The knot. I need to see your knot."

"Oh." I stuck out my foot.

"Other foot."

I stuck out my other foot. She pushed up my jeans leg to look at the knot and nodded. "Good, it's still there. Here, you make me one." She pulled a ball of yarn out of her bag and snapped off a piece with her teeth.

"I don't know how."

"That's okay, I'll show you. First take both ends in your left hand and wrap the whole yarn—no, your left hand—no, that's still your right hand—yes, that's it—now wrap it clockwise—no, *clockwise*—the other way. Okay, now hold the loop under your left thumb and take the two ends with your right hand and loop the top one around your index finger and the bottom one around your pinkie—no, the bottom one, that's the top one—"

This went on for a long time. I wondered whether tying knots would be easier if I had a sense of direction. The cold made my fingers extra clumsy, and people walking past us on Twenty-third Street gave us little amused glances.

"Do we have time for this?" asked Marc. "What are you doing, anyway?"

"Making a knot of protection," said Jaya. "It's very important. It keeps you safe from magic attacks. No, Elizabeth, the other way. You have it backward."

Eventually I produced a lump that seemed to connect the two ends. "Now the rhyme—repeat after me," said Jaya. *"By this charm, be safe from harm."*

*"By this charm, be safe from harm,"* I repeated, pulling the knot tight. "Okay?"

Jaya tugged at it dubiously. It slipped a little, but it didn't come untied. "I hope so," she said. "Your turn, Marc."

"Jaya," he said, "that yarn's pink."

"Oh. You're right. Well, I didn't bring any other color." She snapped off a length with her teeth again, pulled his arm toward her, and began weaving the knot.

Marc crinkled his forehead, but he didn't stop her. I guess Andre gave him plenty of practice indulging little siblings. "You better take Jaya home while I go downtown and deal with this Wallace Stone," he told me.

"If you try, I'll scream and say you kidnapped me," Jaya said. "They'll believe me too—I don't look a thing like you. You have to take me with you."

"Maybe we can find an ogre who'd like to eat her," said Marc.

"Maybe that's what Wallace Stone is," I answered.

old clock

# Chapter 18:
## Marc makes a deal

The building on Otters Alley was an old factory with huge windows and eight buzzers. Marc pressed the one that said *W. Stone.*

After a minute a crackly voice came out of the loudspeaker: "Who is it?"

Marc and I looked at each other in dismay. We'd forgotten to come up with a cover story. Before we could stop her, Jaya pushed her face forward and announced, "It's Jaya Rao. I'm here to rescue my sister."

Silence for a few seconds; then the door buzzed open. We took the clanking old elevator up to the seventh floor and rang the bell.

It only took me a second to recognize Wallace Stone: the repository patron, the man who had tried to take the box of acrobats on Fifth Avenue.

"Well, it's you! Hello again," he said. "Have you brought me back my package?"

"You!" I said.

"Where's my sister?" said Jaya.

He turned to look at her. "My, my, my," he said. "The other one—a matching pair."

"Where is she? Where's Anjali? Give her back!" Jaya filled the hallway.

"I wish I could, but I don't have her."

"Anjali! *Anjali!* Where are you hiding her?" Jaya pushed past him and stuck her head in the apartment door. "Anjali!"

Mr. Stone opened the door wide. "By all means, come in and look around. Bring your friends. You'll see I'm telling the truth. Your sister's not here." He cocked an eyebrow at me and Marc with polite, almost affectionate patience. We all followed Jaya into the apartment.

The smell overwhelmed me for a moment. It was as unmistakable and impossible to pin down as the smell in the Grimm Collection, yet rawer, harsher. It smelled like the false package Mr. Stone had tried to give me instead of the acrobats. Not hyacinths but paint thinner; not loam but wet ash.

Reeling from the smell, I looked around to get my bearings. The apartment was a big loft with a high ceiling. It seemed to be part home, part warehouse. Pedestals, tables, and stands displayed lovely old objects—clocks, paintings, vases, radios—that all looked as if they might be magical. On the computer, some sort of dizzying screen saver whirled and churned sickeningly. It reminded me of the swirling inside the *kuduo*. I looked away.

"Can I get you anything? A soda?" offered Mr. Stone.

"My sister!"

"Excuse me a minute." Mr. Stone went behind a low wall. We could hear the refrigerator open and shut. Jaya stomped around, looking behind furniture for Anjali.

Mr. Stone came back with drinks and cookies. "Root beer? Sparkling water?"

"My sister!"

He poured a glass of root beer and held it out to me. "No, thanks," I said. He offered it to Marc, who shook his head. Jaya didn't even acknowledge the offer—she just glared at him.

Mr. Stone shrugged and sipped the soda himself. "So," he said. "Perhaps we should introduce ourselves. I'm Wallace Stone, but I imagine you know that already. I think you said you were Jaya Rao?" He held out his hand to Jaya, but she put hers behind her. Mr. Stone seemed to find that funny—at least, his eyes twinkled. "And you?" He offered me his hand. "We've met before, of course, but I don't know your name."

I didn't want to shake his hand, but I thought it was probably a good idea to be polite if we wanted to get any information out of him. "Elizabeth Rew," I said.

"A pleasure."

He turned to Marc next and held out his hand. "And you're the great Marc Merritt, aren't you?"

Marc towered over Mr. Stone and didn't offer his hand.

"Now, have some gingerbread and tell me why you thought your sister would be here," said Mr. Stone, holding out the plate of cookies.

"We know she came here this morning, and now she's missing," said Marc, accepting one.

I couldn't resist taking one too and bit off its leg. It was delicious. I tasted ginger, cinnamon, cloves, and some other spice—what was it? Nutmeg? Cardamom? No, something a little more unusual in gingerbread—orange peel, maybe? Not quite: it was a darker flavor somehow, more like, I don't know, caramelized apples or wood smoke. I took another bite. Sweet and dark, like roast duck or cedar pencils.

"Well, you're right—Anjali did come to see me," said Mr. Stone. "But as you can see, she's not here anymore."

"She was here? When? What happened to her?" Jaya chomped the head off a gingerbread man furiously, as if it were Mr. Stone himself.

His eyes flared. "Thank you, my dear. You're about to find out." He cleared his throat and intoned:

*"All who gobble gingerbread,*
*Whether from the feet or head,*
*Be you swineherd, king, or queen,*
*Turn into a figurine!"*

Nothing happened.

Well, Jaya seemed to sort of shudder for a moment, rippling around the edges like a reflection in a pond on a windy day; also, my stomach felt odd. Marc leapt to his feet. But nobody turned into a figurine.

"That's strange," said Mr. Stone. He looked annoyed.

*"Did you miss what I just said?*
*By the power of gingerbread,*
*Whether swineherd, king, or queen—*
*Turn into a figurine!"*

Jaya rippled again. "Stop it!" she yelled, shaking herself like a wet dog.

Marc grabbed Mr. Stone by the shoulders. "What are you doing? Did you just try to turn us into figurines?" he growled, his nostrils flaring.

"Yes, of course. What on earth went wrong? *By the power of gingerbread* . . . Let me see that!" He caught hold of the knot on Marc's wrist. "What is this? Abigail Bender's work?"

"Mine," said Jaya, with a touch of smugness mixed into her fury. "Miss Bender taught me. Is my sister a figurine? Where did you hide her?" She began tearing through the closet, flinging coats on the floor and dumping out the contents of hatboxes.

Marc wrenched his arm away from Mr. Stone. He opened his knapsack and reached in. He held up a burlap sack and said, *"Cudgel, out of the bag!"*

A stout wooden club with a leather handle flew out of the sack, straight at Mr. Stone. He threw his hand up in front of him. The club paused in mid-flight, beating at the air. Then slowly, thrashing and struggling as if it were being dragged against its will, it turned around and lowered itself, handle first, into his hand.

"Thank you, Marc—what a pleasant surprise. The bag too, please." Mr. Stone held out his other hand and the bag twisted itself out of Marc's grasp into his. "Did you really think you could beat your friend's whereabouts out of me? In my own home? How crude." He shook his head sadly.

Marc stared at him in horror.

"What *was* that? What's going on?" I cried.

"The Grimm cudgel," said Marc in a choked voice. "He got the Grimm cudgel!"

"The what?"

"The Grimm cudgel. It beats up anyone you send it after, until you tell it to stop. At least, it's supposed to."

"Marc, Marc, Marc. Don't you know violence is never the

answer?" Mr. Stone seemed to be enjoying himself. *"Cudgel, back in the bag."*

"You thieving piece of—"

"Please—you're addressing a member of the Association of Authenticating Antiquarians, not to mention the Better Business Bureau. I prefer the term 'art dealer.'"

"You sick little creep! You! You're the one who stole that stuff from the Grimm Collection—just like you stole Anjali! Where is it?"

"Perfectly safe, I assure you. My clients are very careful with their collections."

"You'll tell me! I'll make you tell me," roared Marc.

"What about that other page—the one that disappeared? Mona? Did you take her too?" I asked.

"Mona Chen? Slippery little character. No, unfortunately—I don't know where she is. I thought I could get her to help me in my business, but she not only refused to cooperate, she ran away."

"Where is Anjali?" yelled Jaya again.

"Sit down, all of you, and please, stop yelling. Let's settle this like adults," said Mr. Stone. "I have something you want. You have something I want. I'm sure we can come to an arrangement."

"What arrangement? You'll give me my sister back?"

"As I keep telling you, I don't have your sister. But I do know where she is. I sold . . . that is, I placed her with a very good customer of mine, a distinguished collector, who might be willing to part with her if you can make it worth her while."

"Who? Who is the collector? Where is she keeping Anjali?"

"Please. Sit. I'm willing to share that information in exchange for . . ." He paused. "Let's see. You have access to the Grimm Collection, yes?"

"No!" I said. "Do your own dirty work. We're not stealing anything for you!"

"Anything *else,* you mean?" Mr. Stone held up the cudgel bag. I shot a bitter look at Marc, who wouldn't meet my eyes. "But I'm not asking you to steal anything," Mr. Stone continued. "I'm only asking for something that's rightfully yours," he said, turning to Marc. "There's an Akan bronze ceremonial vessel with a puff adder and a hornbill on the lid. Bring me that and I'll tell you where Anjali is."

"You mean Doc's *kuduo*?"

"No!" I said. "Even if we wanted to, we can't take it out of the repository. Doc says no one can except its rightful owners."

"Ah, but that's just the point." Mr. Stone's eyes were twinkling. "Young Mr. Merritt here *is* the rightful owner."

"What are you talking about?" said Marc.

"Nobody told you? You, young man, are descended from great men and women. Chiefs in Africa, in what's now Ghana. The *kuduo* in question belongs to your family. Those prigs at the repository? They have no more right to it than—well, than Jaya here. It's yours to do with whatever you want. Including trade it to me, for information about your friend's whereabouts."

"The *kuduo*? Mine?"

"Exactly."

"He's right," I said. "Doc told me it belongs to your family."

"Why tell you and not me? What's it doing in the repository?" said Marc. "How did they get it?"

"How did they get any of their holdings?" answered Mr. Stone. "The place is rife with trickery, shady deals—"

"That's not true! The *kuduo*'s on loan. Doc said Marc's uncle loaned it to the repository!" I said.

Mr. Stone said, "You think the people running that institution are paragons of virtue? Your people have a proverb, Marc: 'If a bug bites you, it's from inside your clothes.' Believe me, I could tell you a thing or two about a few of your librarians . . . But I won't. I'm a gentleman. Bring me that *kuduo*, and I'll show you where to find Anjali."

He got up and opened the door. "Well, this has been a pleasure. I look forward to further profitable meetings."

"What now?" I said when we got downstairs. We were all three practically shaking with rage at our own powerlessness.

"Now Marc goes and gets that doodoo-oh or whatever it's called and we rescue my sister," said Jaya.

"I don't know if that's a good idea," I said. "I don't trust that guy. What's he going to do with it? Sell it, like he sold Anjali? Or use it somehow, like the cudgel? That *kuduo* is powerful. I think we should ask Doc for help."

"No! That's the worst plan possible," said Marc. "Our only hope of finding Anjali is the *kuduo,* and Doc would never let me take it."

"But you can't take the *kuduo*! It's too dangerous—and it's full of important things! We need help. Jaya, what about your parents? Can we tell them?"

"No," said Jaya. "We have to get Anjali back ourselves. They would kill her if they find out about . . ." She looked at Marc. "About all of this. They would ground her for decades."

"I would rather be grounded and safe," I said.

"Anjali wouldn't. Not when she could be safe and not grounded instead. Let's just go get that thing Stone wants right now and rescue her."

Marc looked at his watch. "Too late now," he said. "The repository's closed, and we don't have the key. We'll have to get it tomorrow."

"Okay. I'll tell my parents Anjali's staying at your place tonight."

"I guess," I said. "I still think it's a terrible idea to steal the *kuduo*."

"Can you think of any other way?"

"Not if you don't let me tell the librarians," I admitted. I still thought that was a better idea, but I could see Marc's point. There was a chance that one of them could be in on the thefts themselves, and even if they weren't, I couldn't imagine them agreeing to trade away the *kuduo*. If that was the only way to get Anjali back, we had to try it. "I'll see you at the repository tomorrow," I told Marc.

Maybe we could even find a way to empty out the contents, like my sense of direction, before we turned it over to Mr. Stone.

Chapter 19:
Embarrassing
reflections

After dinner, my phone rang.

"Elizabeth? It's Aaron, Aaron Rosendorn."

My heart did a little funny flip, like Doc's mini acrobats. Stop it, heart, I told it. You have more serious things to think about than Aaron Rosendorn. "Hi, Aaron," I said. "What's up?"

"Can you come over to my place? There's something I want to show you."

"Really? What?"

"It's just . . . an idea I had."

"Okay," I said. "Where do you live?"

"On West Eighty-first Street, down the block from the Museum of Natural History."

"I have a bad sense of direction these days. I'm not sure I can find it."

"Of course you can. It's not that hard."

"No, really. I get lost in my own bedroom."

"You can at least get to the Museum of Natural History, can't you? The subway goes right to the door. Tell you what, I'll meet you there," he said.

• • •

I found my way to the subway okay and managed to get off at the right stop. Then I had to circle the entire museum before I found the entrance where Aaron was waiting for me.

He was leaning against the pedestal of the statue of Teddy Roosevelt, his cheeks red with the cold. It was the first time I'd seen him since that embarrassing dream.

"So what's at your place? The thing you want to show me?" I asked.

He looked around at the people on the museum steps: a school group, some nannies with their charges, a pair of older men. "Something from the GC," he said, lowering his voice.

"Something you borrowed?" I asked.

He nodded.

"What?"

"Not here," he said.

He steered me by the arm, preventing me from making at least three wrong turns. Even through my coat sleeve, I was very aware of the spot where he was touching my arm.

He lived in an old apartment building from the same period as Anjali's, but less fancy.

"Hi, Aaron," said the doorman.

"Hi, Jim. Is my mom home?"

"No, not yet," said the doorman. "You have the place to yourself." To my embarrassment, he winked at me.

We took the elevator to the seventh floor. Aaron unlocked a door and I followed him down a long, dark hallway, through a cluttered living room, to a small, dark room behind the kitchen.

He held the door open and cleared his throat. "So. Come in," he said.

His room was neater than mine, but not by much. I wondered whether he usually kept it that way. Or had he cleaned it up for me? He took off his coat and I handed him mine. He put them both down on the bed, which was made, if sloppily.

I looked around for somewhere to sit. I had a choice of the bed, a beanbag chair, and his desk chair. I chose the desk chair; Aaron leaned against the wall, his knees bent.

"Did you borrow that invisible chair from the GC? Is that what you wanted to show me?"

He laughed nervously and stood up straight.

I felt nervous too. Something wasn't quite right in the room. Slowly I figured out what: the place reeked of magic, the scary kind. It was laced with undertones of awfulness, the way air freshener might claim to smell like strawberries, but you would never willingly put it in your mouth. It smelled like Mr. Stone's loft or the worst items in the Grimm Collection, the murky picture or the Snow White mirror.

No wonder. There on the wall over the dresser hung the Snow White mirror.

"Is that what I think it is?"

He nodded. "That's what I wanted to show you."

"You borrowed it?"

He nodded again.

"Did you leave a deposit in the *kuduo*?"

"Of course! What do you take me for?"

"What did you leave? If you don't mind my asking."

"My firstborn child."

"But you don't have—"

"My *future* firstborn child, silly."

"Wow." For some reason the thought of that gave me the shivers. I turned to the mirror. "Why did you take this creepy mirror home? Why not just talk to it at the repository?"

"It's not safe to talk to it there. I'm not sure it's even safe to talk to each other there. Things keep disappearing, and I don't know who to trust."

But he thought he could trust *me*.

I felt flattered and a little guilty—I might not have lied to him exactly, but I hadn't been entirely open with him either. I decided to tell him about Anjali's disappearance and our trip to Mr. Stone's. I left out the part where Mr. Stone told Marc to steal the *kuduo,* though. I didn't think that would get a very positive reaction from Aaron.

"Anjali *vanished*?" The concern in his voice was painful to hear. "Why didn't you tell me?"

"What do you mean? I just did."

"But why didn't you tell me right away? Why didn't you call me?"

"I don't know, Aaron. It's not like I was hiding it, it's just . . ." What could I say? I couldn't exactly tell him that it didn't occur to me to tell him, and if it had, I might have been too worried he would blame Marc.

"I can't believe it, Elizabeth! What am I supposed to do?"

"Help us find Anjali."

"I meant, what am I supposed to do about *you*? Can I trust you? I thought I could. The mirror says I can."

"Really?"

"Yes. Watch." He turned away from me toward the mirror. His handsome face looked sinister enough in real life; his reflection was so bitter it scared me. I wondered what he must be seeing in *my* face in the mirror. That mirror could certainly put its own twist on what it saw.

Aaron asked the mirror:

*"Elizabeth, who we discussed,*

*Is she someone I can trust?"*

His reflection listened with a little smirk on its perfect chiseled lips. It looked me straight in the eye and replied in Aaron's voice,

*"Bitsy Rew is brave and true.*

*A pity she's not pretty too."*

"Oh, nice," I said. "For the record, my name is Elizabeth. Elizabeth! Nobody calls me Bitsy. Did you hear that, you vile object?" I started to scowl at the mirror but quickly stopped—I didn't want to think about how my scowl would look once the mirror got through distorting it. I turned to Aaron. "What makes you think you can trust that thing? It's evil!"

"I know, but it can't lie."

"Oh, thanks."

"No, I mean, it's right about you being brave . . . and it does tell people the truth about their looks—you know how it told Snow White's stepmother the minute she stopped being the fairest of them all."

Aaron's reflection was smiling smugly, while Aaron's own face twisted in an awkward combination of embarrassed and angry.

"So you're saying you agree, I'm not pretty?"

"No—I didn't say that! I think it has to tell the truth, but it doesn't have to tell the whole truth. It can't just lie, but it can be as mean and difficult as it wants. It clearly likes to mess around with people and get them in trouble—remember what happened to Snow White's stepmother."

"I don't, actually. What did happen to her?" I asked.

"I don't remember either. Something bad. But that's not the point. The point is, the mirror likes to tease and torment, but it can't just out-and-out lie. So if I have to think about it, it's right: *pretty* isn't the word I would use for you. As far as pretty goes . . . you can be beautiful but not pretty."

"Oh, are you calling me beautiful, then? You're saying that's what the mirror meant?" Did he really think he could get out of the insult by pretending he meant it as a compliment?

Aaron threw his hands in the air. "What is it with you women? There's a magic mirror that can tell you the truth about anything you want to know, and all you can think about is whether you're beautiful!"

"What do you mean, 'you women'? Who's 'you women'?"

"You and Snow White's stepmother, for starts."

"Oh, so you're lumping me in with Snow White's step-mother now? Watch out, I might poison you with an apple."

Aaron's reflection in the mirror looked as if it was enjoying this far too much.

"Don't look at me like that, you!" I told it. "If I weren't afraid of seven years of bad luck, I would smash you to bits." Aaron's reflection in the mirror doubled over laughing. I picked up a shoe from the floor and held it up threateningly. *"You suck. Don't push your luck,"* I said.

The mirror answered,

*"Silly girl, Elizabeth—*

*Don't you know you rhyme with death?"*

"You think you can scare me? You don't scare me one bit!" My voice came out terrified.

Aaron gently took the shoe from me and put it down. "My firstborn child, remember? If you break it, I lose it. Let's just ask the mirror about Anjali."

I pulled myself together. "Okay, if you think that'll do any good." I considered for a while, then said,

*"Anjali, the elder Rao,*

*What is her location now?"*

The mirror answered:

*"In a cabinet of glass,*

*Where only royal blood may pass,*

*From Versailles to the Taj Mahal—*

*There she stands, a real doll."*

"What does *that* mean?" said Aaron. The mirror didn't deign to respond.

"I think it might mean she's a doll."

"Yes, yes, we know she's gorgeous, but where *is* she?"

"No, I mean she's *really* a doll. We think Mr. Stone turned her into a figurine. He tried to do it to us too."

I turned to the mirror.

*"Do you literally mean*

*That Anjali's a figurine?"*

Aaron's reflection in the mirror nodded. *"Don't get your panties in a whirl,"* it answered, demonstrating with an obscene-looking gesture. *"She's a puppet, not a girl."*

"Oh, no, that's horrifying!" I said.

"How are we going to get her back?" said Aaron.

I addressed the mirror:

*"We're terrified for Anjali.*

*Tell us how to set her free."*

Aaron's reflection shook its finger at me teasingly and said,

*"But Liz, your rival's locked away.*

*Here's your chance to seize the day."*

Aaron turned to me, his eyes widening. "Is that true? Is Anjali your rival? Why?"

"Oh, come *on*! Don't tell me you believe that thing! You know it's evil! You said yourself it likes to mess with people."

"Yeah, I guess. She sounded pretty convincing, though."

"Who did?"

"The mirror."

"Why are you calling it 'she'? It was talking in *your* voice."

"No, it wasn't—it was using yours. And now she's smirking at me, just like you do."

Aaron was glowering at me, but his reflection looked like it was about to burst out laughing.

"I bet that's because we can't see ourselves from where we're sitting, just each other. The mirror has to show us what we see reflected. Come over here so it reflects us both," I said. I sat on the bed, across from the mirror. Aaron walked over and sat down beside me, his shoulder touching mine.

In the mirror, his reflection put its arm around my reflection's shoulders. My reflection nestled against him and looked up at him with adoring eyes. His reflection started playing with my reflection's hair. She twisted around, curled her legs up on the bed, and put her head in his lap. I heard myself give an embarrassed giggle. It was almost as embarrassing as what was going on in the mirror.

Aaron looked embarrassed too. He said,

*"Anjali! Is she okay?*

*I'd like an answer, please—today."*

Our reflections put their cheeks together and crooned,

*"She's surrounded by her peers,*

*Royals missing through the years.*

*She's the glory of the hoard—*

*Safe enough, though rather bored."*

Then they put their foreheads together and looked into each other's eyes.

I turned to Aaron and said, "Right. So if we can trust the mirror, she's safe where she is, for now. That's good news, anyway. We have some time to figure everything out."

"While you try to get Marc's attention, with your rival away?"

"Aaron, what is the matter with you?"

In the mirror, our reflections were staring at us with their mouths parted, as if they were watching the climax of an exciting movie. They had their arms around each other.

"Come on, Aaron! Let's try one more time to get something useful out of the horrible thing, and if we can't, let's smash it. Or at least cover it."

"Yes, okay. You ask this time."

I thought for a bit and said,

*"For the last time—answer me!*

*How can we free Anjali?"*

As if they knew this was their last chance to torment us, the couple in the mirror turned to each other with a new intensity. Like a ghastly parody of Marc and Anjali in the magic painting after the basketball game—or my dream that night—Aaron's reflection began kissing my reflection on the neck. She turned to us and breathed,

*"Want to rescue Anjali?*

*Find and use the Golden Key."*

Then she went back to making out with Aaron's reflection.

"Stop it!" said Aaron. The door opened behind us and a woman came in. I saw her in the mirror, staring out at us— evidently the real woman was staring at our reflections in the mirror.

I could see why; they were well worth staring at. They sprang apart hurriedly, straightening their clothes. By the time the real woman turned to look at the real us, our reflections were sitting up very straight, a foot apart, blushing furiously—exactly like us, as if they were reflections in a normal mirror.

"Mom! Can't you knock?"

"I'm sorry. I didn't know you had company." She looked at me expectantly.

"This is—this is my friend from the repository. We were just . . . ," Aaron trailed off.

Aaron's mother held out her hand to me. "Let me guess— Angeline?"

"No, Mom, not Anjali! It's not Angeline, anyway, it's Anjali," said Aaron. "AHHHN-jah-lee. It's Indian."

"I'm so sorry, Anjali. I'm Rebecca Rosendorn." I could see her struggling not to look thrown off balance, wondering how someone so obviously Caucasian had ended up with an Indian name. If I hadn't been so busy trying to get my own balance, I would have felt sorry for her.

"But I'm not Anjali," I said. "I'm Elizabeth. Elizabeth Rew."

"Oh! I'm sorry, Elizabeth! Well, it's nice to meet you. I'll just . . . leave this door open, shall I?" She left the room, with the door gaping wide.

I picked up my coat. "I think I'd better go. I don't think there's anything more we can do about Anjali tonight, and your mom—"

"Yeah, you're probably right." He walked me to the apartment door. "Want me to take you home?" he asked. "Or at least to the subway stop?"

"Thanks, I think I can get there myself."

"Okay—see you tomorrow, then."

"Bye." I concentrated on getting to the subway. It was hard, but it helped keep my mind off what our reflections were doing under that blanket. I made it home with only one false turn.

# Chapter 20:
# The shrink ray

The next morning I went to the repository early and looked for Marc. He was on Stack 6. I looked around to make sure nobody was listening. "Well?" I whispered. "What are we going to do about the *kuduo*?"

"It's done," he said. "I just got back from Stone's."

"You did it? You stole the *kuduo*? You were supposed to wait for me!"

"It's not stealing."

I decided not to argue the point. "Did you at least empty out the deposits before you took it?"

He shook his head. "I couldn't figure out how to get them out, or what to do with them if I did."

Oh, no! Good-bye to my sense of direction! I wondered whether Mr. Stone would be able to take it out of the *kuduo* and use it. Good luck to him if he did—it was never much good even when I had it. Good-bye to Aaron's firstborn and everything else. Not for the first time, I thought Marc was pretty selfish. "Did you at least find out where Anjali is?" I asked. "The Snow White mirror said she's a puppet."

"What? What are you talking about?"

I told him about the conversation with Aaron and the mirror.

"So the spell worked on Anjali! A puppet! At least now we know what to look for when we go rescue her," said Marc.

"So you found out where?"

He nodded. "Stone gave me a name and address. A woman named Gloria Badwin, in the West Village. I'm going there today, as soon as my shift is over—I just have to wait for Mrs. Walker to drop off Andre here."

"Who's Mrs. Walker?" I asked.

"Andre's friend's mom. She's dropping him off here after his playdate, when my shift is over. I'll have to get someone to watch him while I go look for Anjali."

"That's not the only problem. Before we rescue Anjali, we'll need to find the Golden Key, whatever that is."

"The Golden Key? Why?"

I told him what the mirror had said.

"Well, that's easy enough. I'll go get the key right now."

"You know where it is? You know *what* it is?"

"Yeah, it's one of the objects in the Grimm Collection. Wait here, I'll be right back."

I sat down and opened the book I was reading for English. I heard him come in, but I didn't look up. "Did you find it?" I asked.

"Find what?" said Aaron.

My heart tripped over its ankles. "Oh! Sorry, I thought you were Marc."

That was the wrong thing to say. Aaron scowled at me. I tried to think of something better to say. "How's your . . ." His what? His evil mirror? His hastily made bed? "How's your mom?"

He blushed. "She's fine. Look, what are we going to do about Anjali? Have you figured out what this Golden Key is?"

"Something from the Grimm Collection, Marc said. He went to get it."

"You *told* him?"

"Of course I told him! He's Anjali's boyfriend. He has a right to know."

"He's also the guy who's been stealing things from the Grimm Collection, remember?"

Marc walked in before I could answer. "I forgot—you need two keys to get into the GC now. Can I take yours?" Marc asked me.

I reached in my pocket.

"You're not going to give it to him!" said Aaron. "Doc told you never to lend it to anyone!"

"Anjali got kidnapped! I need to rescue her!" said Marc. "Why are you trying to stop me?"

"I'm not—," Aaron began.

I grabbed his arm. "Shh, here comes Ms. Minnian."

Ms. Minnian hurried over to us, her heels clicking on the linoleum. "Have any of you seen Dr. Rust? Or Anjali?" she asked. She sounded very worried.

We all shook our heads. "No—why?" said Marc.

"Nobody's seen Dr. Rust since yesterday, and Anjali didn't show up for her shift. If you hear from either of them, can you come and tell me or Ms. Callender immediately, please?"

"Of course," I said. "Wow, I hope they're okay!"

"I hope so too. Until we find Dr. Rust, we're putting the

Grimm Collection completely out of bounds. We've changed all the locks—your keys won't work. If you get a ★GC slip, send it straight to me." She walked off quickly.

I waited until I couldn't hear her heels anymore, then said, "I guess that means we can't ask Doc for help. But we could still ask Ms. Minnian or Ms. Callender."

"No!" said Marc. "This is just more proof that we can't trust anyone."

"I can certainly agree with that," said Aaron. He glared at Marc to show exactly who he meant by "anyone."

"Do you think Wallace Stone stole Dr. Rust too somehow?" I asked. "We should have warned Doc about Stone—Doc trusted him! Or is Doc looking for the *kuduo*?"

"What do you mean? What happened to the *kuduo*?" asked Aaron.

Now it was Marc's turn to glare at me.

"Answer me," said Aaron. "Where's the *kuduo*?"

After a moment, I answered. "Marc took it. He traded it to Wallace Stone for the address of the person who has Anjali."

"He *what*? He stole the *kuduo*? With my firstborn child in it? And you *knew* about it and you *let* him? I can't believe you!" He stared at me for a moment, then spun on his heel and started to walk off.

"Wait! Aaron!" I grabbed his arm again. "Where are you going?"

"To tell Ms. Minnian and then the police. Let go!" He shook his arm.

Marc stepped between him and the door. "You can't do that. You know you can't. We've got to rescue Anjali—Stone gave me the address and the mirror told you about the Golden Key. Think about it! If we tell the librarians, they won't let us near it and we'll never get Anjali back!"

"They'll get her back themselves."

"You think you can trust them? Maybe Doc's in on it. Maybe they're all in on it!" said Marc.

"Or maybe nobody's in on it except you. You just admitted you stole the *kuduo*! Get out of my way!"

"You think I would let my own girlfriend get kidnapped if I was in on it? Just calm down and *think* for a minute, Aaron! The point is, we know what to do, but if we tell the librarians, they won't let us do it."

"Aaron, he's right," I said. "You know he is. We have to rescue Anjali! Can we please just stop fighting and figure out how?"

Aaron glared at me some more, but he stopped trying to get to the door. "All right," he said. "We'll rescue Anjali. But the moment she's safe, I'm turning Marc in."

"Fine," said Marc. "I don't care what happens to me if Anjali's safe. Let's go get the Golden Key and rescue her."

"Yeah, but how?" I said. "It's in the Grimm Collection and they changed the locks. Our keys won't work. Is there any other way into the Grimm Collection besides the door?"

Both boys looked stumped.

"Not unless you crawled in through the pneum pipes," said Marc.

"Hey," said Aaron. "That's a thought."

"Yeah, right," said Marc. "You may be short, but you're not *that* short."

Aaron gave him a withering look. "We can use the shrink ray in the Wells Bequest. Ms. Minnian didn't say anything about the other Special Collections, just the Grimm Collection—I bet my Wells key still works. I can shrink you down and send you into the Grimm Collection in a pneum."

"There's actually a shrink ray? That's brilliant!" I said.

Marc nodded grudgingly. "I guess that could work," he said.

I thought about it some more. "Okay, so that's how we get into the Grimm Collection, but how do we get out? We would need somebody full size to send us back through the pipes."

"Maybe we can use this Golden Key to get out. Any idea what it does?" said Marc.

"It opens a box. Nobody knows what's in the box," said Aaron.

"Then how do you know it opens it?" asked Marc.

"Didn't you read the Grimm fairy tales? It's the last one."

· "Right, the last story! Of course!" I said.

"Oh. I guess I must have skipped that one. Is it really boring, with lots of oafs and donkeys? I kind of skimmed those."

"No, it's really short. A boy finds a golden key in the woods. Then he digs around and finds an iron box. He unlocks it, but the story ends there, and you never find out what's in the box."

"I don't see how that's going to help us get out," said Marc.

"Maybe the Golden Key unlocks more than just that one box," I said. "Maybe once we're inside the Grimm Collection, we can use something else to let us out. A genie or a wishing ring or something. Or we could put on the invisibility cloak and sneak out when a librarian comes in. I think we should use the shrink ray. I bet we can find a way out of the GC if we manage to get in."

"All right," said Aaron, picking up his backpack. "Let's go."

The shrink ray, a huge machine with streamlined curves, crouched like a gigantic rat in its own section of the Wells Bequest. Aaron picked up its long, curly tail and examined the plug at the end. "Where did I put that extension cord?"

I stared at the machine with rising apprehension as Aaron and Marc argued about who would shrink whom. The argument didn't last long. Wells objects were really Aaron's domain, as he pointed out. He was the only one who knew how to operate it.

"First we'll send some useful stuff down to the GC in pneums, things like scissors and string," said Aaron. "Then I'll shrink the two of you so you fit in the pneums yourselves and send you down. Who wants to go first?"

"I'd better," said Marc. "I'm stronger, so I can help Elizabeth get out of the tube."

We packed a couple of pneums with supplies and stuffed a few more things in our backpacks. Aaron pushed a switch and the machine growled to life. He swung it around to point its nozzle at Marc.

"Hey! Aren't you going to test it first?"

"If you want. What should I shrink?"

I handed him my sweater. It was a hand-me-down from Veronica, and it was too big. In fact, I had thought about trying to shrink it by putting it through the dryer.

Aaron pointed the shrink ray and fiddled with a knob. A

green ray came whooshing out. The sweater writhed like a balloon losing air. In seconds it was down to half its size.

Aaron twisted another knob and the shrinking slowed down. So did the writhing—the sweater waved its arms slowly like something in an underwater documentary, kelp or a sea anemone.

I picked it up. It looked like it would fit a Barbie doll. I was amazed at how finely made it seemed, with its perfect little buttons and blindingly tiny stitches.

"Test the magnifying function—make sure you can get it back to the right size," I said.

Aaron fiddled with the controls and turned the shrink ray on again. This time the light was red. The sweater puffed out, wrinkling into little hills. It looked like lava erupting undersea.

"Okay, stop," I said.

"But it's not done yet," objected Aaron.

"Now! Stop!" I leaned over and flicked the switch to off. The light died down.

"Why did you do that? It's only at 94 percent," said Aaron.

"It was too big to begin with," I said, putting on the sweater. It was still a little loose, but not nearly as bad as before. Maybe I would grow into it.

"Ready, Marc?" said Aaron, switching on the shrink ray.

The green light shot out, but Marc didn't seem to be shrinking. "Is it working?" I asked.

Marc shrugged.

"Give it a minute," said Aaron.

We gave it a minute. Nothing happened. Aaron fiddled with some knobs. Still nothing happened.

"I know!" I said. "It's Jaya's knot—it protects you, remember? I had to take mine off before Doc could remove my sense of direction."

"Oh, right," said Marc, tugging at the knot with his teeth.

"Not that way," I said. "You'll break your teeth. You have to tell it come off. In rhyme," I added.

*"Okay, knot, so here's the gist: get your booty off my wrist,"* Marc told it, rapping like a hip-hop star. The knot came off.

Aaron started the machine again. "Is it working now?" he asked.

"I think so," said Marc. "I feel funny." He sounded funny too.

"Look, it's definitely working," I said. Marc had reached my height and was subsiding slowly, twitching. "Are you okay?" I asked him.

"Yeah . . . it's weird. It kind of tickles inside my bones, where I can't scratch."

"Enough?" I said. Marc was now the height of a soda can.

"Let's check," said Aaron. He switched off the shrink ray and put a pneum down next to Marc. "Can you fit in there?"

Marc slid the door open and tried to wedge himself in. "Too tight," he said. His voice sounded tiny and higher than usual. He was like a doll of himself, with perfect little limbs and itty-bitty shoes. He stepped out of the pneum and stretched gracefully, like a tiny tiger. I wished I could take him home with me and keep him.

Aaron turned the ray on Marc again for a few seconds. "Better?"

Marc tried the pneum again; this time he fit. "Perfect." He climbed back out.

Then it was my turn. I talked the knot off my ankle and went over to the shrinking spot. "Do your worst," I said.

For a moment nothing seemed to happen. Then I felt the itching Marc had described. All at once the world looked as if I'd shaken free of it and was falling down, down, down through exploding space.

The world was so big that I couldn't get my bearings. What were all those looming shapes? Which way was the door? Where was Marc? Was that perilously swaying skyscraper Aaron? How would I negotiate all this with no sense of direction?

The green light snapped off and the insane sensation subsided.

"Elizabeth? Are you okay?"

Aaron's voice sounded strange. I could pick out the individual vibrations. It took me a moment to put them together into words.

"Fine, I guess . . . I'm fine."

"You sure? You look a little . . ." A huge hand came swooping toward me from overhead.

I ducked frantically. "Hey! What are you doing?"

"Sorry. You're just so tiny and delicate . . . I wanted to make sure . . . Here, do you fit in this, or should I make you smaller?"

A pneum barreled through the air and stopped beside me. Aaron's hand held it steady as I slid the door open. It looked crudely made and worn. The plastic was scored with deep scratches, and the felt was battered. Could it possibly protect me as it went banging through the pipes?

Wedging myself in, I pulled the door shut around me, then

slid it open again without trouble and eased my head and shoulders out.

"Aaron? I'm going to close this thing. Can you lay it down with the door facedown, just to make sure I can get out?"

"Sure."

His vast hand! Ugh, with a hangnail on his index finger. He tipped me over with a dizzying lurch, like a Ferris wheel before it really gets started. It wasn't easy getting the door open—I had to throw my weight back and forth to rock the pneum onto its back—but I managed it and climbed out.

"Time for the pipes?" Aaron said.

I nodded.

"Okay, get in your pneums. I'll have to take you up to the MER. There's no direct pipe to the Grimm Collection from here." He brought his face close to us. "Buckle up," he said.

We traveled to the MER in Aaron's pocket, swaying and bumping with each step. "I think I'm going to be sick," said Marc.

"Please don't," I said.

Sarah was on pipe duty in the Main Exam Room.

"Mind if I just get in there for a sec, Sarah? I need to send something downstairs," said Aaron.

"Sure," she said. "Actually, while you're here, could you watch the pipes for me while I run to the ladies'?"

"Of course," said Aaron. We heard Sarah walk away.

"Send me first, and give me five minutes to get out of the way before you send Elizabeth," said Marc.

I heard the hiss as Aaron opened the pipe and sent the two pneums of supplies down. Another hiss and a thump as he sent Marc down. Then a long pause—five minutes is forever when you're in a plastic tube in somebody's pocket, waiting to go crashing through space.

At last, Aaron's hand appeared again and pulled me out of his pocket.

The blood rushed to my head. "I'm upside down!" I yelled.

Aaron lifted me to eye level again, holding me so I was lying on my back, and whispered, "I know. You have to start out upside down or you'll land on your head. The pipes go up before they go down."

"Oh, great," I moaned.

"Sorry," said Aaron. "It's not my fault, it's geometry." He turned me upside down again and pulled the pipe door open. "Well, bye, Elizabeth. Travel safely," he said, and let go.

lasso

Fans of roller coasters and water slides would love traveling by pneumatic tubes. You shoot through the pitch dark, bumping and spinning until you have no idea which way is up—especially if you've left your sense of direction in a *kuduo*. But the worst is when the air pressure suddenly drops away, and so do you, falling with a bone-wrenching thump into a wire basket.

I'm not a fan of roller coasters.

I lay there stunned, facedown, my cheek pressed against the plastic, trying to get used to the light and the silence before I faced the job of rocking the door free. I had just about caught my breath when my pneum lurched.

It was Marc. He slid my door open. "Wasn't that awesome? Better than snowboarding!" He held out his hand and pulled me out.

"Thanks," I said, leaning against the edge of the wire basket.

There was something funny about Marc—he looked different. He frowned at me appraisingly. "You're so tall," he said.

I laughed. "Yeah, six whole inches," I said, but I knew what he meant. Aaron had made us both the right size to fit snugly in the pneums, which meant we were exactly the same height. It was weird being the same height as a basketball star. It made me feel impossibly tall.

The pipes rattled ominously overhead. "We better move before we get hit on the head with a pneum," said Marc.

We climbed out of the basket. Marc gave me a leg up. We might be the same size, but he was still way stronger. We emptied the pneums and stuffed our backpacks with the string, paper clips, and other supplies. Marc tied one end of a length of twine to the basket, tossed the other end off the shelf, and climbed down.

"Come on, Elizabeth," he called up from the floor.

"Ack. It's a long way down!" Rope climbing was never my favorite part of gym.

"Loop the rope around one leg and take your weight with your feet," said Marc. "Good—no, your feet! Not your hands, your feet!"

I scraped my palms pretty badly—it's amazing how rough a piece of ordinary string can feel when you're only six inches tall—but I reached the floor without falling. "Where now?" I said.

"Call number I ★GC 683.32 G65—this way."

Dust flew up and resettled at our feet; it was like walking through feathers and packing peanuts. Was the floor always this dusty?

Marc grabbed my elbow as I made yet another wrong turn. "Over here," he said. He stopped in front of a gray metal locker the height of the Rockefeller Center Christmas tree.

"Great," I said. "How are we going to get the door open?"

"Lasso the handle," said Marc, tying a loop in the string.

He was pretty good at throwing the lasso, but it kept slipping off the handle. "Enough," I said eventually. "It's not working."

"Got any better ideas?" he said. "It's not like I can fly."

"Hey," I said, "what about using some of the objects in here? Like the flying carpet?"

"Huh." He stuffed the lasso into his backpack. "Not the carpet—we could never get it unrolled, and anyway, it's on a high shelf—but the Hermes shoes are on a low shelf."

"The Hermes shoes?"

"You know, the winged sandals. Come on."

Another long, dizzying walk between the vast cabinets. "Here," said Marc, tugging me by the elbow. He stopped beside an open tower of shoes. The lowest shelf came to our armpits. I found myself nose to nose with a scuffed ballet slipper the size of a small rowboat, with dozens of others moored beside it. I *GC 391.413 T94 c. 1—c. 12 read the labels. The twelve dancing princesses' twenty-four dancing shoes.

Marc swung himself easily onto the shelf, shouldering slippers aside. "Come on," he said.

Maybe I could have pulled myself up when I was still doing ballet, but my arms weren't strong enough anymore. "What if I wait here?"

"Fine." Marc piled up some slippers and climbed up two shelves. I heard him moving back and forth up there.

"Found 'em!" He stuck his head over the edge a little farther along. "I'm coming down. Get under cover so I don't hit you with a shoe," he called to me.

I crouched beneath the shelving unit, flinching away from

the dust bunnies. Bunnies, ha—dust ogres was more like it. A tangle of hairs like monstrous, scaly wires. Clumps of green and yellow fibers, lots of pale, flaky stuff, and ugh, was that a fly wing?

I turned my back on the mess and looked out from under the shelf. Overhead I saw the sole of one sandal, wings beating at its heel. Its mate was suspended by its straps, flapping in a panic.

"Easy there," said Marc softly, leaning out of the steady sandal to put his hand on the panicked one. "Hey, boy—nice and easy. Steady now."

The sandal continued to thrash in the air.

"Elizabeth! Can you grab the straps?"

The frightened sandal dove and bucked. Marc threw me one of its leather straps, and I caught the end. That seemed to panic the sandal even more; it flapped away, dragging me along the floor. I hung on, pulling it down with all my weight as Marc landed his own sandal beside me.

"We'd better switch," he said. "Yours is freaking out. It's the left one—the pair must be right-handed."

"Right-handed?"

"Okay, right-footed." He stepped out of the right sandal, where he'd been sitting like a kayaker with his legs stretched out in front of him along the sole and his back against the heel, where the wings attached. He held the straps in one hand like reins.

"Stay," he told the right sandal sternly, handing me its straps and taking mine. He turned to face the shoe I'd been struggling with. "Now, you! Lefty! Are you going to behave for me?" He pulled hard on both straps, and the left sandal subsided beside him, its wings twitching. "That's better. Good boy." He stepped in and sat down, holding the straps with both hands. The sandal gave a little flutter but obeyed. He patted its side.

"Well? Get in and buckle up," Marc told me. I jumped to obey. The man was a born leader.

Unfortunately, his shoe wasn't. It wanted to follow mine, its dominant mate. That would have been fine if I'd still had my sense of direction. As I lifted off, I heard Marc yelling behind me, "Elizabeth! Stop! The other way!"

I tugged at the reins to turn my sandal around. I could tell it was doing its best to obey, but I didn't know how to guide it. Should I pull the left strap to go left and the right to go right, like a charioteer? Should I pull left to go right and right to go left, like a sailboat helmsman? Which way *was* left, anyway?

"The other way! The other way! No, the *other* other way!"

I turned and collided with him.

"This is like having two left feet," he muttered.

I lurched from side to side. Marc fluttered after me. We had rounded a corner into a lane of cabinets that looked just like every other lane of cabinets when Marc shouted, "Stop!" and reached over to catch my reins. "This is it," he said. He reached out with his other hand and turned the handle.

The sandals went wild with excitement, bucking and dragging the door open. It was all I could do not to fall to my death. Marc soothed the shoes and we flew to the fifth shelf.

"I'd better stay with the sandals and keep them calm. Can you find the key yourself?" asked Marc.

"I'll try." Stepping off my hovering shoe a zillion inches up from the hard floor was child's play after the trip in the pneum—or at least, that's what I told myself.

I lost myself quickly in the forest of locks and keys. The smell of magic came off them in waves and puffs. Some were old and rusty, some elaborately carved and jeweled. Some were tiny, no bigger than my finger; others towered over my head. Many shone like gold. Which was the Golden Key?

I checked the labels and followed the numbers in what looked like the right direction only to find I had gone past the key's call number and was wandering through an entirely different sequence of numbers.

"Find it yet?" called Marc.

"Still looking."

This was taking forever. There had to be a better way. I closed my eyes and took a deep breath. The magic smelled stronger to my left, so I went that way. I sniffed my way past an ivory box the size of a coffin and a brass padlock the size of my skull.

A wave of shellfish—oysters?—was coming off a mother-of-pearl casket, masking the smell I was following. I circled it, sniffing. Another heavy reek interfered, like a butcher's shop. I put up my hand to push through a curtain of keys and felt something warm and wet. Blood.

I hastily wiped my hand on my jeans and checked the tag on the bloody key. It was Bluebeard's—it must be the key to the chamber where his murdered wives lay hidden! I shuddered away, trying to ignore the reek of blood, and sniffed for the subtler fragrance I'd been following. Forward . . . around again . . . there!

I had reached the back wall of the cabinet. All I could see

was a blank wall, but the smell was strongest here. I shut my eyes and reached out. My hands closed on something smooth and cold. I opened my eyes and found I was holding a plain gold key the length of my forearm.

It was very heavy, but somehow I didn't mind. I couldn't take my eyes off it. It was like when you dream of walking along a street you thought you'd never find again or like waking up on the first day of spring.

I checked the label. The numbers were right.

"I found it!"

"Great. Let's get going."

"Keep talking, okay? I have to follow your voice." I made my way over to Marc where he hovered on his sandal.

"Wow." Marc couldn't take his eyes off the key either. "Wow, is that it?"

I nodded.

"Can I hold it?"

I handed it to him reluctantly. He leaned back against the heel of his sandal holding it and staring.

"We'd better get going," I said. "Here." I held out my hand for the key.

"I can carry it," said Marc. "It's pretty heavy."

"That's okay, I'll take it," I said.

He gave it back reluctantly. I put it in my backpack—it just fit in the biggest compartment—and buckled up. "Which way's the door?" I asked.

"To the left, but shouldn't we get supplies first?"

"Like what?"

"Lots of things. The cloak of invisibility. The Blue Light.

The Bottomless Purse. Even the Table-Be-Set, in case we get locked in someplace without lunch," Marc said.

"How are we supposed to carry all that? We're six inches tall, remember?"

"Strap it to the sandals. They can carry a full-grown man."

"Yeah, but . . . I don't know, Marc. I don't think it's such a good idea. You know how fairy tales work. They punish the greedy and reward the restrained."

"They give the hero the magic items he needs. Heroes are always stealing stuff. Like the giant's magic harp that plays itself or the goose that lays the golden eggs."

"Yes, but if you remember that particular story, the harp doesn't appreciate being stolen. It yells and gets Jack in trouble."

"Okay, so we won't take the harp."

"You know what I mean. We were told to take the Golden Key. Nobody said anything about lamps and purses. Remember what happened with the cudgel? Come on, let's get out of here."

"Oh, all right," said Marc.

With the usual false turns and accidental zigzagging, we flew to the door. Steadying my sandal, I hefted the Golden Key and tried it in the keyhole.

It didn't fit.

"Now what?"

"I have an idea—I think I we passed something useful near the keys," said Marc. "Wait there." He flew back the way we'd come.

He was gone for a while. I stroked my sandal's wing. While I waited, I took a minute to marvel at my position: six inches tall, riding a winged sandal through a storehouse of magical items. If anyone had told me a year ago I'd be in this position, I would have laughed and then edged away.

At last Marc came back, with a stick a little taller than him propped along his sandal.

"What's that?" I asked.

"The stick from 'The Raven.' It opens any door you hit with it." He flew up and tapped the door with it. The door exploded inward; our sandals got out of the way quickly.

Aaron was there waiting. "Finally!" he said. "Did you get the Golden Key?"

I was so relieved to see him that if I had been my normal size, I would have hugged him.

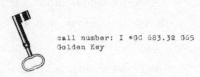

We rode the sandals down the hall to the Wells Bequest. Aaron wanted to carry us in his pocket in case someone saw us, but Marc refused. "Your walking makes me seasick," he said. "It's not that far, and there's nobody else down here."

Aaron didn't argue. Maybe he was being diplomatic, I thought, or maybe he didn't want Marc throwing up in his pocket. In any case, Marc and I followed him at shoulder height. We landed on a shelf.

"Can I have the Golden Key now?" said Aaron.

"Why?" said Marc.

"Well, obviously, we don't want it going through the shrink ray. If it's the wrong size, it won't fit in its keyhole."

"That makes sense," I said.

"No!" said Marc. "I don't trust him. He can unshrink me first, and I'll hold the key while he unshrinks you."

"Come on, don't be ridiculous," said Aaron, holding out his hand. It reminded me of an inflatable raft. "Give me the key."

"I don't know, Aaron. Why not do it Marc's way?"

Aaron gave an exasperated sigh. "Come on, Elizabeth, we don't have time for this," he said. "Give it to me or I'll take it." He reached for my sandal.

"What are you doing, Aaron?" I fluttered away.

"Oh, you think you're a big man, don't you, now that we're small!" said Marc. "Let's go, Elizabeth. We don't need him. We can rescue Anjali by ourselves." He kicked his sandal into the air. We flew for all we were worth, with Aaron underneath, jumping at us and yelling, "Wait, Elizabeth! Stop!"

But I didn't count on my sense of direction. "Left, Elizabeth! Go left! No, the *other* way—LEFT!" shouted Marc. I tried to obey, turning and turning—and found myself flying right into Aaron's arms.

Marc's sandal whirled around. Marc had a powerful grip on the straps, but the pull of its mate was stronger. He crashed beside me into Aaron's sweater-covered chest, a mass of coarse fibers. Aaron grabbed the ends of our straps and held on tight as our sandals bucked and fought, beating the air with their wings.

"Aaron! Let go! What are you doing?" I shouted.

"Quit kicking already! I'm not going to hurt you," Aaron said. He gripped our sandals from beneath by the straps so we couldn't reach his hands. My sandal flapped and I thrashed, but we couldn't get away or even touch Aaron. Is this how lobsters feel when you hold them behind the shoulders so they can't reach you with their claws?

Aaron lifted us to eye level. Such long lashes! "Okay, let's try this," he said. "Step out of these sandals and hand over the key. I don't want to risk hurting you."

"What is *wrong* with you?" said Marc. "You get a little power and you go crazy with it?"

"Aaron! What are you trying to do?" I said.

"You heard how Marc doesn't trust me? Well, *I* don't trust *him,* and I have much better reasons. I'm going to take the Golden Key and rescue Anjali. Then once I know which of the librarians I can trust, I'm going to hand Marc over to them. I'm sorry to do this, but believe me, it's for the best."

"You idiot! Can't you see we're all on the same side? Mr. Stone's the bad guy, not us!"

"I know you mean well, Elizabeth. But you're not seeing things straight. Marc has you enchanted."

"Don't do this, Aaron!"

"Just step away from the sandal."

Marc gave Aaron the look a king might give a swineherd whose smelly animals were blocking his path. "Don't bother fighting, Elizabeth," he said, unbuckling himself from his sandal and swinging the stick over his shoulder like a spear. "He's not worth it. I'll give him the key."

"You? But you don't—"

Marc glared at me. "I said, *I'll* give him *the key.* Get out of your shoe before he breaks your bones. He's enough of a jerk to do it."

Marc unzipped his backpack and took out a key the size of his calf. It was brassy yellow. He held it out to Aaron.

"Thank you, Marc. I'm glad you decided to be reasonable," Aaron said. "The address too, please."

"What address?"

"You know what address. The person who's holding Anjali."

"I'll give it to you after you unshrink me."

"Nope. You'll give it to me now, or I'll never unshrink you."

I saw the muscle jumping in Marc's tense jaw. He got a notebook and a pen out of his backpack, wrote something, and tore out the page. He handed it to Aaron, who held it by the corner like a postage stamp and squinted at it.

"Jeez, can't you write a little bigger?"

"Use a magnifying glass."

Aaron shrugged and put the paper carefully in his jeans pocket. He picked up a large archival fiber bag—the strong-but-breathable kind they use for storing flower bulbs on Stack 8—and lifted Marc around the waist.

"Aaron, what are you doing? He did what you asked! He gave you the key and the address!" I shouted.

Aaron dropped Marc into the paper bag. "Ow!" said Marc.

Aaron ignored him. "I'm sorry, Elizabeth. It's just until I rescue Anjali. It might be dangerous—you'll be much safer here, and I can't risk the chance that Marc is helping Stone. I'll come back as soon as I can, I promise." He picked me up too and slid me into the bag after Marc.

The bag opened again and something big, white, and wet fell in. An enormous slice of apple. We scrambled out of the way.

Aaron's face loomed over us, blocking the light. "That's in case you get hungry," he said. The top of the bag folded down and the light disappeared. After a moment the bag shook and I heard the *clunk-CLUNK* of a stapler. Evidently Aaron wasn't taking any chances.

A lurch, and the bag was rocking and swaying with Aaron's footsteps, swinging Marc and me back and forth against each other. Marc grabbed me tight to steady me and keep me from bashing into him.

Two months ago, if you'd told me I would be lying in the

arms of Marc Merritt, I would have thought you were describing heaven. But this? Of course, being six inches tall and stapled into a paper bag rarely features in visions of heaven.

Marc moaned. "I feel sick."

"Please, please, please," I told him. "Please don't vomit."

He just moaned some more.

"Marc," I whispered, "what was that key?"

"Uh?"

"The key you gave Aaron. I have the real one. What was that one?"

"Oh . . ." He swallowed hard and took a gulp of air. "Something called the Key to . . ." Another lurch. "The Key to All Mythologies. It was in the cabinet with the other keys. I thought we could use it . . ." Another lurch. ". . . to figure stuff out."

"Marc! You agreed not to take anything else!" I hissed. Not that I was such a big Aaron Rosendorn fan at the moment, but I was getting his point about Marc.

Marc moaned again.

At last we came to a standstill. Footsteps receded.

Marc sat up. "Unh," he groaned, but he sounded better.

"You okay?"

"Almost."

"Can you tear the bag open?"

We both tried. The paper was too tough for our shrunken fingers to tear it.

"Do you still have that magic stick?" I asked. "See if you can get us out of here."

Rustling sounds as he hit the bag with the stick. "I think it only works on doors," he said. "Maybe the opening at the top counts as an entrance. Can you help me rock the bag over so we can reach it?"

"Okay," I said. "On the count of three. One, two, three!" We flung ourselves against the side of the bag, which toppled over. I sat up and rubbed my elbow. Marc crawled up to the top, where Aaron had stapled it shut, and hit it with his stick.

The bag burst open with a bang.

Stepping out, we found ourselves on the bottom shelf of a returns cart. It was standing in a vast, empty corridor lit by fluorescent tubes far, far above.

"Let's get out of here before that jerk comes back," said Marc, swinging himself down from the cart and striding ahead of me down the hall.

With our short legs, it took us forever to reach the lobby. We crept along the edge of the room toward the heavy front doors, freezing whenever anyone moved and hoping the page at the desk—Josh—wouldn't notice two soda-can-size colleagues. We had almost made it to the doors when Marc grabbed my arm and put his finger to his lips.

Bad luck. There was Aaron in his coat, presumably heading out to rescue Anjali. He hadn't seen us yet, but when he got closer, he could hardly miss us. The door opened from the outside and cold gusted in. Marc and I looked at each other and frowned, calculating whether it would be safer to run for it or stay still and hope Aaron didn't see us. Marc raised his eyebrows. I nodded. We ran.

It was the wrong choice. "Hey!" Aaron came clomping up

behind us. We heard a scuffle as he tangled with whoever was coming in, but that didn't hold him up for long. "Sorry, sorry," he told them, pushing through.

We had forgotten the stairs! How would we get down? Marc let himself down the first step, leaning on his magic door stick, and beckoned me urgently with his arm. I threw myself over the edge, twisting my ankle as I landed. Marc caught me. We flattened ourselves against the step, barely breathing, and hoped Aaron would step over and past us.

No such luck. The familiar hand, with the familiar hangnail, swooped down and snatched me up.

Anger flooded over me. I grabbed the hangnail with both hands and pulled. It ripped back. Aaron's finger started bleeding.

"Ow!" he yelled, letting go. I plunged through thin, cold air. "Oh no! Elizabeth! Are you okay?" He sounded genuinely freaked.

Was I? I'd landed in a patch of not-yet-melted snow beside the stairs, crashing through the grimy crust to the wet coldness beneath. After a moment of shock, I scrambled out of the snow and ducked through a gap behind the stairs. It was dark and dripping back there. Shapes gathered in the corners.

"Elizabeth! Where are you? At least tell me you're okay!" called Aaron.

I felt something touch my shoulder. I jumped, choking back a scream. "It's all right. It's only me." Marc.

"Elizabeth! Elizabeth!"

"Don't answer him," whispered Marc. Aaron's eye blocked the gap between the building and the steps, the pupil hugely dilated.

"Are you in there? Please come out! Please, I promise—I'll take you both straight to the shrink ray and make you big again."

"Don't believe him," whispered Marc. I stayed as still as I could.

"Don't do this, Elizabeth! Marc! Come out of there!" His voice got louder and softer and louder again. I imagined him hunting for us, checking behind the trash cans, peering down the gutter drain.

"Are you okay?" Marc asked me.

"Not really." My teeth were chattering.

"Come on, let's get out of here." He looked over his shoulder. There was something in his voice beyond the usual arrogant impatience.

I looked to see what he was looking at. A pair of eyes shone. Something twitched.

"A rat!" I forgot about my ankle and scrambled through the gap as fast as I could. Marc followed fast.

Something else followed faster.

"Get out into the middle of the sidewalk," said Marc, pulling my arm. "They stay in the shadows."

Maybe small rats do, but this one was huge, even by normal-size-person standards. It ran parallel to us along the side of the building with a sickening, bobbing gait, its snaky tail whipping behind it, while we ran for the middle of the sidewalk. It reached the point opposite us, against the wall. Then it glanced around, put its head down, and bobbed tentatively toward us.

"Aaron!" I screamed. "Aaron! Help!"

Something whizzed past my shoulder. Marc was throwing stuff at the rat: a shrunken pen, a full-size paper clip. He hit it squarely on the nose. It snarled and compressed its body, but it didn't run away.

I threw my shrunken iPod, no bigger than a grain of rice; it bounced harmlessly off the rat's shoulder. What a waste of an iPod. The rat took three hunched, jumping steps toward us. Marc raised the door stick. I stood rooted to the sidewalk, too scared to run, too scared to scream.

A deeper shadow fell over us. The rat froze. Then it spun in its tracks and ran like an express train, vanishing into the crack behind the steps.

"Elizabeth! Marc! Are you okay?" Aaron knelt down in the street, slush soaking his enormous knees.

"Aaron," I said, almost crying.

"Come on, let's get inside." He held out his hands.

"No way," said Marc.

"I swear—I'll take you right back to the shrink ray. Come on, before someone sees us."

"Don't, Elizabeth," said Marc, but I stepped onto Aaron's hand.

"We have to trust each other," I said.

Marc shrugged, then followed me.

Aaron was true to his word. He took us straight to the shrink ray and restored us to full size, pausing only briefly at the end to argue about Marc's true height.

"Using a shrink ray to make yourself taller is worse than steroids," said Aaron.

"I don't cheat," said Marc coldly. "I think I know my own height better than you do. Another half inch. Now, please."

"Go on, Aaron," I said. "A little more. That's good—right there."

"Thank you," said Marc. "Now let's go find this Gloria Badwin and rescue Anjali. And we'd better do it quickly, because I have to be back here when Mrs. Walker drops off Andre."

inlaid bottomless box

My cell phone rang when I was in the bathroom washing off the worst of the grime. Good thing I hadn't thrown it at the rat. It was Jaya calling to find out where Mr. Stone had said Anjali was. "Meet you there," she said, and hung up.

Gloria Badwin, Esq., lived in a wood-frame house with gingerbread trim on a crooked back street in Greenwich Village, surrounded by brownstones. I would never have found it on my own.

"See if the key works," said Jaya impatiently. "Go on!"

Aaron got out the key Marc had given him.

"That's not it," I said, holding up the real one. "This is."

Aaron wasn't too pleased. "You mean you lied to me?"

"While you were shutting us up in a paper bag, right before you fed us to a rat? Yeah, we lied."

He made a face. "I should have known. This thing is barely shimmering. What's it the key to?"

"Something about mythology," said Marc, shrugging. "Use the Golden Key, Elizabeth."

I tried. It didn't work. "I guess that's not what it's supposed to open. It must be for some other lock."

"Are you sure that's the real Golden Key?" said Aaron. "Let me see."

"You're really going to give it to him? After what he did?" asked Marc.

"I'm sorry about the rat. I really am!" said Aaron. "I rescued you, didn't I?"

"Will you give it back?" I asked.

"Yes. I promise," said Aaron.

I gave him the key. "Oh!" he said, staring at it. He tried it in the lock himself, but it didn't work.

"Convinced?" I held out my hand.

"Yes . . . yes, it definitely has that shimmer. It's so strong! I've never seen anything like it." He continued to stare at it, turning it in his hand.

"Aaron! Give it back now. You promised."

"Oh. Sorry, I was just . . . sorry." He handed it to me.

"You know what?" I said slowly, "you hold on to it." I gave it back to him.

Marc shrugged. "Fine, Aaron can carry it, but I'll be watching," he said. "We don't need it to get in, anyway—I have the magic stick that opens doors."

"No, don't use the stick," I said. "That thing's pretty loud and dramatic. What if she's home?"

"One way to find out," said Jaya, running up the steps. "Ring the bell."

"Stop," Aaron shouted, but it was too late. A sweet double chime was echoing dimly behind the door.

"Who is it?" called a voice behind the door.

We all looked at each other. Once again, we hadn't prepared a story.

"We're students at Vanderbilt and we're doing a project on Manhattan's historic wood-frame houses," said Aaron.

It might have sounded convincing if Jaya hadn't been speaking at the same time: "I'm Jaya Rao, and I'm looking for my sister."

The door opened. "A project on wood-frame houses *and* looking for your sister? You'd better come in."

I recognized Gloria Badwin, Esq., from the Main Exam Room at the repository. She was wearing a pantsuit and pearls, with narrow black pumps. Her lipstick picked up the highlights in her auburn hair, which matched the deep-red leather brief-case standing on the hall table. She ushered us into a living room with chrysanthemums on the coffee table. "Please sit down, and tell me how I can help you," she said.

Marc, Aaron, and I sat down on the sofa. Jaya remained standing, staring with her mouth open. I turned to see what she was staring at: a display cabinet lined with row after row of dolls and figurines.

My first reaction struck me hard—it looked so much like my mother's doll collection! Tears flooded into my eyes. My mother, my mother—I missed her so much! If she were here now, every-thing would be better.

I shook my head. My mother was gone and all I had now were my new friends. And those weren't really dolls; they were enchanted people. One of them could be Anjali!

"Ah, you're drawn to my collection," said Gloria Badwin to Jaya. "Little girls usually are. Aren't my princesses special?"

Jaya was too riveted even to object to being called a little girl.

How could we get into the cabinet so we could find Anjali? I remembered how collectors love to talk about their collections—at least, my mother did. Maybe I could get Ms. Badwin talking and flatter her into opening the cabinet.

"What an impressive group! Is that top one on the left Chinese?" I asked.

"The *benjarong* porcelain? Thai, from the Ban Phlu Luong dynasty. She's a beaut; let me show you." Sure enough, Ms. Badwin unlocked the cabinet and brought out a colorful figurine. "She's in excellent condition, considering that the men who transformed her had to use elephants to hold her down. It's rare to find them with all ten fingers."

"What about the beautiful blue one behind her?"

"My, you really have an eye! Egyptian faience, from the Middle Kingdom."

"And the lacy china one on the next shelf?"

"A Bourbon. Every collection needs one. They're not all that rare, actually—a lot of them came on the market during the French Revolution. Though their heads do tend to come off."

Aaron figured out what I was doing and joined in, with his usual tact. "What about that big doll with the loud colors that looks like a lumpy egg?" he said.

Ms. Badwin chuckled. "Oh, the Russian family—that's a bit of an embarrassment. I keep it to remind me that we all make mistakes." She took out a wooden doll shaped like a squat bowling pin and twisted its middle. The doll came apart. Inside was another doll, which also twisted apart. "See?" said Ms. Badwin, twisting apart the nested dolls until she had a row of five. "A dealer in Leningrad swore the little one here was Anastasia, the youngest daughter of the last tsar. That was long before they identified Anastasia's bones. Well, of course I didn't *really* believe him, but I *wanted* to believe, so I took a chance. I paid three thousand dollars for the set of five. Dollars! Hard currency! Of course, the real Anastasia would have been worth a thousand times that. How they laughed at me when I got to West Berlin. A fake, but a very clever one—the eyes are just the right royal blue. I suspect there might be a drop of genuine Romanov blood in her. You fooled me, little lady!" She held the smallest doll up and waggled her finger at it, then put the dolls back together, nesting them.

Jaya was having trouble sitting still through all this. I grabbed her wrist and squeezed it to keep her quiet.

"I must say," Ms. Badwin continued, "it's very nice of you young people to listen to me go on like this. We collectors can get a little obsessive, I know. Not everyone would be so patient. But I imagine you take a family interest—most of you royals are related somewhere along the family tree." She turned to Jaya. "Was the raja of Chomalur your great-grandfather, dear, or your great-great-grandfather? The dealer told me when I bought your sister, but I can't remember."

"You bought Anjali from Mr. Stone?" Jaya was almost choking with fury.

"Yes, he's a very reliable dealer—she came with all her papers. I'm meticulous about provenance. Well, you have to be, especially these days. I have a friend who's always snagging what she calls bargains on eBay, but all her Tang dynasty specimens turned out to be looted and had to be returned. And between you and me, that Maltese she brags about so much isn't royal at all—it's just a duchess. But you didn't come here to hear all this. Where are my manners? Can I offer you anything? Some gingerbread, maybe?"

"Yes, actually, that would be great, thank you," said Aaron.

I kicked him. I tried to be subtle about it so Ms. Badwin wouldn't see. He kicked me back, much less subtly. I managed not to say "ow."

"Excellent! Back in a jiff," said Ms. Badwin. She left the room.

"What are you doing, Aaron?" I hissed. "You know it's not safe to eat anything here!"

"Getting her out of the room, you dimwit. Quick, let's find Anjali!"

Marc rushed over to the cabinet. Jaya was already there, pushing princesses aside. "There she is! Marc, can you reach?" She pointed to a painted clay puppet in the back of an upper shelf, the kind with strings to control the arms and legs. It was wearing a cloth sari, and it had Anjali's eyes.

"No, no. Don't touch." Ms. Badwin had come back. She was holding—I know this sounds lame—a magician's wand. It looked like it came out of a magic kit, the kind an uncle might give his six-year-old nephew. She reached for Marc with the wand.

"Watch out!" yelled Aaron, throwing himself in front of Marc. The wand hit Aaron full in the face, leaving a red welt across his cheek.

"Very noble. Now get out of the way, please," said Ms. Badwin.

Aaron grabbed for Ms. Badwin's arm, the one with the wand.

She whipped it away and jabbed the wand between his legs. He crumpled, moaning.

Ms. Badwin reached across him and tapped Marc on the shoulder with the wand. Nothing happened.

Marc reached into the cabinet and grabbed the puppet with Anjali's eyes. "I got Anjali! Run!" he yelled. I grabbed Aaron by the arm and hauled him to his feet.

"Run if you like. You won't get very far. The door's locked," said Ms. Badwin, twisting one end of the wand. "How do I put this thing in reverse? It's a royalty tester, but it should also work to—ah, got it."

She reached out and tapped Marc on the shoulder again. He dropped Anjali and collapsed, shrinking like a lump of metal and falling to the floor with a heavy clunk. He appeared to have become a small brass statuette.

Jaya dove for her sister.

"Marc!" I yelled. "What did you do to him?" Aaron and I threw ourselves at Ms. Badwin, but she held us off with her wand. Neither of us wanted to become dolls.

"Don't worry, it's much better this way," said Ms. Badwin, picking Marc up and putting him in the cabinet. "He'll last far longer, maybe millennia. I don't normally collect princes, but you have to admit, this one's hard to resist. With any luck I'll be able to trade him for a female version. I don't have any west African princesses, which is a real hole in my collection. And it will be nice to have both Raos." She spun around and struck Jaya with the wand.

Jaya convulsed and wavered, but she didn't transform. My knot! She must still be wearing it.

Ms. Badwin shook the wand. "Shoddy thing. I knew I shouldn't have cheaped out and bought the imported model," she said, twisting the end again.

"Jaya, grab that wand!" If she could get it before her knot of protection gave out, maybe the three of us could overpower Ms. Badwin.

"No violence please, children," said Ms. Badwin, easily shaking Jaya off and continuing to fiddle with the wand. "My liability insurance doesn't cover . . . Wait, I thought I had already turned this up . . . Oh, here . . ."

"Quick, give me my backpack," said Jaya urgently, handing me the puppet. She fished frantically in it, throwing things on the floor.

Ms. Badwin rapped her again. This time Jaya's outline shook like Jell-O and she almost dropped her backpack.

"I hope you two won't be disappointed, but I'm not planning to add you to my collection," Ms. Badwin said to me and Aaron. "Some people collect scullery maids and swineherds, but I stick to royals. I have to be selective. Not that you aren't very fine examples of the common horde . . . Ah, I think this will do it." She reached out for Jaya again with the wand.

Jaya jumped back. She had something in her hand, which she snapped open—a fan. She waved it energetically at Ms. Badwin and yelled, "Get lost!"

A ferocious wind sprang up.

Papers blew off the desk. The chrysanthemums blew off the coffee table. A window burst and the curtains blew out of it. Ms. Badwin's hair blew straight out behind her, exposing black roots.

The wand blew out of her hand. Then the wind blew her away.

Jaya stopped fanning. The curtains fell limp and the papers fluttered to the floor like autumn leaves. We rushed to the window and looked out. There was no sign of Ms. Badwin.

"What was that?" said Aaron.

"A fan my auntie Shanti gave me." She glanced at me. "Okay, she gave it to Anjali, but I borrowed it. We're supposed to share it."

"Is that the one I saw in Anjali's room? It didn't do that when you fanned me with it," I said.

"You have to give a command. And fan really hard."

"Where's Ms. Badwin?" said Aaron.

Jaya shrugged. "Lost, I hope."

"Let's get out of here before she finds herself, then," said Aaron.

"Good idea," I said. I took Marc out of the display cabinet and stowed him in my bag. He had been turned into a three-inch-tall brass figure of a man beating a gong with a stick. Its features were very stylized, but it was still obviously Marc.

Anjali was bigger and much lighter.

"Here, I'll take her," Jaya said. "She's my sister."

I handed Jaya the puppet and picked up Marc's backpack. "Let's go."

"What about the other princesses? We can't just leave them here. What if Ms. Badwin comes back?" said Jaya.

"How can we possibly carry them all?" Aaron asked.

Jaya took another familiar object out of her bag: the inlaid box from Anjali's shelf. "We can use this," she said. "It's bottomless, so they should fit." She opened it and began packing in princesses.

"We don't have time for that," said Aaron. "We don't know when Ms. Badwin could come back."

"It'll go faster if you help."

"Jaya! Come *on*."

"We can't leave them here," said Jaya, tucking a delicate Japanese ivory into the box. "They're people, just like you."

"She's right," I said. "Plus, she's stubborn."

"And I'm royal, so you have to obey me."

"Yeah, a royal pain," said Aaron, but he went over to the cabinet and started reaching down princesses for us.

Jaya finished packing and snapped the box shut. "Get that wand," she told Aaron. "Maybe we can use it to turn them back into people."

"Good idea." Aaron reached for the wand.

"Don't touch it!" I yelled, but it was too late. He already had it in his hand.

"Why not?" he said.

"I thought you might turn into a doll. I guess it only works on royalty," I said. "Maybe you really are a swineherd, like she said."

"Yeah, right." He draped a throw from the couch over the broken glass on the windowsill and climbed out the broken window. Jaya followed.

I sat on the sill and swung my legs over. "Why can't we go out the door?" I asked.

"You heard her—it's locked."

"So? We have the door stick."

"Just jump already. It's faster," said Jaya.

"Don't worry, I'll catch you," said Aaron.

He tried, but we both fell over. For the second time that day, I landed with a crash in a pile of dirty, half-melted snow. At least this time I was wearing a coat.

"Was that entirely necessary?" I asked.

"Sorry! You know how I sweep girls off their feet." He grinned at me and held out a hand.

I struggled to my feet, sloughing off slush.

"We did it! It's over! We rescued Anjali!" said Jaya, making the puppet clap her hands.

"Not quite over," I said. "Anjali's still a marionette, and Marc's a brass figurine, and we haven't used the Golden Key yet. And I'm freezing, and my leg hurts. And what about Marc's little brother? Somebody has to take care of him now that Marc can't."

"Let's go back to my place and figure out what to do," said Aaron. "We can ask the mirror."

"*That* horror?" I said, but I followed him to the subway. Jaya trailed after, making Anjali jump over all the fire hydrants along the way.

feather

Aaron's mom came home soon after we arrived. "Hello, Elizabeth," she said, poking her head in Aaron's door. "And you must be Anjali?" She looked puzzled. Clearly she wasn't expecting the object of her son's obsession to be a ten-year-old toting a puppet.

"How do you do, Mrs. Rosendorn? I'm actually Jaya. Anjali is my sister," explained Jaya.

"It's nice to meet you, Jayda. You can call me Rebecca."

"It's Jaya, Mom," said Aaron. "Close the door when you go, okay?"

She hesitated, but I could see her deciding that nothing too adult would happen with a ten-year-old in the room. "Okay, sweetie. Don't forget you promised to do your laundry before Monday." She shut the door.

Jaya made Anjali wave at the closed door. She was pretty impressive at manipulating the strings.

"Let's see if we can turn Anjali back into a person," Aaron said, taking Ms. Badwin's wand out of his backpack and tentatively poking Anjali.

Jaya put Anjali's hands on Anjali's hips. "No good, I'm still a puppet," she said in a parody of Anjali's sweet, high voice.

"Try the other end," I said.

Aaron turned the wand around and poked Anjali again. Nothing happened.

Jaya shook Anjali's head no and put the puppet down. "Let me try," she said, grabbing the wand.

"No, Jaya! Drop it!"

Her outline wavered, but the knot of protection held. "Why did the wand work on Marc, anyway?" she asked. "I made him a knot of protection."

"He had to take it off," I said. "We needed to use the shrink ray on him to get the Golden Key."

"Why didn't you tell me? I could have made a new one."

"You're right. It was a mistake."

Jaya liked being told she was right. "We all make mistakes sometimes," she said generously.

Aaron was fiddling with the wand. "Didn't Gloria Badwin say something about putting this thing in reverse?" He twisted the end cap one way, then the other, until we heard a click. He tapped Anjali again. The end of the wand glowed bright green.

"I wonder what that means?" he said. "Jaya, can you get me one of the other princesses?"

Jaya opened the box and fished out a lacy china shepherdess and an Incan figurine in a feather headdress. The wand glowed the same bright green as Anjali when Aaron touched the Incan girl. It glowed greenish amber when he touched the china doll.

"Does green mean royal? See if you can find those Russian dolls," said Aaron.

Jaya felt around in the box. "Here."

Only the innermost doll, the supposed Anastasia, gave a hint of green. The four outer nesting dolls tested red—completely nonroyal, presumably.

"Interesting," said Aaron, tapping me. The wand read red. "I guess you really are a scullery maid, not a princess."

"I'm a student and a page, thank you very much. I never claimed to be royal," I said. "Give me that—I bet you make it turn red too."

He did. The two of us fiddled with it until we were satisfied we'd seen both settings. It could identify royalty or, in reverse, transform princes and princesses into figurines. But no matter what we did, we couldn't make it transform figurines into princesses.

"'Shoddy thing! I knew I shouldn't have cheaped out and bought the imported model,'" Jaya made Anjali say in Ms. Badwin's voice.

"You should be an actress, Jaya—you're really good at that," I said.

Aaron rolled his eyes, but I could see he was amused. "Now what? Time to ask the mirror for help?" He pointed to the wall, where his blanket was still hanging.

I shuddered. "Ugh, do we have to?"

"What is this mirror, and what's so terrible about it?" asked Jaya.

"It's Snow White's stepmother's. It's evil. It manipulates people, and it gloats," I said.

"How bad can that be? I'm used to dealing with people like that," said Jaya. She pulled the blanket off the mirror.

It reflected a fairly normal version of me and Aaron—maybe

a little meaner-looking than usual—but it showed Anjali as a human girl, puppet size.

"Hey, look at Anjali!" said Jaya. "How can it do that? It's a mirror! Doesn't it have to reflect things the way they are?"

"It can't just make things up," I said, "but it reflects the truth as it sees it, so it must know Anjali is really a person. But it has a horrible vision of the world. Like I said, it gloats. And you have to talk to it in rhyme, and it never gives you a straight answer." I fished out the little brass figurine that was Marc and put it down next to me. The mirror reflected it as a tiny human Marc.

I told the mirror:

*"Our friends Marc and Anjali—*
*Tell us how to set them free*
*And how to use the Golden Key."*

Anjali's reflection in the mirror answered:

*"You found the key, now find the lock.*
*You found the royals, now find Doc."*

Marc's reflection continued:

*"You lost the vessel. Get it back.*
*Get your feet on the right track.*
*First go nowhere, then go home.*
*Return the mirror and the comb.*
*Elizabeth will lead you there—*
*And say good-bye to pretty hair."*

"What does that mean?" I cried. "Where do we look for Dr. Rust? Where do we look for the lock? How can I lead anyone anywhere without my sense of direction? What are you talking about, you maddening mirror?"

It didn't answer. Of course not: I hadn't rhymed.

"And why should you care about my hair?" I added.

*"Your hair, though fair, is not that rare.*

*Without the comb it can't compare,"* explained Aaron's reflection in the mirror.

"I don't know why it's talking about your hair, but the lost vessel has to be the *kuduo,"* said the real Aaron. "We need to get it back from Mr. Stone. It has your sense of direction. Not to mention my firstborn and everything else. Maybe something in there can turn Anjali back into a girl."

"Even if we do get it back, I still can't use my sense of direction. Something went wrong with the . . . with the object I borrowed from the Grimm Collection, the one my sense of direction was a deposit for. I think maybe Mr. Stone stole the . . . the real object."

"You mean the mermaid comb? The one that makes you pretty?" said Jaya.

"Yeah," I said, blushing. I longed to kick her.

"You traded your sense of direction for something to make you pretty? Is that what the mirror is raving about? That was so not necessary," said Aaron.

"Thanks, Aaron, that makes me feel a lot better," I said.

The reflections in the mirror were laughing at us. My reflection was batting her eyelashes and fluffing her hair; Aaron's was swooning at her. I wanted to kick them too.

"So if Mr. Stone has the real mermaid comb," said Jaya, "when we get it back, you'll get your sense of direction back too."

"Maybe. We definitely need the *kuduo,* but I don't see how we're going to get it. Nobody can take it except its rightful owner, remember? Dr. Rust said it's on loan from Marc's family.

That means only Marc can steal it, and he's not in any shape to steal anything right now. He's a brass weight," I said.

"That's not true—Marc's not the only member of his family! What about his brother?" said Jaya.

"Who, Andre? No way—it's too dangerous! He's only three."

"So what?" said Jaya. "Why can't a three-year-old be a hero? Andre has a right to help rescue his brother."

"I think she's right," said Aaron. "It's like that Akan proverb the librarians like to quote: 'We send the wise child on the errand, not the one with the long feet.' Besides, we need him. We just have to be really careful and make sure he doesn't get stolen."

"I'm not sure about that," I said, "but he does need *us*. Marc said his friend's mother was dropping him off at the repository— right around now. We can't just leave him there. We'd better go get him."

Aaron and Jaya waited outside when we got to the repository while I went in for Andre.

He was sitting at the front desk with Sarah, playing with the rubber date stamps. He had ink on his hands. "Hi, Libbet!" he said.

"Oh, Elizabeth," said Sarah, looking up. "Are you going upstairs? Can you tell Marc his brother's here?"

"Marc left a little early, actually," I said. "I'm here to pick up Andre for him. He says thanks for looking after Andre."

"Oh, okay."

"Come on, Andre," I said, "let's go find your brother." I buttoned him into his coat.

Jaya and Aaron were waiting on the steps. "Good, let's go get the *kuduo,*" said Aaron.

"Wait," I said. "We need to explain to Andre and see if he agrees." I squatted down and put my hands on the little boy's shoulders. "Andre," I said, "a bad person turned your brother into a toy. Now we're trying to turn him back into a boy. We need to get something from the bad person's friend. Do you want to come with us and help?"

"My butter's in trouble?" asked Andre.

"Yes. Can you help us help him?"

Andre nodded. "Yes. I wanna help."

"Great," said Jaya. "But first you all need knots of protection." She took some yarn out of her bag and started weaving it around Andre's wrist. At least this time it was yellow.

I found the door stick in Marc's backpack and used it to get into Mr. Stone's loft. The sun had set; it was dark inside. The only light came from a streetlight that cast shadows through the long row of windows. Dim shapes loomed, and the place reeked of magic. Andre held my hand tight.

Jaya found the light switch and flipped it on.

"My butter's boots," remarked Andre, pointing.

"Hey, he's right!" said Aaron.

I picked them up and sniffed. Carrots—no, sheep—no, blueberries you pick for yourself on a mountaintop after hiking all afternoon. "They smell magic. I wonder if they're the real ones or just temporary copies?" I kicked off my shoes and slipped my feet into the boots.

"What are you doing?" said Aaron. "We have to find the *kuduo* and get out of here."

I finished tying the boot laces and took the tiniest of itsy-bitsy baby steps. "Yow!" I'd shot across the room and smashed my shoulder against a window, shattering the glass. I was lucky I didn't fall out.

Aaron ran over, kicking through broken glass. "Are you okay, Elizabeth?"

"Yeah, I'm fine. I guess it wasn't such a great idea trying to walk around in these things, especially without my sense of direction," I said, starting to unlace them. It was cold by the broken window, with the winter air blowing in.

"Is that the *kuduo*?" asked Jaya, pointing to an ornate marble casket.

"No, the *kuduo*'s brass," I said, pulling off a boot. "It's round and it has a puff adder and a hornbill on the lid."

"A what and a what?"

"A snake and a bird."

"Hey, Elizabeth," said Aaron, "come over here quick." He was looking into a crystal ball on a tall iron tripod.

I hopped over on my stocking foot to take a closer look, careful to avoid the broken glass. Inside the ball was a small figure, groping around as if blind. It looked like Dr. Rust. Stars of light drifted across the surface of the ball. "Oh my gosh! Dr. Rust is in there!"

"You mean the librarian?" said Jaya, coming over. "Trapped in a crystal ball?"

"It looks that way," I said.

The three of us peered at the ball. Andre came over to see what we were looking at, and I picked him up.

"Do you think if we smash it, we can free Doc?" I asked.

"Let's try," said Jaya.

Aaron grabbed her arms. "No!" he said. "You don't know what'll happen. Maybe if you smash the ball, you'll smash Doc."

"Pretty ball," said Andre. He reached up and touched one of the drifting stars.

A blinding light flashed from the surface of the ball. Jaya yelled, and I pulled back, with Andre in my arms. Across the room, a huge, dark shape loomed in the broken window. I saw wings silhouetted against the orange sky and choked back a scream.

A vast bird with a crush-and-tear beak and talons like kitchen knives leapt from the windowsill and flew straight for Andre.

The bird! The bird from Anjali's window—the bird from the park!

I hugged Andre close, huddling my body around him and waiting for the talons to slice through me. What could I do to save him? What could I do to save myself?

Then I remembered the feather Mr. Mauskopf had given me when I told him about the bird. "When your need is great, give it to the wind," he had said. I fumbled in my pocket, felt the soft feather, and pulled it out. The wind of the bird's wings swept it away.

Well, that was useless. I felt the talons grasp my coat.

Then another dark shape loomed in the window and launched itself at the bird, grabbing it by the throat. The new shape wasn't a bird, but an enormous dog—an enormous dog with wings. I stared at it, recognition dawning. It was Griffin—Mr. Mauskopf's dog, the Beast, as the librarians all called him. Griffin had wings!

"It's Griffin," I yelled. "My teacher's dog!"

Mr. Stone's loft was large by New York standards but nowhere near large enough for a fight between a lion-sized winged dog and a condor-sized bird. They smashed through the air, knocking over lamps and toppling statues. Drops of blood spattered the walls. Griffin held on to the bird's throat while the bird slashed and clawed at whatever it could reach.

The fight didn't last long. The bird caught the tip of Griffin's tail in its beak, but Griffin gave a twist and shook it by the throat. It gurgled and stopped struggling. Griffin dropped it and it fell like a baseball mitt and lay flopping on the floor, with blood streaking its neck and one wing lying at an impossible angle.

"Way to go, Griff!" I yelled.

Griffin gave a short, pleased bark. He hooked his tail around something and flung it across the floor toward me.

"The *kuduo*! You found it!" I knelt so Andre could reach it without leaving my arms. "Get that box for me, sweetie?" I said.

He clutched the *kuduo* in his little arms. "Okay, Libbet, I got the box," he said.

The bird squawked. I looked up. Mr. Stone was standing in the doorway.

"Miss Rew, Miss Rao. I knew you'd be back. But what have you done to my bird? This is really too bad." He strode over to the bird. It lifted its head and snapped at him. "You shouldn't have done that," he said.

He lifted his hand and threw a blast of light at Jaya.

It bounced off, but her outline wavered. "Stop that! I hate that!" she said, shaking herself.

He lifted his hand again.

"Run, Elizabeth! Get the *kuduo* away! I'll hold him off," shouted Aaron, picking up a nearby object and throwing it uselessly. He was brave, I thought, but he had terrible aim.

"But I'm only wearing one boot!"

"Just go!"

"My seven leaguers! You took my seven leaguers? You irritating children! Where's the other one?" said Mr. Stone, looking around. "Oh, there." He strode to the window.

I ran to stop him, but I must have used the wrong foot, because I found myself hurtling through the air, cold darkness whipping past.

I ran with Andre in my arms.

For a second I was confused; then a rush of exhilaration swept over me. The speed, the air! Was this how Marc felt when he leapt for the ball and spun above the basket?

I landed on my socked foot and glanced around. Tall brick buildings. The Bronx, perhaps? Queens?

Before I could get my bearings, Mr. Stone appeared behind me. He was wearing the other boot. "Stop, Elizabeth, it's pointless to run," he said.

Pointless or not, I ran. The air, the speed, the motion—forward! forward!—the world melting to background, ice to my one-footed gliding as I threw myself into the thrill of speed. My mismatched footwear gave me a syncopated rhythm: a step and a leap, a step and a leap. I had no idea where I was going. I followed my feet. At every other step the world reassembled: a town square, a highway, a front yard, a frozen lake, a forest, a parking lot. Mr. Stone was always there, a step behind me.

"You won't get away," he called. "I have the other boot."

I didn't care. I was in love with motion. The pneum ride had made me sick with its headlong helplessness, but this was different—I was in control.

"Faster, Libbet!" yelled Andre happily, banging on the *kuduo* lid with his fists. A step and a leap. A step and a leap. A mountainside, a snowy beach, a cabin, a frozen stream lit only by the moon.

"Stop!" shouted Mr. Stone. "Where are you going?"

"Nowhere," I called back, running.

A pale, moonlit wasteland all around us. I paused to catch my breath. Mr. Stone was panting hard, Andre laughing. In the moonlight the ground sparkled like stars or shattered glass. No houses, no trees, no roads—just the glittering ground and the moon.

"Elizabeth," said a gravelly voice. I spun on my bootless foot, feeling tiny pebbles through my sock, and saw a small woman dressed in layers of cloth. A familiar woman—the one I'd seen dozing in the Main Exam Room, the one I'd given my sneakers to long ago, it seemed, on the day Mr. Mauskopf assigned me the paper on the Brothers Grimm.

"Where am I? Where is this?" I said.

"Nowhere. Nowhere special," she said. "Have you come for your sneakers?"

Pale white light filled the air, like the moon shining behind a cloud, but there were no clouds. The sky blazed with zillions of stars, more and more dense wherever I looked. I recognized constellations from the freckles on Dr. Rust's face: a triangle, a cartwheel, a butterfly. They seemed to be spinning slowly—or was I the one spinning? I couldn't tell.

"Put me down," said Andre, scrambling out of my arms. He set the *kuduo* on the ground so he could draw pictures in the sparkling dust.

Mr. Stone looked bewildered and rumpled. He lifted his arm and made a gesture as if throwing something at me, but nothing left his hand.

"That won't work here, Wallace," said the homeless woman.

"Grace!" said Mr. Stone. He made another threatening-looking gesture.

"Neither will that. Give me the boot."

"And be stuck here? Not a chance!" Mr. Stone turned and ran, but the boot took him no farther than boots usually do. He tripped and landed in a heap.

"The boot, Wallace," said Grace, holding out her hand. Slowly, as if against his will, Mr. Stone unlaced the boot and handed it over.

Grace turned to me. She had looked sad and tattered back home, but here she was clearly nobody to pity. She looked strong and calm and powerful. Even her clothes hung straighter.

"Your boot too, Elizabeth," she said, holding out her hand to me. I pulled off my boot and handed it over. "Thank you. Here." She held out my old sneakers, with my old tube socks, now clean, tucked neatly under their tongues.

"Who are you?"

"I'm Grace Farr. We've met before."

"Yes, but . . . Where—what is this place?"

"I told you. Nowhere."

"But how did we get here?"

"Ah, that's simple enough. You're missing your sense of direction, aren't you? Nowhere's about the only place you *can* go. Or could, without your sneakers. With them, I think you'll find you have no trouble getting home."

"Why? Are they magic? Did you enchant them or something?"

Grace smiled. "No. You did, by giving them to me."

"Libbet?" Andre was pulling at my sleeve. "Libbet!"

"What is it, sweetie?"

"Libbet, I gotta go."

"We're going soon—oh! You mean *go*." I turned to Grace. "Is it okay—?"

"Of course."

"Go ahead, Andre," I said, turning my back to give him some privacy.

"And then you'd *both* better go. They need you at the repository."

"What about Mr. Stone?"

"Oh, I don't think you'll need to worry about him again."

"All right." I hoped it was safe to believe her. "How do we get home?"

"The same way you got here: just follow your feet. Your sneakers will take you—that's their magic. Don't forget your *kuduo*."

I turned back to Andre. "All done?"

"I made a sun," he said proudly, pointing to a wet circle in the dust.

"Wow, I can see that," I said.

When I turned around again, Grace was gone. I could see Mr. Stone in the distance, growing dimmer.

Andre picked up the *kuduo* and I picked up Andre. I put on my backpack and began to walk, choosing the direction at random.

call number: I *GoS 584.34 U55
summer flowers

# Chapter 25:
## The Garden of Seasons

I walked for what seemed like hours. A strength of purpose flooded up through me from my sneakers. Andre fell asleep in my arms, hugging the *kuduo*. He felt as light as a paper doll. The stars seemed to be falling around us, like glittery specks of dust.

After a while I found I was walking through trees with dim, bare branches. The air began to take on a tinge of pink, and the specks of dust in the air grew rosy. They rested on my shoulders and Andre's hair, like flower petals. They were big for dust, soft like petals, and lightly cupped; when I looked closer, I saw they were, in fact, petals.

The tree branches took on a greenish tinge. Little leaves sprouted. I heard the sound of running water on our left—or was it our right?—and went to meet it. Dragonflies darted. A deer flashed its tail and soared out of sight. Andre woke up and yawned. "Where are we?" he asked.

"I don't know. I don't think we're Nowhere anymore, but I don't know where we are."

Ahead of us a fountain tossed water in the air. Leaning against the fountain, looking bored, sat Aaron. Nearby, Jaya was doing a headstand.

"Elizabeth! There you are!" she shouted, flopping over and

sitting up. "What took you so long? We've been waiting here for*ever*!"

Andre scrambled down and ran over to her. "Look, it's Jaya!" he said.

"What are you doing here?" I asked. "Where are we? How did you get here?"

"We used the Golden Key, of course."

"On what?"

"The door. It's a gate, on this side."

"Hello, Elizabeth," said Aaron. "I was starting to worry you'd never show up. You have petals in your hair."

"Where are we? What is Jaya talking about?"

"We're in the Garden of Seasons."

"*This* is the Garden of Seasons?"

He nodded. "The mirror said that's where we would find you. So we used the Golden Key to open the door—you know, down in the Dungeon, near the elevator. From that side it's just like all the other doors in the repository, but from this side it looks like an iron gate in a stone wall. How did *you* get in?" Aaron continued. "You don't have the key. Is there some other way in?"

"We didn't come through any walls or gates; we came straight from Nowhere," I said. I looked around for a wall, but I didn't see any. I had a weird sense of familiarity, as if I'd spent hours and hours here, although I knew I'd never set foot in the Garden of Seasons before.

The fountain filled the air with the scent of water. Water and autumn leaves. Water and autumn leaves and lilies of the valley. And earth. And snow . . . Suddenly I recognized this place: the scenes from the Tiffany windows! I stood up straight and spun around slowly, looking. The frost-rimed rocks to the north, the blossoming trees to the east, the thick, bird-spangled greenwood to the south, the sunset-red forest to the west.

"You came straight from *where*?" said Jaya.

"Nowhere—that's where we wound up when I ran away from Mr. Stone. The homeless woman who hangs out in the Main Exam Room lives there. Grace."

Andre plopped down next to me and started playing with twigs and pebbles, making them walk around and talk to each other. "It's sparkly in Nowhere," he said, looking up. "I made a sun."

"Where's Mr. Stone?" asked Jaya. "Is he still chasing you?"

I shook my head. "I left him in Nowhere. I think he's stuck there for good."

"I made a *sun,*" insisted Andre.

"Yes, you did!" I said. "And the stars turned into flowers, and now it's summer and it's daytime too. Did you do all that?"

"Yeah," said Andre proudly.

I mussed his hair, which had a few leaves and petals in it. "You're a pretty powerful young man, then, Andre," I said. But maybe he was right—maybe he did do all that. I couldn't say for sure that he hadn't.

"So where's the flower, then?" asked Jaya.

"What flower?"

"The one the mirror said would be here when we met you. The one that's going to disenchant Dr. Rust."

"What are you talking about?" I said.

"The mirror said we'd find you here with a flower."

"What? Back up. What happened after I left?"

"The enormous dog flew off somewhere," said Jaya. "I don't know where he went. The gigantic bird was in pretty bad shape. Doc was still stuck in the crystal ball, and it made a blinding light whenever we touched it, and that made the bird screech, so I shut my eyes and put the ball in the bottomless box. Then we went back to Aaron's and asked the Snow White mirror what to do."

"What did it say?"

"It told us to meet you in the Garden of Seasons. It said we needed a flower to break the enchantment. *Meet Betty in the magic bower and break the prison with a flower.* We figured it meant here."

"*Betty?* My name's Elizabeth! Someday I'm really going to smash that wretched thing."

"Sorry. I'm just telling you what it said."

"I wonder what flower it's talking about. Could it be the one from 'Jorinda and Joringel,' in Grimm?" I said.

"Remind me," said Aaron.

"It's the one where a witch turns Jorinda into a bird, and Joringel finds a magic flower. When he touches Jorinda with it, she turns back into a girl."

"That sounds useful," said Aaron. "Maybe we could use it on Anjali and Marc. Where is it?"

"I have no idea," I said.

"It must be here somewhere," said Aaron. "The mirror never quite lies. We just have to find it."

"What does it look like, then?"

Aaron shrugged.

"Is this it?" asked Jaya helpfully. She plucked a dandelion from the lawn.

"Of course not, that's a dandelion," said Aaron.

"How do you know it's not a magic dandelion?"

"What makes you think it would be?"

"What makes you think it wouldn't? Anything could be magic here," she said.

"Okay, fine," he said. "Test it. Get the globe with Doc in it out of the bottomless box."

Jaya opened the box and stuck her arm in up to the shoulder—which looked strange, since the box was only three or four inches tall—and fished around. "Hey, this feels like Anjali." She hung her from her strings on a bush and tapped her with the dandelion. Nothing happened.

"Just find Doc," said Aaron impatiently.

Jaya went back to fishing in the box. "I'm looking—there's a ton of stuff in here. Wait, I think this is Merritt . . . No, here he is," said Jaya. She pulled out the brass figure of Marc beating a gong.

"It's my butter!" shouted Andre, dropping his leaves and pebbles. He grabbed the figurine from Jaya and kissed it again and again. "You found him!"

Jaya went back to fishing around in the box.

"Please get on with it, Jaya," said Aaron. "We need *Doc.*"

"Calm down! It's not so easy. There's a lot of stuff in here and it's all tangled up," said Jaya. "Okay, here we go. I think."

A blast of white light, like concentrated moonlight, shot upward from the box as she lifted out the globe. Dimly through the light I could see what looked like Doc, still in the globe.

I heard a screech overhead and something huge came plummeting down from the heavens and fell heavily at our feet.

Andre ducked behind Jaya. "The birdie that got hurt," he said, pointing.

He was right. It was the bird from Mr. Stone's. Its throat had stopped bleeding, but blood stained its feathers and its wing still lay at an impossible angle. It shrieked and shrieked.

"Put down the globe, Jaya! I think that's what's making the bird scream," I said.

She dropped the globe on the grass and the light went out. The bird stopped shrieking, but it went on making soft growling noises.

"Do you think touching the globe summons the bird?" Aaron asked.

"Must be," I said. "That poor bird looks terrible!"

The bird was trembling. "The birdie got a big ouchie," said Andre, still keeping Jaya safely between himself and the bird.

I dipped my bandana in the fountain and used it to wipe away some of the blood.

"What are you doing that for? It tried to kill us, remember?" said Aaron.

"Can't you see it's in pain?" I rinsed the bandana and dabbed at the wound in the bird's neck. It growled, but it didn't bite me. "Nice birdie. There, there," I said, washing its wounds.

"Nice birdie? Way, way, *way* too nice, Elizabeth," said Aaron. "Never mind the bird, let's find that flower and disenchant Doc."

"Okay, here goes," said Jaya. She flourished her dandelion like a stage magician's wand, then tapped the globe with it.

Nothing happened.

"I guess it wasn't a magic dandelion," said Aaron.

"You don't know that," said Jaya. "Maybe that's just not what its magic does."

"Whatever," said Aaron. "Let's go find more flowers." He walked off around one side of the fountain.

I filled my water bottle at the fountain and poured some in the bird's beak. I found an orange left over from lunch in my backpack and put it near the bird's head. The bird snapped it up in three bites, peel and all, spurting juice on the grass. I shuddered to think what that beak might have done to my hand.

"Hang in there, I'll be back soon," I told it.

"Bye-bye, birdie," said Andre, putting Marc down in Anjali's shadow and taking my hand.

The fountain spouted in four directions; each spout let out a torrent that turned into a stream. Ducking under the first one before it hit the ground, we went into the woods. It was fall there, like in the western Tiffany window—the perfect, peak-leaf October moment when every maple tree is aflame with orange and red. We found purple asters, and Indian paintbrushes with tall, fuzzy black stems that hurt my hands to break, and a rose. It smelled wonderful, but it didn't disenchant Doc when we got back to the fountain and tried it. Neither did any of the others.

The bird had gotten up and was perched on the edge of the fountain, its head tucked under its good wing. It seemed to be sleeping, which I took as a good sign.

Next we went around behind the fountain, ducking under two torrents this time to the winter side. The stream from the fountain froze into complicated icicles. Shivering, we found witch hazel, winter sweet, and white, waxy bells on an ever-green. None of them disenchanted Doc. The bird didn't wake up when we hit the crystal ball with a flower and made the ball flash light—it just stirred uneasily on its perch.

"Any luck?" asked Jaya, coming back from the spring sector with her arms full of daffodils and crocuses, tulips, branches of forsythia, and hot-pink azaleas.

I shook my head.

Aaron came back from his search with armloads of summer flowers, which he tossed on the grass beside the globe. He started poking it systematically.

"Roses don't work," I told him helpfully.

"Oh. You can have this one, then." He thrust the rose he'd been hitting the crystal ball with under my nose and wiggled it.

"Stop it! That tickles!" I said, shaking my head to get away.

He went on wiggling the rose. I grabbed his wrist. He twisted it away from me. "Hold still," he said, and tucked the rose in my hair.

"Thanks," I said.

"Will you guys quit it with the mushy stuff and concentrate?" said Jaya.

"What mushy stuff?"

"Just test the flowers already."

None of them worked.

"I guess we better go find more," said Aaron.

Andre had gone back to playing with the grass near the fountain. "Pretty flower," he said, waving a minty-looking weed with tiny white blossoms on a tall stalk.

It wasn't particularly pretty, in fact. I doubt I would have noticed it myself.

"What've you got there, Andre?" asked Jaya.

"My turn," he said. He ran over to the crystal ball and thumped it with the flower upside down in his fist.

The bird gave a loud squawk. The ball burst open like a popped bubble. Drops flew everywhere and sprayed the grass. Doc sprang upward like a spaghetti pot boiling over, regaining full size so fast that I could barely see it happening.

"I popped the ball!" said Andre.

"Well done, young Merritt," said Doc. "*Circaea lutetiana,* yes? Enchanter's nightshade?"

Andre nodded solemnly.

"Thank you. I was getting very uncomfortable in there."

"Wow! Way to go, Andre!" I exclaimed. "Welcome back, Doc. Are you okay?"

"Yes, I think so, thank you. You've brought the *kuduo,* I see. Good job! Ah, and there are Anjali and Marc. He makes a great-looking *mrammuo,* doesn't he?"

"What's a *mrammuo?*" I asked.

"An Akan brass weight. The Akan people measured their gold by weighing it against *mrammuos,* brass weights in the shape of men and animals, so naturally one of their princes would take that form. Interesting subject, the gong beater. A symbol of dutiful public service. I wonder if it's prophetic?"

Something was different about Doc's face, but I couldn't figure out what. "How did you get stuck in that bubble?" I asked.

"Someone trapped me."

"But who?"

"I didn't see—they came up behind me. One of the librarians, I think. I was in my office."

"So Mr. Stone was right! He told us not to trust the librarians. He told us not to trust *you*," I said.

"I bet it's Ms. Minnian," said Aaron.

"Why," I said, "because she wears her hair in a bun?"

"Because she never smiles."

"I would hate to think it was Lucy—or Martha, or any of them," said Doc. "But I'm afraid it probably is. I imagine Wallace Stone had some hold over whoever it was."

I stared at Doc's face. Doc's freckles! That was what was different—they were gone.

"We're safe here for the moment," continued Doc, freckle free. "Let's deal with Anjali and Marc first."

"Let me do it," said Andre. He ran over to the brass figurine and hit it with the enchanter's nightshade. Nothing happened.

"Good try, Andre, but it's not that kind of spell," said Doc. "Enchanted princes and princesses are a special case."

"How do we disenchant them?" I asked.

"The customary method is the Kiss of True Love."

Aaron and I looked at each other. "You better kiss Anjali," I said.

"If you kiss Marc."

"Elizabeth! Are you in love with Merritt too?" said Jaya. "Even though he's dating my sister?"

"No!" I said. "Anjali's my friend, and Marc—well, Marc's a prince. I would never dream . . ."

"Go ahead, kiss him," said Aaron. "You know you love him. All girls do."

"You first," I said.

"Both at once, when I count to three," said Jaya. "One, two . . ."

I lifted Marc, hot with embarrassment. In spite of being a little brass weight, he looked so much like himself that it felt like one of those dreams where you're doing something you would never do in real life with someone . . . well, one of those dreams.

"Three!"

I closed my eyes and kissed. The metal was cold on my lips.

I opened my eyes. The brass figurine of Marc hadn't changed.

Aaron was holding the puppet Anjali. "Did you kiss her?" I asked him.

"You weren't lying. You really don't . . . ," he said.

"Did you kiss Anjali?" I asked again.

"No, not yet."

"Cheater! What are you waiting for?"

"I was watching you. I wanted to see if—I wanted to know—"

"Go on, Aaron! Kiss my sister already! I want her back," said Jaya impatiently. "Even though she's really annoying and bossy," she added.

Aaron shrugged and lifted the puppet to his lips.

I found I was holding my breath.

He kissed Anjali.

Nothing happened. She stayed a puppet.

I let out my breath slowly. My heart, I discovered, was pounding. Aaron looked at me. I looked away.

"Not just any kiss will work," Doc said, "only the Kiss of True Love."

"Great," I said. Despite myself, I felt my heart soar. Aaron didn't truly love Anjali after all! "The Kiss of True Love—where are we going to find *that*?"

"The Marc Merritt fan club?" suggested Aaron.

"He said the Kiss of True Love, not the Kiss of Puppy Love," I said.

"What if Andre kisses Marc?" I asked. "He really does love him."

"That won't work," said Aaron. "He already did, and it didn't. We need the Kiss of True Love, not the Kiss of Brotherly Love."

"You know who loves Anjali and Merritt? They love *each other*!" said Jaya. She picked up the two figurines and smushed their faces together. "Mwah, mwah, MWAH!" she shouted.

"Oh, like *that's* going to work," I said, rolling my eyes.

"No, wait—look!" Aaron grabbed my arm.

The air around Anjali and Marc grew thicker, like a fog of diamonds. I felt the rose stir in my hair. A smell of roses filled the air, as if all the roses in the Garden of Seasons had hurried over to watch. Colors swirled in the mist. It intensified, slowly, slowly, until I could hardly stand to look, and just as slowly it dispersed.

There stood Marc and Anjali, full size, holding hands and gazing into each other's eyes. They looked perfectly human—or, at least, as human as a couple in love can look.

# Chapter 26: The willpower of a librarian

garden gate

"Butter!" Andre threw himself at Marc's legs. Marc looked down. He didn't say anything, just opened his arms wide and swept Andre up in a huge hug, grinning his head off. What I felt for Marc might not be true love, but I had to admit he was incredibly handsome, especially with that smile on his face.

Marc turned to Jaya. "Thank you," he said.

"Yes, good job, kid," said Anjali, hugging her sister. "Although I could have done with a *lot* less of the whole moving-me-around-like-a-puppet thing."

"I liked you as a puppet," said Jaya. "And you have to admit I'm a good puppet master. You would still be a puppet if I weren't."

"Welcome back, both of you," said Doc.

"Thank you," said Marc. He cleared his throat. "Hey, Aaron. I, um, I'm sorry I didn't trust you. You tried to save me from Badwin back there. I owe you." It's hard to look dignified and repentant with a crowing three-year-old on your shoulders, but he did it.

"Yeah, well," said Aaron. He sounded embarrassed. "It didn't work, did it?"

"That's not the point. She could have killed you. Thank you."

"Yes, thank you, Aaron," said Anjali. She leaned over and kissed his cheek. He turned bright red and looked at me.

I felt a sudden breeze, as if I were fainting.

"Elizabeth, watch out!" Jaya yelled.

The enormous bird had opened its eyes and leapt out of the tree straight at me. I ducked and threw my arms over my face. It landed on my shoulder—it was like having a motorcycle land on you—and reached for my head with its vast, hooked beak.

I was too scared even to scream. I shut my eyes. Why hadn't I left well enough alone? The bird was dying before I helped it. Was this my reward?

It was taking the bird an awfully long time to tear me to pieces. I peeked at it.

"Crawk," it said. With its vicious beak, it began gently combing my hair.

"You seem to have made a friend, Elizabeth," said Doc.

The bird looked at me with one yellow eye. It was the size of a cereal bowl.

"I expect she likes being scratched under the chin," said Doc.

"But its neck—her neck," I said. "She's hurt."

I was wrong. The wound was gone. My fingers found nothing but soft feathers.

"You washed her wound with fountain water, didn't you? The water here has healing powers."

"Creek," said the bird softly, taking my earlobe in its beak and twirling my earring around with its tongue. It tickled.

"You're kind of heavy, bird. And that tickles. Dr. Rust, what *is* this bird?"

"I'm not sure, probably a crossbreed. She looks like a roc, only a whole lot smaller."

"Smaller!" It was the biggest bird I'd ever seen, or even heard of.

Doc nodded. "Rocs are the size of a house—a big one. Our friend here would fit nicely in a Manhattan studio apartment. And she has those scallops on her wings and the pink cere. A cross between a roc and a parakeet, maybe."

"A parakeet? Those little birds they sell for ten dollars at the pet shop?"

Doc nodded.

"You're a pretty big parakeet," I told the bird.

"Crock," she agreed.

"That still tickles."

"Why is Polly being nice now, when she tried to kill us before?" asked Jaya. "Isn't this the monster bird that was chasing you?"

"Wallace Stone must have put her under a spell, and the fountain water must have broken it," said Doc.

"But why was she following me?" asked Anjali.

"I bet Mr. Stone sent her to try to kidnap you, to sell you to collectors," I said.

"Could be," said Dr. Rust. "Or to throw us off his trail so we wouldn't guess he was the thief. I'm ashamed to say it worked. I really believed he was on our side. That reminds me. Where's that *kuduo*?"

"Here," said Marc.

"Thanks." Doc took the lid off, said a few words I couldn't quite make out, and tipped the contents out on the grass. "Let's see if we can figure out who trapped me in that bubble. I bet Wallace Stone was using something in here to control them."

The contents piled up in a shining mound. I saw my sense of direction—bright, complex, and embarrassing—come tumbling out. "Oh!" I said, before I could stop myself.

Andre banged on his brother's shoulders. "Let me down," he said. Marc swung him to the grass, and Andre ran over to look at my sense of direction. He reached out one hand and poked it. I felt momentarily dizzy.

"Don't worry, Elizabeth," said Doc. "With Wallace out of the picture, I'm sure we'll find that comb, so you can get your sense of direction back."

The flow of *kuduo* contents slowed. Doc shook the box a little and pulled out something flat and dark, then something fluffy like cotton candy, then something sharp, which he put down carefully on the grass. Something shining oozed out next. It looked infinitely vulnerable and undefined, like a thought before you put it into words. "Oh!" said Aaron, chokingly.

"So that's your firstborn! I can't believe you traded *that* for the Snow White mirror." I still felt shocked by this.

Aaron bristled. "Not traded! It was a deposit—and not for the mirror, for the chance to save Anjali! I thought it would be safe!"

"It is," Doc reassured him. "You kept the mirror safe, right? Then there shouldn't be a problem getting it back . . . Ah, here we go, I think."

Something hard and angular clattered out of the *kuduo*. It lay on the grass, denting the dandelions. Doc picked it up and twisted it this way and that.

"What is it?" asked Anjali.

"Somebody's willpower."

"Whose?"

"I'm not sure—I expect it belongs to whoever locked me up in that bubble. We'll find out soon. I'll use it to summon them. They have to obey whoever controls their willpower." Doc wrapped a corner of the thing around a finger and pulled it tight. "Okay, they're on their way now."

"Here?" I asked.

Doc nodded.

"Are you sure that's safe?" asked Anjali.

"Oh, I doubt they wanted to hurt me. Their willpower was in Wallace Stone's hands, and now it's in mine. I won't let them hurt anyone. Who has the Golden Key? Aaron? Would you mind letting whoever it is through the gate?"

"Not at all," said Aaron.

"Meanwhile, perhaps the rest of you could put this stuff back in the *kuduo,* since I have my hands full." Doc gestured with the willpower.

"I'll do it," said Jaya eagerly. She began picking things up and stuffing them indiscriminately into the *kuduo.*

"Gently, Jaya. Some of that stuff is . . . sensitive."

Anjali and I went over to help. I found it uncomfortable work. Every one of the objects alarmed me, some so much that I hesitated to touch them. Jaya had no such scruples.

"What is this?" she asked, holding up a long, translucent, sweater-shaped thing. I had trouble focusing on it.

"Is that the elusive cloak of invisibility?" I asked.

"No, somebody's sense of privacy, I think," said Doc.

"I wonder how it works?" said Jaya, turning it inside out and poking at the folds.

"Quit it, Jaya! That's none of your business," I said.

She laughed—"It obviously doesn't belong to *you*! Your sense of privacy is working just fine!"—and tucked it into the *kuduo*.

"I'm helping too," announced Andre. He picked up corners of things and held them out.

"Thanks, Andre," I said, gathering up the rest of something large and orange and stuffing it into the *kuduo*. It didn't look like it would fit, but it did.

"Oh, there's Aaron's firstborn," said Anjali.

"Baby," said Andre, poking it with one finger.

"I'll deal with that," I said, quickly scooping it up. I held it for a minute before sliding it into the *kuduo*. It trembled a little—or was that me?

"And here's your sense of direction," said Anjali, holding it out to me. It whirled over the edges of her fingers.

"Would you mind dealing with it? It makes me light-headed just to look at it."

"Of course." She folded it neatly and fitted it into the *kuduo*.

In a little while, Aaron's head appeared on the other side of the fountain. He walked toward us, ducking under the two waterspouts. Somebody was with him. We all sat up straight.

"Martha," said Doc, holding up the willpower. "Is this yours?"

"Oh! You got it back! Thank heaven!" Ms. Callender almost threw herself at Doc, then stopped and looked around at us uncomfortably.

"Please sit down, Martha." Dr. Rust sounded stern but not angry.

She sat awkwardly on the grass. Her round face was wreathed in worry.

"Did you leave this as a deposit? I didn't find a slip," said Doc, gesturing with the willpower.

She grimaced, but she didn't say anything.

"Oh, I get it. You can't answer me. Wallace Stone must have put a curb on your tongue. Let me fix that." Doc twisted the will back the other way.

Ms. Callender sighed and relaxed. "That's much better! Thanks, Lee."

"So, can you talk now? About Wallace, I mean."

"I think so."

"What happened to the call slip, then?"

"I filled one out and filed it, but Wallace made me tear it up when he got the *kuduo* and got his hands on my will," said Ms. Callender. "I'm so sorry! I had no idea . . ."

"None of us did." Doc held up the willpower. "What was this a deposit for?"

"That's almost the worst part. It's so embarrassing." Ms. Callender hesitated. I felt so bad for her, I wanted to hide. Why should she have to confess in front of all of us?

But Doc said, "Go on," and she did.

"It was Table-Be-Set, the French one. I thought I was being so smart! I set my will to restraint and left it in the *kuduo,* where I couldn't change it. That way I could eat delicious food, but I wouldn't overdo it. It was supposed to be a diet plan."

"A diet. I guess that makes sense."

Ms. Callender nodded sadly. "It was working too, until Wallace Stone got his hands on my will. He still has that nasty sense of humor. I've been eating corn chips nonstop ever since—and I don't even like corn chips."

"What happened to the table, do you know? I assume he took it?" Doc asked.

"It should be easy to find out, if we can only catch him. He keeps meticulous records. He has a lot of powerful things. We have to stop him!"

"Don't worry—the pages caught him already. Elizabeth led him to Grace's place and stranded him there."

"You did? You angel!" She gave me a big hug.

"Anytime," I said, embarrassed.

"So can you find the objects he stole from the Grimm Collection?" asked Doc.

Ms. Callender nodded. "I saw his records—he was making me help with the paperwork. He sold a lot of the objects, but he kept track of where they went. It might take a while, but the lawyers should be able to get them back—we have a clear title."

"How did he do it?" asked Anjali. "We couldn't figure out whether he was stealing the magic out of the objects or replacing them with copies."

"He used a dereifier. At least, he did before he got ahold of my will. The latest few objects he just made me steal from the collection, but the earlier ones, before he got his hands on the *kuduo* this morning, he had his interns borrow them from the collection and then he copied them with the dereifier."

"What about Zandra, the page who got fired? Was she working for him?"

"Yes. He was mad that she failed the Grimm Collection

key test. She only had access to the stacks, not the Special Collections."

"What about Mona Chen?" asked Doc.

Ms. Callender shook her head. "He tried to get her to work for him. He threatened to get her family deported, but she refused and disappeared with them. I imagine they're hiding. He was furious about that too."

"That's a relief," said Doc. "We'll have to figure out a way to let her know it's safe to come back."

"So he just told you all this?" I asked. "Wasn't he worried you'd try to stop him?"

"He answered all my questions and boasted about everything. He had my willpower, so he thought he was safe. He always did like to gloat."

"But wait a minute," said Aaron. "How did Mr. Stone make the copies? I thought you couldn't copy magic with a dereifier."

"Not fully and permanently, but you can approximate it for a while," said Ms. Callender. "They're working on some pretty advanced dereifiers up at MIT. Wallace managed to make fairly convincing temporary copies. That's why they lost their magic after too many people checked them out."

"So if my mermaid comb is a fake, where's the real one? Will I get my sense of direction back?" I asked.

"I think it's in Hollywood now. I'm sure we'll get it back eventually, but I wouldn't hold my breath. They have deep pockets and stubborn lawyers. I'm sorry, Elizabeth."

"I'll take you wherever you need to go," offered Jaya. "I have a great sense of direction."

"Thanks, Jaya," I said sadly.

"The sooner we get started, the sooner we'll get it back," said Doc. "Your sense of direction and everything else. You still have the Golden Key, Aaron?"

Aaron held it up.

"Good. Marc, will you carry the *kuduo*?" Doc started around the fountain, under two spouting streams, and led us through the winter wood, Polly flapping loudly overhead. We came to a high wall that seemed to circle around forever. Through a low wrought-iron gate I could see the flat, fluorescent white lights of Stack 1, the Dungeon. Aaron took out the Golden Key and opened the gate.

Polly settled on the top of the gate and looked at us expectantly.

"Not you, little roc," said Dr. Rust. "I'm sorry, but you can't go home with Elizabeth. You'll have to stay here for now."

"Crrrick," said the bird, putting her head through the gate. She sounded angry.

"It's nicer in the garden. And Elizabeth will come visit you," said Dr. Rust.

"How will I get in?" I asked. "I mean out? Do I need to borrow the Golden Key? Or will my sneakers work?"

"You can use the Golden Key, when you can find it. It doesn't always let itself be found."

"Good-bye, Polly. I'll come soon," I said. "It's not everybody who gets to be friends with a former terrifying monster who lives in a magical garden!"

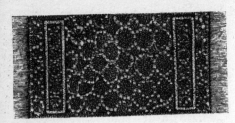

# Chapter 27:
## A carpet ride

The rest of the weekend was something of a letdown. Not that I would have expected my parents to notice my adventure; I made it home in time to help with dinner, after all. But after being shrunk down to the size of a soda can and almost eaten by a rat, defeating a crooked art dealer, helping rescue a prince and a princess from an obsessed collector, and traveling to Nowhere and back, I almost resented being expected to peel potatoes. At the end of the fairy tale, the scullery maid usually gets a promotion.

Monday at lunch, Marc waved me over to sit at his table with the basketball stars and their girlfriends. "This is my bud Elizabeth Rew," he said, draping his arm around my shoulders. "We work together after school. She saved my life when I got in trouble with the boss."

"Hey, Elizabeth," the team said, nodding at me. The girlfriends smiled politely.

Then they all went back to talking, and I felt very out of place. Still, it was the thought that counted.

After lunch, Mr. Mauskopf stopped me in the hall. "Nice work," he said. "Lee Rust told me about your adventures. It would have been even better if you'd stopped Marc from stealing the *kuduo,* of course—the arrogance of princes! And you both should have come to me at once for help. But still, you and your friends rescued Lee from a tight spot and did the collection a great service. I'm proud of you."

"Thank you, Mr. Mauskopf," I said, blushing.

My phone rang that evening. "Elizabeth? It's Jaya. What do you think I should do with all these princesses? There aren't any princes to kiss them. But they've got to be bored out of their minds, just sitting there."

"What does Anjali think?"

"She's no use. She told my mom she was going to your house and went off to hang out with Marc."

"Oh. I'll ask Doc about the princesses next time I'm in the library."

"Thanks. Do you think maybe I should play with them?"

I thought about it. If I were a doll, would I want a frenetic ten-year-old bumping me around as she acted out her fantasies? "Maybe you could play some music for them? Or put them where they can see the TV?" I suggested.

"My parents won't let me have a TV in my room. Oh, I've got to go, my mom is calling."

At the repository, I spent a long time looking for Doc's office. "Did you get the mermaid comb back yet?" I asked when I finally found it. Then I noticed something odd. "Your freckles! They're back," I blurted out.

Doc nodded. "They're what connects me to the Garden of Seasons. In the garden, they're stars in the sky. Out here, they're only freckles on my face."

"That's . . . cool," I said. "How do you get star freckles?"

"They came when I took the job. Now, your sense of direction. I'm sorry to say we don't have the comb back yet. I expect it will take at least a year, maybe longer. In the meantime, I thought you could use this. The board of governors approved the loan for as long as you need it." Doc handed me a ring made of some gray metal—it looked like iron or steel—with a silvery, mirrory stone in it.

I put on the ring. "Thanks. What does it do?"

"If you think about what you desire, it shows where to go to find it. Try it."

I thought about lunch. I felt the ring gently pulling me toward the door. I thought about my friend Nicole. The ring pulled me gently toward the door. I thought about the skating rink in Central Park. The ring gently pulled me toward the door.

"Whatever I think about, it pulls me toward the door," I said.

"Are you thinking about things in this room?"

"No."

"Good, then it's working. You have to go out the door first before you can go anywhere else."

That made sense. "Would it have led me to Anjali when we didn't know where she was? What if I think about world peace? Not the school, I mean—the ideal. Will it lead me to where I can make it happen?"

"No. It's magic, but it's not a miracle maker. It just shows you a starting place, based on your own understanding of what you want. You have to do the real work. As the Akan proverb says, 'Your beauty may take you there, but it's your character that brings you back.'"

"Oh. Too bad. Well, still—thank you."

"I thought it was the least we could do."

"What about everybody else who borrowed the fake objects, the ones Mr. Stone made with the dereifier?" I asked. "Will they ever get their deposits back?"

Doc nodded. "They got them back already. You're the only person who still had one of the replacements checked out after it went dead. I guess that's because we gave you an extra day on your loan. The replacements were set to last through three patrons and run out on the fourth day after the third patron took them out."

"Good," I said. "And what about the real objects, the ones he copied? Did you find them?"

"Some of them. There were some at Wallace Stone's apartment, waiting to be sold. We've been contacting his clients. Most of them were appalled to learn they'd bought stolen goods. They're returning them. A few people are fighting, but we have some very good lawyers among our alumni. I'm confident we'll get them back eventually."

"Oh, I almost forgot," I said. "Jaya Rao wants to know what to do with the princesses, the ones Gloria Badwin collected."

"Ah, yes, the princesses. That's quite a problem." Doc sighed. "Tell her to bring them in and I'll put them under a sleeping spell for now—I can use the Sleeping Beauty spindle. We'll keep them here while we figure out what to do. Most of them would be pretty confused to find themselves in twenty-first-century America, even assuming we could disenchant them."

"Won't the Kiss of True Love work?"

"In theory, yes. But Gloria Badwin liked antiques. It may be hard to find someone who truly loves a princess who last walked the earth over a hundred years ago. On the other hand, they tell me true love lasts beyond the grave, so perhaps there's hope."

I wondered whether a ghost could administer the Kiss of True Love.

"Speaking of love," Doc continued, "here's the Golden Key if you want to visit that bird of yours. Bring it back before you leave the library."

Anjali called me on Thursday to ask if I would take her to the basketball game on Friday. "You could come over here and hang out, maybe get caught up on homework, and have dinner with my family," she said.

Jaya insisted on coming to the game with us. "If I hadn't saved you, you would still be a puppet, and Merritt would be three inches tall. He wouldn't be playing a lot of basketball then, would he? I want to see him play!"

"Oh, let her come," I said.

Anjali sighed and shrugged yes.

Just before the game started, Aaron showed up. This time he was wearing a purple-and-white scarf, and he cheered whenever Marc scored. The game was satisfying but not that exciting—we were up by six points by the end of the first quarter and never lost the lead after that. When Aaron left to go to the bathroom after the third quarter, Katie from my French class leaned over to me and said, "Is that your boyfriend? Because he's really cute."

"Who, Aaron? No, he's just a friend."

"He is not! He's *totally* your boyfriend," said Jaya.

"No, he's not. We work together after school."

"Don't listen to her. He likes her. They argue all the time, and he's always putting flowers behind her ear."

"Jaya! He does not!"

Katie smiled. "I get it. Cute but taken. Aren't they always."

Back from the bathroom, Aaron sat down behind me. He put his hand on my shoulder and said in my ear, "You can lean on me; I don't mind."

I leaned back, my face aflame. Seemingly absently, he played with my hair. I wished I had a working mermaid's comb; still, he seemed to like my hair okay as it was. Jaya smirked. I tried to watch the players and ignore her, but it was hard to concentrate.

A roaring all around me made me aware that the game was over and we had won. "You hungry?" said Aaron. "Want to go get something to eat?"

"I think a few of us are going to Jake's Joint," I said.

"You can come too," said Jaya.

"You're not coming, Jaya," said Anjali.

"I am so!"

"No, you're not. It's late, and you don't want Mom and Dad to get mad and say you can never come to a basketball game again."

"Please? Just one soda?"

"I'll take her home afterward," I offered.

"Oh, all right, you can come, but only for one drink."

Aaron walked next to me to the diner. He pulled out a chair for me.

"What a gentleman," I said. "Is it safe for me to sit down? Or is an invisible elf going to pull my chair away at the last minute?"

"You never know until you try," he said.

He didn't pull the chair away, but he did eat my pickle a little later. "Hey!" I objected.

"Sorry—were you planning to eat that? It didn't look like you were."

"You could have asked."

"You could have stopped me."

"Lovebirds," said Jaya, slurping the end of her soda.

"Okay, Jaya. That's your one soda. Time to go," said Anjali.

"But I'm not done yet!" protested Jaya, making loud bubbles with her straw to show there was still liquid in the glass. "See?"

"Stop making those disgusting noises, or I won't take you to the game next time."

"I liked you better as a puppet," she said, but she got up and put on her coat.

I got up too. "Ready?" I said.

"You sure you want to take her, Elizabeth? I can do it myself," said Anjali.

"No, that's fine," I said. "You stay here with Marc."

"Come back afterward, then?"

I shook my head. "I have to get home. My stepmother will kill me if I leave the dishes till morning."

Anjali made a sympathetic face.

"Thanks, Libbet," said Marc. "See you Monday."

Much as I usually hate having my name shortened, I didn't object. If Marc Merritt wanted to give me an affectionate nickname in front of everybody who was anybody at Fisher, that was fine with me. Besides, it reminded me of the adorable Andre. "Give your brother a hug from me," I said.

Aaron stood up and put on his coat too. "I'll walk you," he said.

"Yes, come on, Aaron!" said Jaya, winking at me.

"Thanks—but I can find my way okay now," I said, dying of embarrassment.

"No, she can't," said Jaya. "You have to come with us."

I didn't argue, but I showed them both the desire ring once we were outside. Jaya wanted to try it on. "Hey, that's neat!" she said. "Is Madison Square Garden really that way?"

"The subway is—you would have to take it downtown. Can I have my ring back now?"

We reached the Raos' building. "Bye, Jaya," said Aaron.

"Bye, Aaron! Bye, Elizabeth! Have fun!"

Aaron and I walked in silence to the subway. "I'll see you next week," I said.

"See you next week." He looked as if he was going to say something else, but he didn't.

"Okay, bye, then."

"Bye."

I had to concentrate very hard to get the ring to take me to the right train platform. Whenever I let my mind drift, I found it pulling me west—following Aaron as he rode the bus across the park.

The next week it was suddenly spring. The snow, already melting, gave a last sigh and trickled down the drains. Crocuses poked up their purple noses around the sidewalk trees. Teachers started talking about midterms.

On Wednesday, Ms. Callender put me on Stack 7, the art collection, with Josh. It was pretty quiet, which was good—I had a French dialogue to memorize. My ring kept wanting me to go upstairs, where Aaron was stationed on Stack 10, Science and Medicine, but when I went to look for him on my break, he wasn't there. So I walked over to Central Park instead and communed with the snowdrops.

Saturday evening I was doing my math homework when I heard a tapping at my window. It sounded like a branch blowing against the pane. I glanced up and glimpsed a dark shape. A chill ran through me.

Don't be ridiculous, I told myself—Mr. Stone is stuck in Nowhere and the dark shape that used to hover terrifyingly in windows is a friend now.

The tapping came again. "Polly?" I said, throwing the window open, "is that you?" I wondered how she got out of the Garden of Seasons.

"Hey, Elizabeth." It was Aaron. He was sitting cross-legged on a flying carpet.

"Aaron! What are you doing there?"

"I just was wondering, what are you up to?"

"I'm doing my math homework, why?"

"Want to come for a ride?"

"You mean now?"

"No, yesterday. Of course I mean now."

"Um . . . sure." I put on an extra sweater and hauled the window open wide.

Aaron mushed the carpet up against the side of the building and held out his hand. "Careful," he said.

His hand was cold but steady. I stepped out and sat down quickly. The carpet wobbled like a water bed.

"Okay?" asked Aaron. "It's easier to keep your balance if you stay low." He sent the carpet into an upward glide.

I lay down and looked up at the sky. A fullish moon made the clouds glow. Aaron lay down beside me on his side. I turned over on my side too. He put his arm over me awkwardly, then took it away. After a minute I moved back and leaned against him.

"Are you warm enough? I brought blankets."

"I'm fine. Where are we going?" I asked.

"Anywhere you like. Green-Wood Cemetery? Battery Park? The Hudson?"

"How about The Cloisters?"

"You got it."

The wind blew my hair back and ruffled the carpet fringe. I turned over on my stomach and peered over the edge, watching the buildings zip past underneath us. Aaron put his arm over my back again.

"So what did you leave as a deposit? For the carpet, I mean."

"My sense of humor."

"Come on. That's the oldest joke in the repository."

"Naturally it would be, since I've lost my sense of humor. I can't tell a funny joke now, can I?"

"Your sense of humor doesn't seem any different to me. What *did* you leave as a deposit?"

"My powers of persuasion."

"No, you didn't. You got me to come with you."

"That didn't take much persuasion."

"Come on. What was it really? Your firstborn again?"

"No way. I'm never leaving my firstborn again as long as I live. That was too horrible."

"Yeah, I saw," I said. "It looked so . . . vulnerable."

Aaron nodded uncomfortably. He moved his arm away. I changed the subject. "What's that down there? The East River?"

"No, silly, the Hudson. I guess that means you didn't get your sense of direction back?"

"Doc says they're working on it. The ring helps, but it's not the same thing," I said.

"Too bad."

"Yeah. It's okay, though, my sense of direction was never all that hot . . ." We passed over a necklace of lights strung across the river. "What's that down there?"

"The George Washington Bridge."

"Oh, of course . . . So if you got your firstborn back, you must have returned the Snow White mirror?"

"Yeah—I couldn't get that horrible thing out of my bedroom fast enough," said Aaron. "Here we are. Hang on, I'm taking us down."

Peeking out again, I saw The Cloisters—the museum of medieval art that sits on a hilltop in Fort Tryon Park, at the northern end of Manhattan. Aaron put his arm around me and held me tight against the carpet as we banked and glided down toward the castle-like cluster of buildings. We landed with a gentle bump in the high garden overlooking the river.

The still air was mild after the wind of our flight. The moon made the bare trees look as if they'd been cast in silver. Shadows played across Aaron's face, emphasizing his cheekbones. His lips were a beautiful shape.

He brought out a thermos. "Want some cocoa?"

"Sure, thanks."

I sniffed at my cocoa. There was something in it besides chocolate. Cinnamon? No, vanilla? Not quite . . . "What is this smell?" I asked. "You didn't enchant the cocoa, did you?"

He gave an evil chuckle. "What, you're worried it's my secret aphrodisiac? And now that I've got you alone . . ."

My heart pounded. I hit him on the shoulder. "Come on, what is it really?"

"Ginger."

"Oh."

We sipped in silence for a while, watching the lights across the river.

"So what did you really leave as a deposit?"

"My ambition."

"You? Never."

"My sense of t-t-timing?"

I shook my head. "Uh-uh."

"My most precious memory—of the moment I met you?"

"Fine, don't tell me."

He put down his cocoa mug, took the empty mug out of my hand, and put it down. He leaned forward—much too far forward—and fell, taking me down with him. "My sense of balance," he whispered into my hair.

I pushed at him. "Ow, get off, you're on my arm."

He shifted his weight but didn't move away. "My inhibitions," he whispered into the other ear.

Then he kissed me.

He tasted of chocolate and ginger and apples. Spring air, books. New grass. Magic.

"Hey, you're not bad at that," I said.

"Neither are you."

He kissed me again. Then I kissed him.

"You know," I said, "you almost let a rat eat me."

"I'm glad it didn't."

Shadows went across the moon. I pulled a blanket around me. We kissed again.

The trip home went by like a flash. I lay back in Aaron's lap looking at the sky while he stroked my hair back from my forehead. His hands were cold, or maybe my face was hot.

"Aaron?"

"Mmm?"

"What was it really? The deposit."

"My color vision."

"Really?"

"Yeah. I figured I don't use it much at night anyway."

"Oh. So why didn't you just say so?"

"Because you're so much fun to tease."

"Oh, *I'm* fun to tease?"

"Yes, you're fun to tease."

"Mmm." We kissed again, this time upside down.

The carpet slowed down and gave a little bob. Aaron looked up. "Too bad. We're here already," he said.

I sat up. There was my room, with my desk lamp still on. I knelt and pulled the window open. "Well, thanks for the ride," I said. "This was . . . fun."

"Yeah, it was." He put out his hand and helped me through the window—which wasn't strictly necessary, but I didn't mind.

I put my head back out the window. "Bye, Aaron," I said.

"Bye, Elizabeth. Maybe we can hang out in the daylight sometime," said Aaron. "You know, I don't think I know the color of your eyes."

"Yours are brown. With gigantic red blood vessels at the corners. And you have cavernous nostrils, they look like a bear's den, and a monster hangnail on your right index finger. Or is it your left?"

"Shut up," he said, kissing me one last time.

I leaned out the window and watched him until the carpet vanished over the rooftops.

I would like to say the prince and princess lived happily ever after, along with the swineherd and the scullery maid. And, in fact, things did get easier for Anjali and Marc—thanks to Jaya, who spilled the beans by answering Anjali's phone in front of their parents and telling Anjali her "boyfriend" was calling. After some recriminations—Mr. and Mrs. Rao thought Anjali should have mentioned Marc's existence herself—they invited him over for dinner and pronounced him a "nice young man."

"They're just using reverse psychology," Jaya told me. "They think Anji's dating Merritt to rebel, so if they tell her they approve, she'll get bored and break up with him."

"How do you know they don't just actually like Marc?" I said. "He's pretty likable."

"I know my parents. They're crazy for reverse psychology. They're always trying it on me."

"Maybe that's because you're so perverse."

"No, I'm not."

"Yes you are, silly, you just proved it."

"I think I know my parents better than you do, Elizabeth Rew!"

"Whatever you say," I told her. I was glad the Raos allowed Anjali to date Marc, no matter why—and even gladder that she still went to the basketball games with me, even though she no longer needed me for cover.

As for the swineherd and the scullery maid, I was so used to the princess being somebody else, I had trouble getting used to being the heroine of my own story. In a few short weeks, I had gone from having nobody to eat lunch with to having a basketball-game buddy and even—wonder of wonders!—a boyfriend. It took me a while for my self-image to catch up with my new status. But "happily ever after" doesn't begin to describe it. Not a week goes by when Aaron and I don't have three or four little squabbles and at least one full-out fight.

Still, for a smug, pigheaded ogre, he's pretty darn cute, and he hasn't stuffed me in a paper bag and fed me to a rat again—at least, not yet.

And my sense of direction? I'm still waiting.

# *Acknowledgments*

If ever a book had a fairy godmother and a Prince Charming, they were Christina Büchmann and Andrew Nahem. I'm deeply indebted as well to the assorted witches, magicians, and librarians without whom my mice and pumpkins would never have had a chance of transporting anyone anywhere: my editor, Nancy Paulsen; my agent, Irene Skolnick; my mother, brother, father, and stepfather, Alix Kates Shulman, Ted Shulman, Martin Shulman, and Scott York; and David Bacon, Yudhijit Battacharjee, Mark Caldwell, Elizabeth Chavalas, Cyril Emery, Vida Engstrand, Rob Frankel, Erin Harris, John Hart, John Keenum, Katherine Keenum, Sara Kreger, Shanti Menon, Christina Milburn, Friedhilde Milburn, Laura Miller, Laurie Muchnick, Alayne Mundt, Lisa Randall, Maggie Robbins, Bruce Schneier, Jesse Sheidlower, Andrew Solomon, Greg Sorkin, Jaime Wolf, and Hannah Wood. Thanks also to my tenth-grade social studies teacher, the late Ira Marienhoff, who stopped me in the hallway one day with the words, "You! Polly! You look like a young lady who needs a job. Call this number." And to Stanley Kruger at the New York Public Library, who hired me when I did.

**POLLY SHULMAN**, who also wrote *Enthusiasm*, has written and edited articles about books, infinity, edible jellyfish, planets, circuses, and many other subjects for *The New York Times*, *Science*, *Salon*, and other publications. She is an alumna of Yale, where she majored in math. She puts cayenne pepper in her chocolate cookies and reads forgotten books with frontispieces. In high school she worked as a page at the New York Public Library's main branch, where the librarians trusted her with the key to the special materials storage cage. She lives in New York City with her husband.

Visit her online at **www.pollyshulman.com**.